Under Open Skies
# Born to Run, Live to Be Free

Under Open Skies

# Born to Run, Live to Be Free

Daris Howard

**Publishing Inspiration - St. Anthony, Idaho**

Publishing Inspiration
St. Anthony, Idaho
Copyright © 2014 by Daris Howard

This book is a work of fiction. Names, characters, places, organizations, and incidents either are products of the author's imagination or are used fictitiously. Any resemblance to actual persons, living or dead, events or organizations is entirely coincidental.

Cover art by Mark McKenna

ISBN-10: 1629860042
ISBN-13: 978-1629860046

Manufactured in the United States Of America

www.publishinginspiration.com

# Table Of Contents

## Dedication

I dedicate this book to my daughter, Elliana, who loves horses and was the motivation for me to finish it.

# Chapter One
# Horse Attack

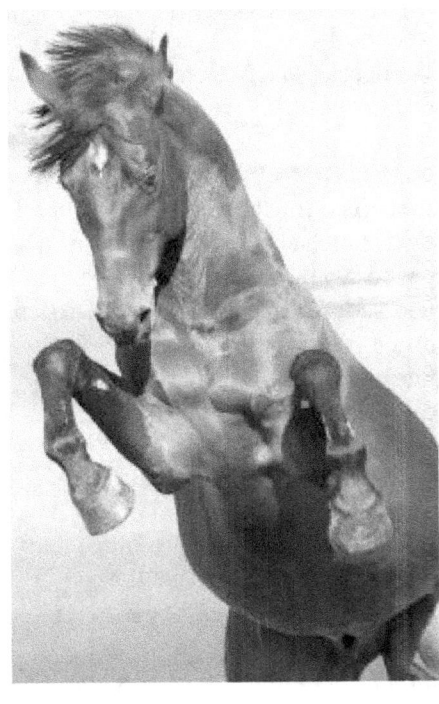

It was Sunday morning, and it was beautiful, as most June days are in Utah. My wife, Hannah, and I, along with our two little girls, had barely come home from church when our phone rang. When I answered it, I heard Brenda's voice on the other end of the line, quivering with anxiety. "I am sending a horse to you, and he is dangerous and could kill you, so be careful."

"Brenda, are you sure you want to have that kind of horse again?" I asked.

"It's a long story," she replied. "I'll tell you all about it when I get there. But meanwhile, take every precaution. I don't want you getting hurt, even if I lose the horse. Just put him in the pasture with the old mares and the gelding."

"What if the gelding fights with him?"

Brenda said, "That old horse has been a gelding so long, he probably doesn't realize he's not a mare."

I wasn't so sure. From what I had seen watching him, he seemed to think it was his herd.

Brenda told me some more about the new horse. She said his name was Cashmere.

"Cashmere? Like in a sweater?" I asked.

She laughed. "Yes, like the sweater."

She then went on to tell me that Cashmere was not only on his way already, but that the men that she had shipped him with had called her from a rest stop in Ogden and had said they would be in Logan in about an hour. "You are to meet them at the gas station at 5000 West Main," she said.

When I hung up the phone, Hannah was standing behind me. She had heard my end of the conversation, and the worry showed in her face.

Her voice quivered slightly as she spoke. "Brenda didn't go and buy a mean stallion again, did she?"

I shrugged. "I don't know the whole story yet, but it sounds like it."

"But the last one . . ."

Her voice trailed off in anxious concern. We both remembered the last one, but no one remembered more than I did.

****************************

I met Brenda not long after I had arrived in Cache Valley. When I came to Utah State University to attend graduate school, the professor responsible for hiring graduate students who would teach college algebra called me to his office. Even though I had sent my application by certified mail months before the deadline, he claimed it had arrived late, and for that reason I hadn't received the teaching fellowship they had promised. He said I could teach three classes instead of the normal one to increase my salary, but that would still only bring my pay up to half of what the others received on their fellowships only teaching one class.

I was able to do some maintenance and ground work at our apartment to pay part of the rent, but we were still struggling to make ends meet. I continually searched for extra work on the job board at the university, but what work I could find only lasted a weekend or two. But then came the day I saw Brenda's ad.

*Wanted: An experienced horseman to help take care of spirited race horses. Weekend work and evenings needed. Must be able to haul hay and do other heavy lifting and hard work.*

It sounded like the perfect job, and I was afraid someone else would get it. I hurried to one of the university's courtesy phones. I only reached an answering machine, so I left a message that included my home phone number.

When I arrived home later in the evening, I anxiously asked Hannah if anyone had called. She paused to think a moment. "Yes, come to think of it, there was a call. Some lady named Brenda said she was returning your call."

I quickly dialed the number, and this time I found her at home. She said I was the first to call and could have the job if I wanted it. I gladly accepted, and we set up for me to meet her on Saturday at the hay barn.

I arrived at the barn early. When the appointed time arrived and passed, I became concerned that I was at the wrong place. I rechecked the address, and I was sure I was at the right place. Almost an hour went by when, finally, a big tan pickup pulled up.

A lady stepped out and approached me. She carried herself with great confidence. She reached out her hand and took mine. "Are you Tom Johnson?"

I nodded.

"Sorry I am so late," she said. "For some reason I forgot where I told you I would meet you, and I have been waiting at the pasture. It finally dawned on me that I had told you to meet me here. It is my fault, and I want you to count this hour in your wages." I told her there was no need for that, but she insisted.

We visited briefly, and then she wanted to see how good I was at loading hay. She backed her pickup to the stack, and I loaded a good, tight load. She had me climb into the cab with her, and we drove to the horse barn.

She backed up between some corrals and showed me where to stack the hay. When I finished, she produced a tarp from behind the seat of her pickup, and I strapped it over the stack.

She motioned toward the corrals. "Now, come meet my babies."

Knowing I was going to be meeting some horses for the first time, I had asked permission of the apartment owner to take any good apples that has survived under the snow beneath the old tree in the yard. "Sure," he had said. "Take all you want. They will just go to waste anyway." So, I had filled my coat pockets full. I asked Brenda if it was okay if I gave the horses some, and she nodded.

As we approached the first corral, one of the most beautiful paint mares I have ever seen came over and stuck her head above the top pole.

"This is Patches," Brenda said. "I moved her in here so we can feed her a little grain to sharpen her up before I have her bred."

I offered Patches an apple, and she happily took it. I scratched her behind her ears while she ate, and she turned her head so I didn't miss any spots.

We moved to the next corral, and a big black quarter horse lumbered up. "This horse is Jackie," Brenda explained. "She is supposed to have been bred, but I'm sure she should have had her baby by now, so I think it never took. She is fat enough to have twins, but I think it is just that: fat. I'll probably have her bred again when I have Patches bred."

I fed Jackie an apple and petted her nose briefly before we moved on. When we reached the final corral, a young Arabian stallion snorted and pawed the ground. "This is Dader," Brenda said.

Dader watched us suspiciously for a time, and then slowly approached. He cautiously reached his head between the pole rail fence. I held out an apple to him, and he slowly moved toward it like he would take it from me. He moved closer and closer, and then, at the last instant, he turned his head and clamped his teeth around my wrist.

He jerked back hard and fast, catching me by surprise and slamming me hard into the pole fence, holding me there. I dropped the apple as he clamped his teeth even tighter. Brenda yelled and waved her arms, and he finally let go. He then started eating the apple as calmly as if nothing had ever happened.

"I'm sorry about that," Brenda said. "He can be as friendly as anything one minute, and then the next, I just don't know. I can't tell if it's meanness, or if he is playing. But whatever it is, be careful with him."

After I pulled my arm back through the fence, Brenda wanted to see if anything was broken. Much of my forearm was bruised and turning blue, but nothing was broken.

Since we didn't have any ice, I went and stuck my arm in the water trough for a while until the swelling and pulsing pain subsided. Brenda thought I might want to knock off for the day, but I desperately needed the money, so I told her I would be fine.

I hauled some more hay, having pleasant visits with Brenda as we drove. I learned that she had two daughters and lived with one when she was in town. She was a consultant for companies seeking government contracts, and she was usually gone all week and only home on weekends. Sometimes she would be gone for two, three, or four week stretches at a time.

"That is where you come in," she told me. "I will need someone to take care of my horses. Just plan on doing it all of the time, and I will check on things whenever I get into town."

When I finished with all of the hay for the week, we made sure there was good bedding in each of the small horse barns attached to the three corrals. I was cautious as I put straw in Dader's barn, but he acted like I didn't even exist and like nothing had ever happened before.

When that was all done, Brenda took me out to a pasture on the northeast side of town, near the mountains. There were a few mares and an old gelding grazing there.

"These are mine, too," Brenda said. "They should be fine until we get more snow; then you will need to start bringing hay out here. Also, their old barn needs some work, and I want you to fix it up."

As we finished for the day, I grabbed a piece of paper and a pen from my pickup and wrote a list of everything Brenda wanted me to do. There were barns to repair, hay to haul when needed, and lots of fences to fix. Those things, along with the feeding, would be enough to continually keep me busy.

For the next few weeks everything went well. Brenda joined me on the weekend and often found more things she wanted to have done. She brought me lots of old tin, nails, and other things to use in repairing the sheds. One weekend she showed up with rolls of old, used net wire. I spent most of that day trying to straighten it enough for it to be usable.

Most of the time when I climbed into Dader's pen to clean out his small barn, he ignored me. But on the fourth weekend, as I started this task, he stood at the other end of his pen snorting and rearing. I kept an eye on him, but he didn't come any closer. I wondered if Jackie or Patches was in heat, ready to be bred, and that was making him anxious.

The next two weeks he did the same thing, but always kept his

distance. On the seventh weekend, Brenda was gone, so I was working alone. As usual, I climbed into Dader's pen to clean, and, this time, he didn't seem anxious at all. He stood at the other end, chewing on a little bit of hay I had given him.

I started cleaning. I had turned my back on him for only an instant when I heard a loud, angry snort directly behind me. I spun around to find him rearing with his front hooves directly over me. How he moved across the corral that fast, and without me hearing him, I had no idea, but the look in his eye told me he was not playing.

I had no time to prepare before he came down, hitting me hard on my right shoulder with his hoof. The force of the blow slammed me to the ground, knocking the air from me, causing me to drop the pitchfork. Although I was too dazed to think, the adrenaline surged through me, and my heart started racing.

He rose again to strike, and although my thoughts were jumbled and cloudy, I somehow knew that if he came down on me, he'd kill me. I rolled, and his hooves crashed down where I had lain. Again he rose to strike, but now my mind was starting to clear, and, along with the adrenaline increasing my speed, my thoughts raced for a way out of my predicament. That was when I saw the pitch fork. I rolled again, and once more his hooves crashed down where I had been. But this time I rolled toward the pitch fork.

As he rose to strike once more, I reached out and grabbed the fork, and in a single motion swung the back of it, hitting him on the side of his head. The force of the blow was barely enough to twist his body one way and mine the other. His hooves came down so close to me that I felt them brush against my skin.

The blow caused him to tremble and pause for the few seconds I needed to scramble to my feet. But I was still cornered, and once again he rose to strike. But from a standing position, I could defend myself much better.

With my mind now clear, I considered using the prongs of the fork to force him away, but I hated to mar this beautiful animal. It was not because I felt any good will toward him, but it was because he belonged to Brenda, and I loved my job. So instead, as he rose to strike once more, I turned the back part of the fork and hit him as hard as I could, swinging it into the side of his head.

This time it was he that stumbled. The force of the blow turned his whole body a couple of feet, and when he landed, he went down on

5

one knee. He quickly came up onto his feet and stood back to face me. I didn't even let him rear up to strike again, but once more swung as hard as I could, hitting him on his shoulder.

He spun away from me, and as he did, he kicked out with his back hooves, narrowly missing my head. He retreated to the other end of his corral, and I moved to the gate. I climbed it and just threw myself over it, landing on the ground on the other side.

That was when the pain in my shoulder engulfed me. It was so bad I started to shake. I wondered if it was broken. Still, my reasoning told me it probably wasn't, or I would not have been able to swing the fork like I had, or to have climbed the gate.

As I lay there on the ground, in the light dusting of November snow, an old man was suddenly standing over me.

"Son, are you all right?"

I nodded, and he knelt down beside me. "I watched the horse attack you from out my window. You are lucky to be alive."

He pointed to the house next door and told me that was where he lived. "I came to help as fast as I could, but it was all over by the time I arrived."

Because I continued to shake, he was concerned that I was in shock. I told him I felt I was fine, but when I tried to sit up to show him, everything started spinning, and I flopped onto my back again.

He wanted to call an ambulance, but I told him I didn't have money for that and would be fine once my head cleared. He found an old horse blanket and laid it over me. I lay there for a few more minutes. Finally the shivering began to subside, as did the throbbing in my shoulder, and my mind felt more alert.

As I sat up a second time, everything spun just briefly, and then settled. I eventually stood, tested my arm, and was sure nothing was broken, though I figured some muscles were sprained, if not torn.

The old man looked concerned as I worked my arm to loosen my shoulder. He followed me as I turned to finish the feeding. "Well, aren't you a stubborn young buck. If I had taken a blow like that, I would have said to heck with the horses and headed home."

"I am a married college student, and I really need this job," I told him. "Besides, I love horses."

"Well, I do, too," he replied. "But a horse like that young stallion will never be any good. If he will attack like he did, there is only one place for him, and that is heading down the road."

I must admit that I agreed with him that Dader needed to be sold.

As I continued to work, the old man kept an eye on me, concerned because of my injury. He sat down onto a bale and talked. He told me his name was Cyrus. He was retired, and liked to come over and visit the horses. He had worked for a lot of years as a ranch hand on a big cattle ranch across the valley, and he missed it. He said he often brought apples

6

and other treats for the horses. He told me that he especially liked Jackie, and I wondered if that was part of the reason she was so fat.

Cyrus told me he had been bitten by Dader just like I had been, and he didn't feed him apples anymore. "I saw that nasty beast bite you, and hoped the owner lady would sell him because of it, but she didn't."

I told him that she wasn't sure if Dader was mean or just playing.

"Oh, he ain't playing," Cyrus assured me. "I'd never turn my back on him. I'm sure he was trying to kill you today. Of course, I don't need to tell you that."

I nodded. That was one thing I knew for myself.

"You don't mind me coming over here, do you?" Cyrus asked.

I told him that it was fine with me, and I was sure Brenda didn't mind.

He talked to me the whole time I worked. I learned about his years working on the ranch and how, when he left that job, he became a mechanic. "Always pretty much worked with my hands," he said. "None of that book learning for me. Couldn't stand to be locked up inside a classroom for hours on end."

I smiled and told him I understood because I, too, had worked as a mechanic for a couple of years. But I liked both the learning and working with my hands.

When I finished what chores absolutely had to be done, I decided I would have to leave any extras for another day. My shoulder was throbbing, and I wanted to get home and put some ice on it. Cyrus thought I should have it checked, and when he reached out to shake my hand, and I grimaced when I lifted my arm, he just shook his head. "You don't want no permanent problems with that."

I had had sports injuries and was sure there was nothing a doctor could do other than tell me to immobilize it. When I got home, Hannah was very concerned. My whole shoulder was black from bruising. The ice cooled the burn I felt in it, and the throbbing slowed. I took a cloth and wrapped my arm tightly against me to keep me from moving it.

I used it as little as possible, but come Monday morning, I had to teach. The higher I raised it, the more it hurt, so I wrote as much as I could on the lower half of the chalk board. But by the end of the week I was beginning to get some more motion in it.

That next Saturday, besides doing the regular chores, I also worked on fixing the horse sheds for winter. I also cleaned the horse barns, all except Dader's. I tossed some straw over the fence into his barn, but decided that, with my sore arm, I was not about to try to face him. Cyrus joined me not long after I arrived and visited almost the whole time.

The work went well. Every night after school I fed the horses, and Cyrus almost always came to visit. The second Saturday after Dader's attack, I was in the middle of feeding when Brenda showed up.

She was pleased at how well the horses were doing. I was about to tell her what happened with Dader, but before I had a chance, she noticed I was favoring my right arm. When she asked me the reason, I told her the story.

She seemed very concerned. "I will take care of him today. You worry about the other horses."

I told her I didn't think she should go in there, but she laughed. "Don't worry about me. I'll be careful, and I've never met a horse I couldn't handle."

I went to my work cleaning the other horse barns. I had barely begun when I heard Dader snort. It triggered an instant memory, and something inside of me said "run!" I threw myself over the fence and sped across the yard, grabbing a shovel on my way. In seconds I was at Dader's pen where I could see Brenda on her back and Dader starting to rear above her.

I vaulted the gate, landing on my feet next to Brenda just as Dader started coming down toward her. Brenda threw her hand over her face to protect herself. I swung the shovel with all my strength, catching him in the side of his shoulder. It twisted his body just enough so that he mostly missed her, though one hoof struck her arm.

Dader crashed to his knees. I dropped the shovel, grabbed Brenda under each arm, and pulled her back to the fence while Dader was scrambling to his feet again. I thought he would go to the other end of the corral, but he rose to strike again. I stepped up between him and Brenda and scrambled to reach for the shovel. I grabbed it, but was unable to use it for defense before his hooves hit me.

I was slammed back into the pole fence, but was able to stay on my feet and keep hold of the shovel. He had barely started to rear again when I slammed him across the nose with the shovel. He stumbled backward, but then started to rear again. Again I slammed him across his muzzle, and again he stumbled back. Twice more he started to attack, and each time I slammed him across his face.

The last time I did, I heard the shovel handle crack and wondered how long it would hold out and what I would do if it broke. But just then he retreated to the other end of the corral, snorting and pawing. Keeping the shovel in one hand, I helped Brenda to her feet with the other. Dazed, she stumbled her way to the gate with me holding one arm around her while keeping the shovel at ready in the other, never letting Dader completely out of my sight.

Brenda reached out and grabbed the gate to climb over, but gasped in pain. I could tell something was wrong with her hand, so I set the shovel against the fence where I could grab it quickly, and I started unhooking the gate.

Whether Dader saw me put the shovel aside and thought it was his chance to renew his attack, I don't know, but once more he moved toward us, rearing and snorting. I quickly grabbed the shovel and only had to raise it to cause him to retreat. I was finally able to unlatch the gate, and Brenda slipped through it. I followed and then quickly relatched it.

We were both breathing hard as we dropped to rest on a hay bale. She turned to thank me, even as the tears from her pain rolled down her face. "If you had been even a second later, I'm sure he would have killed me. How did you know to come to my rescue?"

I couldn't even answer that. I only knew that something in me had said to run.

I just shrugged. "I guess you must have a good guardian angel."

She nodded. "Maybe, counting you, I have two of them."

I smiled. "How's your hand?"

She felt it with her other hand. "I think it's broken."

"I'm sorry I couldn't move him enough to avoid his hooves hitting you."

"I'm glad you did as much as you did. My hand will heal."

That was when Cyrus showed up. "Man, are you two lucky. I've never seen a stallion so dad blamed set on killing someone. I wouldn't keep a horse like that."

"Don't worry," Brenda said. "He has spent his last day here."

I asked Brenda if she wanted me to drive her to the hospital, but she shook her head. "As long as I have one good hand, I can drive myself. You finish with the horses, but stay away from Dader. He won't be here long enough for us to mess with him anymore."

She was just ready to leave when she stopped. "Tom, you're bleeding! Are you all right?"

That was the first time I realized there was blood rolling down the side of my face. I just shrugged. "It must have been from his hooves or the fence or something when he hit me. But it doesn't feel like it is anything serious."

It took a while to convince her of that, but eventually she headed to the hospital, once more stubbornly refusing my offer to drive her. As her pickup left the yard, Cyrus turned to me. "That is one strong-willed woman."

"Yeah," I replied. "But she is a good lady."

"And you are just as stubborn," he said. "You ought to get yourself home before you bleed all over the place."

"I need to finish feeding first," I replied.

Cyrus just shook his head as I tore a piece of my shirt to try to stop the bleeding. I soaked it in cold water under the hydrant and held it to my forehead. Each time I thought the bleeding had stopped, I pulled the cloth away, and it started again. Finally I gave up and hurried with the chores and headed home.

By the time I arrived at our apartment, the blood had dripped down my face and onto my shirt. Hannah just gasped when she saw me. I assured her I was okay, but she wanted to see the cut. I slipped into the shower, and then we bandaged my head.

When I went the next evening to feed, Dader's pen stood empty. Brenda was already there, her hand now in a cast. When I asked her what she had done with him, she said, "He's gone. That's all that matters."

\*\*\*\*\*\*\*\*\*\*\*\*\*\*\*\*\*\*\*\*\*\*\*\*\*\*\*\*\*\*\*\*

All the memories of Dader came back as I hung up the phone from talking with Brenda. I changed my clothes and prepared to meet the men bringing in the new horse. It had been seven months since Brenda had gotten rid of Dader, but it was as fresh in my mind as if it had just happened.

My oldest daughter, Kaylynn, who was only three, pulled on my pant leg. "Me go wif you?"

In the past five months I had taken her with me quite often when I just needed to feed. I had bought her a small plastic bucket and would put some apples in it that she could carry to the horses. She knew their names and thought all horses were named Jackie or Patches, depending on the color. If she saw a horse that was a solid color, she would say, "Wook, there's a Jackie." If it was more of a spotted horse, she would say, "There's a Patches."

She loved the horses. She had learned to hold an apple out in the flat palm of her little hand, and the horses were always careful to only use their lips to pull it into their mouths. She would giggle as their lips tickled her palm.

But I couldn't have her with me if I was going to be working with a dangerous horse. I scooped her up into my arms. "I'm afraid Daddy needs to go alone today."

"But me want see Jackie and Patches."

"I'm not going to see Jackie and Patches," I said. "I'm going to take care of another horse."

She kept begging until I firmly told her no. As I prepared to leave, Hannah expressed her concern again. I promised to avoid taking chances. I kissed her goodbye. "Don't worry. I'll be fine."

But as I left, I wished I really felt the confidence I had expressed.

## Chapter Two
## A Wall And A Horse Named Cashmere

As I traveled to meet the men bringing the horse, I listened to a news report. The commentator was talking about the different events that had occurred on that day throughout history. "And, exactly one year ago on this day, June 12, 1987, Ronald Reagan gave one of the most famous speeches ever given. Standing before the Brandenburg Gate of the Berlin Wall, he challenged Russia to tear down the wall. Here is a part of that speech."

Then I listened to Ronald Reagan's distinctive voice. "We welcome change and openness; for we believe that freedom and security go together, that the advance of human liberty can only strengthen the cause of world peace. There is one sign the Soviets can make that would be unmistakable, that would advance dramatically the cause of freedom and peace. General Secretary Gorbachev, if you seek peace, if you seek prosperity for the Soviet Union and Eastern Europe, if you seek liberalization, come here to this gate. Mr. Gorbachev, open this gate. Mr. Gorbachev, tear down this wall!"

I remembered hearing those words the year before. I had been coming home from a hard day at the university, and President Reagan's speech had thrilled me. I wondered if the Soviets and the East Germans would really allow freedom to their people. When I arrived at home, that was all Hannah and I could talk about.

"I don't think there is anyway in this world that it is ever going to happen," I had said.

"But just think," she replied, "what it would be like if those people were able to move about freely. What if those who were separated from the ones they loved by that wall were able to be reunited with them?"

"I don't know," I answered. "I think it is just an impossible dream. Granted, our relations with them aren't as bad as during the height of the Cold War. But it is still no utopia."

"But the Soviet Union is talking about reforms," she said.

"Yes, I know, but it might just be a show to make them look good."

"Maybe," she said, "But it never hurts to hope. We can dream of a world where everyone is free."

At church that next Sunday and at the university the next week it was the topic of every conversation. But as time went on, hope began to fade. Nothing happened, and I doubted anything ever would.

It was now a year since that speech, and the news commentator played that segment of the speech a second time, and then asked, "Are we any closer to seeing those freedoms Reagan talked about a year ago? Will the East Germans ever be free to go where they want and be what they want?"

"Fat chance," I said out loud as I shut off the radio. I couldn't stand to listen to any more. I understood in some ways how those in East Germany felt and had an affinity for them. Granted, I was not hedged in by a wall built by the government to stop me from traveling, but I felt imprisoned by my circumstances. There were things I wanted to do, places I wanted to go, and things I wanted to be, but I didn't have the means to do so.

Every weekday I had to be to school by 6:30 in the morning, and after teaching, taking classes, and studying for twelve hours, I would work much of the evening, barely earning enough for my family to have food and a place to live. Then, at night when I arrived home, I would often have to study until the early hours of the morning, getting very little sleep and having very little time to spend with my family.

On Saturdays, I would get up and go to work, and then come home and study some more. It seemed like a never-ending, exhausting cycle.

Hannah worked hard, too, trying to sew our clothes, make all of our food homemade, and do everything else she could to conserve what little money we had. There were times I would have liked to buy her some special present, or take my family on a vacation, or just take a drive up the canyon. But even the extra gas to drive up the canyon might mean the difference between having enough money to buy food or not.

Feeling so trapped and imprisoned by my own circumstances, I could easily empathize with the plight of the East Germans, and I often wondered what it would feel like to really be free.

As I turned onto the road the gas station was on, my thoughts returned to the new horse and my assignment. By the time I arrived at the gas station, the men were already there. They were hard to miss. They were towing a bright red, six horse, slant trailer. I approached the large pickup that was pulling it, and a man rolled down his window.

I knew they couldn't have been there very long unless they were already there when Brenda called, but they were impatient and let me know they didn't like waiting. They felt I should pay them extra for their time, but I told them they would have to take it up with Brenda since I came the minute I received word.

Grumbling, they started their truck engine, ready to follow me. I climbed back into my little pickup and led the way to the pasture. A third vehicle, a small car, joined in behind them.

As we pulled up to the gate of the pasture, the car stopped with us. I stepped out and went back to talk to the driver of the pickup pulling the horse trailer.

"This is the pasture we are going to put him in."

The man laughed a cynical laugh. "What's this 'we' stuff? Boy, I saw them load this horse. I was only paid to haul him. You couldn't pay me enough to get close to him. As far as unloading him, you are on your own."

I looked at him and at his partner in the passenger seat. They just grinned at me. I didn't know what else to do, so I just nodded. I did talk them into backing the trailer as close to the gate as possible without blocking traffic on the road. I figured I might be able to wrap the gate around the side of the trailer so that when the horse came out it would be natural for him to go into the pasture.

When the trailer was in position, the two men in the pickup climbed out. One of them told me they were both heading off to get a well-deserved cold beer and would come back in an hour or so to see if there was anything left of me. With that, they both laughed, climbed into the waiting car, and drove away.

I opened the pasture gate and pulled it around to the side of the trailer. I found some twine in my pickup and tied the gate loosely to the horse trailer. If the horse would come out and go into the pasture, I could then put the gate back up and that would be that. There was a small gap on the other side of the trailer, between it and the fence, but it was small enough it would be hard for a horse to squeeze through it. On the other hand, I could use it as an escape route if he tried to attack me.

Once I had everything in place, I went to the front of the trailer and opened the small door. It was only meant for a person to reach through and unhook a horse that might be tethered there. Because of the door's size, I couldn't see him well. But I could tell he was big since I couldn't see to the top of him from my position. I was not about to lean through the door to look at him, afraid that he might crush me. I could see the bottom of his head and knew he couldn't be tied since there was no halter.

There was a closed gate in the trailer behind him. It was opened by a lever on it. I did not plan to be inside when it opened, so I would have to figure a way to pull the lever from the outside. I went to my pickup and found some more twine. I was grateful that I always carried some. I strung the twine through the side of the trailer where I could easily pull it. I then opened the back door and went inside.

I still couldn't see him well, but in the shadows, I could tell he was a massive horse. The sheer size of him sent chills down my spine. He whinnied and snorted. He could not turn, but stomped, rocking the whole trailer from side to side until I could barely keep my balance.

I tied the end of the twine to the release bar on the gate and made my way back outside. I was about to release him when I remembered I had some crab apples. I figured it would be safer to give him one when he was trapped rather than after he was free.

I went back around to the small door and cautiously held an apple through it. He stopped his snorting and moved his nose toward the apple. Just as he reached out his lips to take it, the memory of Dader grabbing my wrist got the better of me and my courage failed. I dropped the apple and jerked back.

He didn't seem to menace me at all, so I picked it up and held it out again. Once more he reached for it, and once more I dropped it at the last minute. Finally, the third time, I held it long enough that he was able to pull it from my open hand.

He grabbed it with his lips, just like Jackie and Patches did,

gently, and tickling the palm of my hand. As he munched it, I reached up and cautiously petted his nose since I couldn't see much more of his head than that.

When he finished the apple, he gently nuzzled my hand, begging for another one. I was glad I had stuffed my pockets full.

I handed him another one, and again he took it as gently as any horse I had ever worked with. I was still cautious, and wanted to make sure I didn't let my guard down. I petted him, and he nuzzled me for some more.

But I thought maybe it was time to let him go. The other horses were now milling around. They could smell him, and he could smell them, and they whinnied to each other.

I went around to the other side of the trailer, made sure everything was in position, and pulled the twine holding the bar. When I heard the bar snap free, he must have heard it too. He let out a whinny, then a snort, and immediately started backing up.

The internal gate moved out of his way, and almost instantly he came out of the trailer. He blinked in the light briefly, and then he reared, stretching himself, happy to be free of the small enclosure.

I stood tight against the trailer for safety as I looked on in awe. Once he stepped out into the light, I could see how massive he truly was. I had never been close to a horse that was as tall as he was. I didn't even know race horses grew that tall. Although I was at a distance from him, I was sure he was taller than I was at his shoulders. I figured he was at least 18 hands and maybe even 19 hands tall.

When he reared, he could have put the whole front half of himself on top of the horse trailer. I also realized, with great concern, that the simple pasture fence only came about three quarters of the way up his side. He could almost step over it.

The other horses seemed to want to meet him. The mares did, anyway. The old gelding laid his ears back and showed his teeth – not a sign of friendliness. He also threw his body in front of the mares, blocking them from approaching this new stranger.

Cashmere, for his part, paid no attention. He bucked and whirled and snorted like a calf let out to pasture in the spring. Suddenly he turned and headed down the fence line, moving at breakneck speed. The other horses turned and followed him, falling behind quickly.

"Oh, my heck!" I said out loud. "He can really run!"

Each side of the pasture was about a quarter of a mile, and he ran one side of it in about 20 seconds. I knew the fences weren't that good, and as he approached the fence in the distance I was afraid he would go through it or over it, but he turned and headed along the next fence line.

I was engrossed with watching him when I suddenly realized that I should be putting the gate up. But it was hard to take my eyes off of him. With his tail in the air he was an impressive sight. I had never seen a horse that could run that fast. Not even close. Our old horse had been a race horse in her early years, and I had thought she was one of the fastest horses there was, but he would have left her in the dust.

I struggled to untie the gate from the trailer. My anxiousness was flustering me, making it so I couldn't undo the knot in the twine. I was still fumbling with it when he turned along the third fence line. By the time I got the knot undone and pulled the gate around into place, he had turned down the last side. His whole body was stretching out as if he was moving down a race track, his head bobbing slightly up and down in rhythm to his step.

I could only hook the bar around the gate post from inside the pasture, and he was coming fast. I thought of dropping the gate and running, but he, and maybe some of the other horses, would get out onto the road and be gone. I stepped through and pulled the bar fast, but my anxiousness made me lose my grasp. I grabbed it again and pulled, hooking it into the wire that held it. I turned to scramble through the gate, but it was too late. He came sliding to a stop right in front of me.

If I thought he was big before, he now seemed monstrous as he stood over me, looking down at me. My heart raced as I trembled. If he rose and struck at me I would have no way to defend myself.

But he reached out his big nose and nuzzled me, breathing a hard breath from his run into my neck. It tickled, but I couldn't laugh. I was too scared. I didn't respond, so he nuzzled me harder. I reached out a trembling hand and touched his nose. "Good boy . . ." I was trembling so hard my voice quivered and didn't sound like my own. I stroked his nose and tried again. "Good Cashm . . ." Somehow Cashmere just seemed too formal and stuffy, especially when he was nuzzling me like I was his best friend. "Good Cash," I said, abbreviating his name. My voice sounded surer and more like my own.

As he continued to nuzzle me, my courage started to return. He seemed to enjoy me petting him, and I knew he was begging for another apple. I pulled one from my pocket, and he took it and started munching it. I petted him along his neck. He leaned his head down so I could scratch his ear.

I continued talking to him as I rubbed the dirt from his coat. "Are you really as mean as they say? Are you just trying to get my confidence so you can take me off guard, or were they just putting me on?"

I rubbed all down his front leg, and he lifted it as if he was experienced at having his feet worked. As I touched his front knee, he quivered slightly. His front knees were the main thing that stood out about him. They were huge, about the size of small basketballs, and his right leg was slightly turned inward. He had had some kind of accident, probably broken knees, and they hadn't healed properly. But what had happened, and why both of them? The more I looked at them, the more I wondered and the more questions I had. Was it some kind of abuse, or was it just neglect?

But, through all of my petting and rubbing him, never once did he make an aggressive move. When he finished his apple, he nuzzled me again, begging for another one.

"All right," I said, "but just one more for now. I don't want you getting a tummy ache." I pulled out the apple, and he carefully reached for it.

The other horses came lumbering up, finally making it back from the other end of the pasture. As they approached, he looked at me like he was asking my permission. I gave him a little push. "Well, go run again, if that's what you want."

He didn't need any more invitation. He turned and flew across the pasture, his head high and his tail arched. He was the essence of majesty as he covered the distance to the far side of the pasture.

The other horses turned to chase him, but they weren't even half way across the pasture by the time he reached the far side. About then they gave up and quit the chase. He turned and headed down the far fence line. His speed continued to amaze me. Somehow, just watching him, it was as if I was on his back, the air flowing through my hair, his muscles and hooves pounding underneath me. Watching him gave me a feeling I couldn't understand.

I didn't even think to scramble through the fence until he turned down the last fence line. Somehow, I wasn't scared. It was as if I sensed a gentleness in him different from what I had been told.

As before, he slid to a stop in front of me, his sides heaving. He reached out his nose and breathed blasts of hot air into my face as I stroked his nose. He nuzzled me again, and I finally reached in my pocket for an apple. "If you get a tummy ache, don't blame me," I told him.

He ate while I rubbed dirt from his coat. I wished I had a brush. And then I remembered that I did have one in my pickup. When he went for another one of his runs, I slipped through the fence, retrieved it, and was waiting for him when he returned.

As I brushed him, he just seemed to revel in it. He closed his eyes and took in the pampering. As I continued, he suddenly went from a blackish gray to a coal black as the dust fell out of his coat. I tried to brush his mane, but part of it was matted, making it impossible to work through. I knew he hadn't been brushed in a long time. I still got out what knots I could.

I wondered if I dared work his tail. I gradually worked my way to his withers, and tested what he would do as I brushed just a bit down his back leg, ready to jump away if he kicked. But he didn't kick. He seemed to enjoy that, too. I eventually did get hold of his tail and started brushing a few knots out of it. I had just finished it and had moved to the other side when the little car with the three men pulled up.

The man who had been driving the pickup stood there, beer in hand, with his mouth hanging open. I just continued to brush Cashmere, and eventually he spoke.

"What the heck did you do to that horse?"

"What are you talking about?" I asked.

"When they loaded him in California, they had 30 men on ropes, and he pulled them all around the horse yard. He nearly killed some of them, and they almost had to give him a sedative and winch him into the trailer. And now, here you are, brushing him like a kitten."

I just shrugged. "I don't know anything about what happened in California. But he seems to like being brushed."

"But what did you do to make him gentle?" the other one asked. He looked at the beer in his hand then back at me. "You didn't give him something funny to drink, did you?"

I laughed. "Of course not. He's just gentle."

"I'll be danged if I believe that," the first man said. "You must have done something."

"I didn't really do anything," I replied. "I fed him a few apples, let him out, he ran a bit, and then I started brushing him."

"Maybe it is the apples," the first man said as the others nodded in agreement. "Do you have any more?"

I pulled one from my pocket and tossed it to him. The man approached the fence, holding out the apple at arm's length. "Here, boy. I have an apple for you."

Cashmere saw him, turned toward him, and reared, snorting and whinnying, his ears laid back against his head. I jumped back, shocked at his sudden anger. As he rose high in the air, the man fearfully fell back so fast that he tumbled to his back. Cashmere screamed out threateningly again and reared once more, and the man scrambled far away from the fence, cursing and screaming. "That there is the meanest, wildest horse ever. And you, boy, are a fool to think otherwise!"

"Cash?" I said, and he settled down and turned back to me. I was trembling, but he nuzzled me like nothing had ever happened, so I petted him. I pulled another apple from my pocket and gave it to him, then continued to stroke his neck.

"I just think he doesn't like you," I said.

"Thank you! Thank you, Mr. Einstein, for that brilliant observation!" the man shouted. "Did you figure that all out by yourself, or did it come to you from the fact that he just tried to kill me?"

The third man, the one who drove the car, joined the conversation for the first time. "So how come he acts all friendly with this young man, but wants to kill you?"

The first man was all annoyed. "Why don't you tell me, and then we'll both know?"

The second man, the one that had been in the passenger seat of the pickup, now spoke thoughtfully. "You know, it almost looked to me like the horse thought he was protecting the young man from you."

"Yeah, like holding out an apple is somehow threatening somebody!" the first man said.

"How about someone else tries?" the second man said. "Maybe it's just you he hates."

The first man shrugged. "Whatever."

"Maybe you smell funny or something," the second man said.

The third man laughed. "There ain't no doubt about that."

"Ha, ha. Very funny," said the first man. "Maybe one of you would like to try."

They debated this for a minute, neither of the other two wanting to, but finally the second man said he would.

I tossed him an apple, and, trembling, he approached the fence. "Here, Boy. Here's an apple for you."

Again, Cashmere rose, squealing, and the man quickly retreated.

They reasoned that maybe it was because they drove him, so the third man tried, but the result was the same. "Well, doesn't that beat all," the third man said, after he had taken up a position a safe distance from the fence. "It's like the horse thinks this young man belongs to him, or the horse to him, or something."

They sat there watching as I continued to brush Cashmere, each trying to come up with an explanation as to his behavior. No one had a final conclusion, and I was as much at a loss about it as anyone.

Eventually they tired of it all and climbed into their vehicles and left. I finished brushing Cashmere and stood back to look at him. Once he was brushed, he was an especially handsome horse. I had thought he was a blackish-gray, but he was actually a pure, shiny black, with a small white blaze down half of his nose. He also had four white stocking feet. He nuzzled me, and I pulled out one more apple. "It's the last one, buddy."

I crossed through the fence and walked to my pickup. When I did, he suddenly panicked. He ran up and down along the fence, whinnying to me. I made my way back to the fence, and he stuck his nose over. "It's okay, buddy. This is your home now. I will come take care of you now and then."

He whinnied his concern, but just then one of the mares pushed her way around the old gelding and trotted over to Cashmere. "Now he can make some friends, and all will be okay," I thought.

# Chapter Three
# The Fight

After the first mare got past the gelding, nothing seemed to hold back the others. They surged around him on both sides. He didn't like it and nipped at them. One of them nipped back, and another spun and caught him hard with a hoof to his chest. He backed off.

But as the mares gathered around Cashmere and started sniffing and nuzzling him, the old gelding, whom Brenda called Tor, became visibly angry. He started pawing the ground, rearing, snorting, and trumpeting a challenge to Cashmere.

As for Cashmere, he didn't seem too sure that he liked the attention. He kept backing away. But the more timid he became, the more irresistible he seemed to the mares. They nuzzled and sniffed him. Finally, he turned, pushed his way out of the center of the huddle, and headed full speed across the pasture. The mares took off after him, but within seconds he was far ahead.

When he reached the far fence and turned, they also turned. Each time he reached a new fence and turned, they turned right where they were as if they were running at his side. It was as if they were making a miniature lap around the pasture as he was making a bigger one. As he ran the last stretch to the gate where I was, they raced there as well, reaching it at about the same time.

The mares started nuzzling him again, and I swear I saw him roll his eyes. I didn't know if it had to do with the fact that they were all past breeding age or if he was just more interested in running, but after another few minutes of their attention, he turned and headed around the pasture again. This continued again and again until the mares grew tired of chasing him and just waited for him to come back.

The whole time Tor continued snorting and rearing, throwing out his challenge. He became more and more annoyed that Cashmere didn't seem to get it, so he tried something new.

As Cashmere would take off for his lap around the pasture, Tor would take off after him, as if he was chasing him away. Tor quickly fell behind, and would then turn and come back triumphantly with his head held high as if he had scared off this new stranger.

But I could see the angst in his eyes each time Cashmere came around the last turn heading back toward the gate.

After a few times of thinking he had chased him off, only to have him come back, Tor decided it was time to throw down the gauntlet. As Cashmere came around the last corner, Tor moved into his path. Cashmere was coming so fast he plowed through Tor like he wasn't even there, sending him rolling.

That was it. Tor had had enough. He struggled back up and moved in like he was going for the kill. He smashed his way through the mares and threw himself against Cashmere. Cashmere seemed unfazed. But then Tor rose on his back feet, and, like a boxer, struck out with a hoof, catching Cashmere in the nose.

Cashmere was surprised and backed up. Tor seemed to feel he had this newcomer on the ropes and rose again, striking Cashmere in the face once more. But Cashmere still seemed reluctant to fight.

I didn't know what to do. I was afraid one of them might get hurt, and I wasn't sure what I would tell Brenda, but I knew a human wouldn't fare too well trying to break up a horse fight.

Cashmere moved to the side, and I realized he planned to just take another loop around the pasture. But Tor had other ideas. He was going to finish this fight once and for all. He quickly moved to block Cashmere's running path.

This seemed to anger Cashmere more than being hit in the face. As Tor rose to strike again, Cashmere did as well. His long, sleek body rose almost another half higher than Tor's pudgy one. Tor struck out, but he couldn't come anywhere near Cashmere's head. Tor's hooves only pawed open air near Cashmere's underbelly. But Cashmere struck downward, hitting Tor on top of the head, dropping him to his knees.

The mares had moved back, and their whinnying and snorting sounded like cheerleaders cheering their favorite fighter. The way they swung their heads and pranced, I think they wanted Cashmere to win, though they seemed reluctant to antagonize Tor in case things turned out in his favor.

I thought that Tor would quit after being knocked to the ground, but he seemed to know that if he lost this battle, he would lose his position forever, and he quickly scrambled up.

Cashmere had moved to make a run again, but once more

Tor blocked his path. Being stopped from running a second time, Cashmere seemed determined to stay and finish the fight.

Both horses squealed, rose, and struck out. Tor's hooves again missed their mark, and once more Cashmere knocked Tor to his knees. Tor wasn't anything if he wasn't persistent, and again and again he struggled back up. But each time he rose to fight, he put more distance between himself and Cashmere. This only worked to Cashmere's advantage, since Tor couldn't reach Cashmere, but Cashmere could still strike Tor.

Finally, they both rose one last time, and when Tor struck out, Cashmere not only struck down on Tor's head, but threw his whole body at him. Tor not only went down, but the force rolled him onto his back.

I was afraid Cashmere would strike while Tor was down, possibly killing him, but he didn't. Instead he simply reared and squealed as if asking Tor if he had had enough.

And Tor had had enough. He rolled to his stomach, struggled to stand, and, weaving like he was drunk, wobbled his way to the far corner of the pasture. He hung his head, and I felt sorry for him.

Cashmere, having cleared that up, quit rearing, and just threw his head up and down a few times. But when the mares moved in to surround their new champion, Cashmere didn't like it and turned for another run.

The mares again took up the chase, but, falling behind, just turned and disgustedly walked back to the gate. When Cashmere came around the corner near where Tor was, Tor dropped his head further, submissive in his loss.

Cashmere just flew past him, acting as if the fight had never happened. When he came back to the gate, the mares immediately surrounded him again.

Cashmere seemed to have taken all of the attention he could stand from the mares. He snorted at them and shook his head at them, but it just seemed to make him all the more enticing. He kept backing away, but soon he was in the corner with nowhere to go.

He suddenly stopped shaking his head and snorting, and looked past the mares toward Tor. Cashmere seemed to be thinking. Suddenly he busted his way past the mares and headed straight for Tor with the mares trailing after. I felt some anxiety, wondering if Cashmere was going to attack again, even though I couldn't think of any reason why he would.

When he reached Tor, the old gelding trembled in front of him. Cashmere stopped and flipped his head up and down and whinnied. It wasn't an angry whinny, but more of a friendly, anxious invitation. Tor raised his head, confused at this friendliness.

I said to myself, "Cashmere, what are you doing?"

Cashmere grew more anxious and desperate in his whinnies as the mares approached. Finally, just as they moved up close, Cashmere moved around to the other side of Tor and pushed him toward the mares. Tor seemed as confused as I was. It was as if Cashmere was saying, "You want them, you got them."

The mares tried to push past Tor, but Cashmere kept Tor between him and them as much as possible. Then, suddenly, he broke free and headed around the pasture again.

I wondered if he would ever get tired of running, but he never seemed to. He would only give himself time to rest, and he was ready to go again. The mares followed him for some distance and then gave up. When Cashmere made his lap, he continued on to the gate where I was.

He put his head over the fence and I stroked his nose. "Are those old mares annoying you? Can't run with all of their attention, can you?" He threw his head up and down as if agreeing with me.

The mares saw him at the gate and started in his direction. Tor didn't try to stop them, other than whinnying, asking them to stay. A couple of them started toward Cashmere, but then turned back to Tor. I think they must have had enough of Cashmere's rejection.

The other two continued on to the gate where we were and started nuzzling Cashmere. He took it only for a few minutes, and then turned and headed to Tor. Once more he positioned himself on the other side of Tor from the mares.

I laughed. "You are trying to lead them back to Tor, aren't you, boy?"

And that was exactly what he was doing. The two mares followed him over, and, as soon as they arrived, Cashmere took another loop around the pasture.

I shook my head. "Aren't you ever going to get tired of running?"

This time the mares didn't even leave Tor. He moved out with the mares gathered around him and started eating grass. When Cashmere finished his loop, he came back to the gate. Once more, I scratched his nose. "Well, Old Buddy, I thought I had seen some interesting animal dynamics, but this one takes the cake."

I had watched them for way too long and knew I should get to other work. I scratched his nose for another minute. "You be good here, Buddy, and I'll be back later today to check on you."

I started to leave, and he grew anxious. He started whinnying to me. I went back and petted him just a bit more. "You'll be okay. I've got to go take care of the other horses."

I climbed into my pickup, and I almost feared his concern would cause him to go through the gate to get to me. I started down the road in my pickup, and he ran the whole way beside me inside the fence until he came to the edge of the pasture. Even with my window closed I could hear him calling to me as I continued on my way.

As I drove along, I suddenly thought of Hannah. She was so anxious when I left. I thought I had better give her a call. I pulled into a gas station. I searched my wallet and the pickup and finally found a dime.

I went to the phone booth and dialed my home number.

"Hello?" Hannah answered.

"Hello, Hon," I said.

"Are you all right?" she blurted into the phone.

"Oh, yes. I'm fine. In fact, that is why I am calling. I thought you might be concerned."

"What happened? Did he try to attack you? Is he mean?"

I laughed. "Not to me. With me he is as gentle as a lamb."

"What do you mean 'with you?'"

"I'll tell you all about it when I get home. I still need to feed the other horses before I come."

"Okay. It will be good to have you back safely home."

I could sense the relief in her voice as she said that. I hurried over to the other horses and took care of them. When I finished, I decided I should go back around by the pasture and check to make sure everything was well there. The fences weren't good enough to hold Cashmere if he decided to go over them. I filled a small bucket with grain, and then considered that I might make the other horses jealous, so I filled a second bucket.

When I arrived at the pasture, Cashmere was grazing beside Tor with the mares all around. The instant he saw me, he was on his way over. The others followed. I climbed through the fence with the two buckets of grain. I poured a small pile on the ground for Cashmere, and then I moved over a little and poured the rest in a line.

Cashmere started eating his, and the other horses came over and started eating the other. One mare came over to share Cashmere's, but a quick squeal from him told her to go back to her own.

As he ate, I rubbed my hand along his back. All of my previous brushing was pretty much for nothing. With all of his running, the sweat had mixed with dust, and he was dirtier than before.

I got my brush from the pickup and brushed him for a minute. When he finished his grain, he continued to stand there, reveling in the attention. Whenever I quit, he would turn with his head and give me a nudge as if to tell me to keep going.

By this time, Tor and the mares had moved back to their grazing. When I climbed through the fence to leave, Cashmere once more threw his head up and down and whinnied.

I scratched his head. "Don't worry, boy. I'll be back again."

Once more he chased along as I left.

When I arrived at home, Hannah was still quite anxious. She had to hear the whole story. After I had told her most of it, she asked, "Then is he really as mean as they say?"

I told her about how the other men came up while I was brushing him, and how he acted toward them.

"What if he turns on you someday?" she said, the anxiousness

24

telling in her voice.

"That's the funny thing about it. I almost feel like he thought they were bad and he was protecting me from them. He never wants me to leave. It's as if he is attached to me for some reason."

"Why?"

I shrugged. "I don't know. Maybe I'll know more when Brenda comes and tells me what his story is." I suddenly remembered something. "Speaking of Brenda, I had better call her and tell her how it all went."

I called the number she had left, and after it rang quite a few times, the pleasant voice of a lady came on the line. "Hollywood Marriot. This is Marianne speaking. How may I help you?"

I told her that I had called the number Brenda had given to me, but it rang through to her.

"She must be out presently," Marianne said. "Would you like me to leave her a message?"

"Yes. Please tell her that Tom Johnson called."

She said she would, and I hung up.

When I put the phone in its cradle, I felt a tug on my pants. I looked down at my little daughter. "Me go wif you? See Jackie and Patches?"

I picked her up in my arms. "Sweetheart, Daddy will take you again when he is sure it is safe. We have a new horse, and I want to check him out for a while."

She didn't seem to like my answer, and buried her head in my neck and cried. "Well," I said, "maybe we could all go, and you could see the new horse out in his pasture."

"Are you sure it will be safe?" Hannah asked.

"Sure. We'll just stay outside the fence."

I helped Kaylynn get her shoes on while Hannah bundled up our one-year-old daughter, Caroline, whom we called Linny. I grabbed a handful of apples, we loaded into our pickup, and we were on our way.

As soon as we arrived at the pasture, Cashmere thundered his way over to the gate by where we parked. Hannah looked up at him through the pickup window and gasped. "My heavens! He's huge!"

As I got out of the pickup, she called after me. "You aren't going to get near him, are you?"

"It's okay. Watch."

I walked up to the gate, and he reached his nose toward me. I rubbed his nose. He could smell the apples, so I pulled one from my pocket. He threw his head up and down, begging. I broke one into pieces and held it flat in the palm of my hand. He gently took it from me with his lips, tickling my palm.

Kaylynn started to call, asking to join me. I went back and pulled her from her car seat.

"Are you sure?" Hannah asked.

I nodded. "It will be all right."

When I got close enough to the fence so that he could reach her, he put his nose down to us and sniffed her. His breath blew into her neck, and she giggled. "Jackie," she said.

I smiled. "Horsey. Cashmere."

Kaylynn repeated what I said. "Hosey. Casmer."

Seeing how gentle he was with Kaylynn, Hannah checked to find that Linny was asleep, and then she decided to join us. I wondered if he would react to her as he had to the men. But when she stepped from the pickup and started to walk in our direction, Cashmere pricked up his ears. He didn't get upset, though he seemed excited, snorting and whinnying. Hannah backed up to safety behind the pickup.

When Hannah moved away, he became more excited, whinnying as if he was calling to her.

"What is it with this horse?" Hannah called.

"I don't know," I replied. "But he's not acting mean like he did with the men. It's more like he is calling to you. I think he wants you to come."

"Well, I think you better stay away from him. He seems unpredictable."

"No," I said. "It's not that he's unpredictable, but there seems to be something about who he trusts and what he wants. Come closer and see what he does."

Hannah slowly came out from behind the pickup, and Cashmere calmed down. His whinnies grew softer. He leaned out far across the fence, as if trying to reach to her. She paused a few feet away, and he started whinnying anxiously, as if begging. Still holding Kaylynn in one arm, I went to Hannah and put my arm around her. "Come on. It will be okay. Walk with me."

Reluctantly, she moved toward the gate with me. Cashmere started breathing excitedly. "Good boy, Cashmere," I said.

I kept talking to him as we moved closer, keeping Hannah close beside me with my arm around her. His whinnying subsided, though he breathed strong breaths. When we were close enough, he shoved his nose into Hannah's chest, as if trying to hug her with his head. This scared Hannah, and she backed up. "He's trying to shove me away."

"No, he's not," I said. "He's trying to tell you he likes you. It's almost like he thinks he knows you already. Kind of like he did when I first met him."

I reached my hand out and petted his nose and told her to do the same. "Move slowly and don't jerk back, especially out of fear."

"Oh, right!" she muttered. "I can hardly keep myself from running right now."

I put my hand right by hers, and slowly we reached out together. Finally we touched his nose. After she had stroked his nose a couple of times, his breathing slowed and he nuzzled her.

I broke up an apple and handed her a piece. She reached out with it, but just as his nose touched her hand, she dropped the apple and jerked her hand back. Cashmere immediately snorted.

"No, no, Cashmere," I said, trying to speak calmly. "It's okay."

Once more I gave Hannah a piece of apple, and this time, though she was trembling, she held the apple until he had taken it from her hand. She laughed as his lips tickled her palm.

I had her feed him a few more pieces of apple, and he just kept nuzzling her.

"I would like to try something else, now," I told Hannah. "Would you try staying here if I move away?"

"I don't know. He's still kind of scary."

We stayed there together for a little while longer, than she agreed to try it.

"As I move away, just keep talking gently to him," I said.

I took Kaylynn, and we moved away while Hannah fed him another piece of apple I had left with her, and he continued nuzzling her for more.

"What is it with him?" Hannah asked. "I've never seen a horse act like this."

"I'm not sure," I replied. "With the men he reared and snorted and all sorts of things. With you, it is more of anxiousness, like he was calling you, wanting you near, upset when you would leave. It was kind of like that when he saw me. It's like he felt we are good and those men are not."

Hannah continued to stroke his nose. "He's so big and beautiful."

"You ought to see him run," I said as I joined her again.

"I'd like to."

I pushed him. "Go. Go run, Buddy."

He didn't move, other than to lean back over the fence.

Hannah laughed. "He's not going anywhere as long as he thinks we still have apples."

I tucked the last two apples deep into my pocket. "Now, go run."

He didn't move, so I pushed him again. "Go run, and I'll give you another apple."

I pushed him a couple more times, and then, suddenly, he turned and headed across the pasture, his tail and head high. He flew along the fence line.

"Wow!" Hannah exclaimed.

Kaylynn started clapping. "Hosey Casmer pritty!"

"Yes," I said. "The horsey is pretty." I laughed as he turned along the fence on the far side. "He's also a bit of a show off."

As he came rushing back to the gate, Hannah backed away. But he slid to a stop and reached his nose over the fence.

I handed the apple to Hannah. "You reward him."

She did, and he ate it and reached out and nuzzled her for another one. "Push him and tell him to run," I told her. She did, but he didn't move. I waved my hand lightly. "Go, Cashmere. Go run!"

He immediately raced around the field again and came back, breathing hard. I pulled the last apple from my pocket and handed it to Hannah. She fed it to him, and he munched it for quite a while, happily chewing every piece. Without us saying anything, he turned and ran around the pasture again. When he got back, he reached out his nose expectantly.

"Sorry, Boy," I said. "I don't have any more apples." He seemed disappointed, but appeared to understand.

As we continued to pet him, Hannah suddenly noticed his front knees. "What happened to his legs?"

I shrugged. "I'm not sure. It looks like some kind of injury that didn't heal correctly. Maybe Brenda can tell us more when she comes."

We petted him a little bit longer, and then decided to head to the zoo. As we left, he grew anxious, and whinnied and whinnied. As we drove off, he raced along the fence as if trying to stay with us. As we drove beyond the end of the pasture, I looked in the rearview mirror. I could tell by the way he was moving his head that he was whinnying to us, even though I couldn't hear him.

We drove to the zoo and parked as close to a tree as we could, hoping for shade. The zoo was one of our favorite places to go. It had a little box at the front for modest donations. Since we were college students, we couldn't afford too much, but we always put in some. We had brought popsicles with us.

Once we got to the zoo, Linny woke up. The four of us went in and found a bench. We sat down and Hannah, Kaylynn, and I started eating our popsicles. Kaylynn soon left hers and headed over to watch the peacocks. We enjoyed feeding the fish and the deer the pellets that we could buy for a dime, but our topic of discussion always came back to Cashmere.

All too soon the sun was dropping behind the horizon, and Kaylynn was asleep in my arms. We loaded into our pickup and headed on our way home. As we drove, Hannah expressed the thought that was foremost on our minds. "I can't wait until Brenda gets back and can tell us more about that horse."

## Chapter Four
## Running Free

The phone was ringing when we arrived home. I hurriedly unlocked the door and ran to answer it. I heard Brenda's panicked voice on the other end of the line.

"You had me so scared. Since you left a message at the hotel desk I have been calling and calling thinking something was wrong. I even called the Logan hospital to see if you had been admitted."

"Well, you know, Brenda," I joked, "an increase in your heart rate is good for you now and then."

"Yeah, but a heart attack isn't. So tell me how it all went!"

"It went fine. I had them back up close to the gate, and then the men left me alone to unload him."

"They left you to do it alone? Those useless cowards!"

I laughed. "It's okay. I think it turned out better that way."

"What do you mean?"

I told her the whole story, including how I fed him apples and brushed him. She was really quiet until I got to the part about brushing him.

"You got in the pen with him?"

"Yes. He really liked the brushing I gave him."

"He didn't try to kill you?"

"Oh, no. Not at all. He sure didn't like those guys that drove the truck, though. When they came back with their friend, he wanted to attack them."

"What happened?"

I told her all about it, and then said, "I've never seen any horse act like he does. If it is anyone besides me or Hannah, he gets upset." I then told her about taking Hannah and my girls over there.

She expressed her concern, and I assured her that I kept them outside the fence. "But it is interesting," I continued. "He seemed to immediately like us and is upset when we leave. He sure didn't have that same opinion of those men."

"Well," Brenda said, "there might be a reason. I can't really explain it on the phone, because I need to show you something, but please be careful."

I promised I would, and then I asked her a question. "Brenda, what is the deal with this horse, anyway? All he seems to want to do is run."

"What do you mean?"

I told her about his running and about the fight with Tor. I told how he had tried to push Tor to the mares so they wouldn't interfere with his runs around the pasture. "There are just so many strange things about him. Can you tell me more?"

Brenda laughed. "All in good time. All in good time. My phone bill won't hold up under all the things I need to tell you about him."

"When will you be back?" I asked.

"In three weeks, if everything goes as planned," she replied.

As we hung up, I knew it was going to be a long three weeks.

Through the next two weeks I went out each evening to feed the horses. I went to the pasture each night to take the horses a little grain, but mostly I knew it was just an excuse to see Cashmere run. I couldn't explain the feeling, but there was a thrill that ran through me as I watched him, and Cashmere seemed friendlier to me every day.

The second weekend after he had arrived, after I had taken care of the other horses, I loaded up a little grain and some fencing tools and headed over to the pasture. Cashmere and Tor were grazing side by side as if they were best friends. A person wouldn't have any reason to think they had ever fought at all. The mares, for their part, just acted like Cashmere was another horse, and he seemed to like it that way.

As soon as I pulled up, the horses came running, with Cashmere at the lead. I poured out the grain, spreading it out so everybody could have their share.

I grabbed my fencing tools and walked along the fence line. The fence along the road was actually the best one, but there were a few staples missing. I tacked them back up and then climbed through the fence to check out the other three sides.

I hadn't gone too far when I realized I was being tailed. I turned, and Cashmere was right behind me. Once I stopped, he nuzzled me.

"Okay, okay," I said. "I do have apples for you. But you've got to go run to get one."

As if he totally understood what I said, he took off for a lap around the pasture. I marveled again at his speed and grace. With his head high and his tail arched, he was amazing to watch. He slid to a stop in front of me, breathing hard. "Show off," I said, as I pulled an apple out of my pocket and broke off a piece for him.

I began working my way along the fence, stapling up the wire, and stretching the net fence back into place where the winter snow had bent it over.

Soon Cashmere was back by me. He started nuzzling me again. I tried to ignore him, so he pushed harder. I still ignored him, and he pushed me so hard I lost my balance and landed on the fence.

"Hey! Watch it!"

He whinnied like he was laughing.

"Oh, you think that's funny? Ha, ha. I'm laughing. Not!"

He took off for another lap around the pasture and came panting up to me. He nuzzled me, his heavy breath blasting my face.

"Wow! What have you been eating, a dead skunk?"

Still, I pulled the broken apple from my pocket. "You think you should get this just because you did a run? I didn't tell you to run. You did that on your own."

He nuzzled me as if to tell me to quit teasing and give him the apple. I held it out in the palm of my hand, and he carefully pulled it into his mouth.

I rubbed my hand along his back and shoulders. "I do have to admit that I like to see you run. But I don't get anything done when I'm just watching you."

I went back to work and continued my way along the fence. Soon he joined me again, begging for more.

"Hey! Do I look like an apple tree to you?"

He nodded his head and whinnied.

"Well, for your information, I'm not."

I started back to work, trying to ignore his persistence. I pulled the wire up tight, put a staple over it, and reached for my hammer. It wasn't there. I was sure I had set it down right next to me. I looked all around me, still trying to keep the wire up in place. Cashmere made a funny whinnying sound, and I thought he was begging for another apple. "Not now, Cashmere," I said, turning to look at him. "I need to find . . ."

I stopped. He had my hammer in his mouth. "Okay, Cashmere," I said, "bring me the hammer."

He responded by backing up and curling up his lips like he was laughing. "Cashmere, seriously, I have work to do. Give me my hammer."

He whinnied like he was saying, "Come and get it."

I dropped the wire and tossed the staple back in the bucket. I started walking toward him, and he started backing up. I increased my speed, and just as I was almost to him, he flipped around and took off with my hammer still in his mouth. Instinctively, I took off running after him, but I quickly fell behind, and I knew catching him was impossible.

But he couldn't run very fast carrying a hammer in his mouth, so he soon dropped it and made a run around the pasture. I retrieved the hammer and walked back to my fence while Cashmere finished his lap. He joined me and nudged me for an apple.

"Hey, I'm not giving you an apple. You were a naughty horse, stealing my hammer."

He backed up and leaned his head to one side and slightly down.

"Oh, don't give me the puppy horse eyes," I said. "You aren't even sorry you took it." But he continued to look at me like he couldn't believe I didn't give him an apple for his run. Finally, I set down my tools, broke an apple into pieces, and gave him one. "But don't think I will be rewarding naughtiness."

I put the hammer on the ground and put my foot on it so he couldn't steal it. I lifted the wire into place and reached for a staple, but the bucket wasn't there. I didn't even search for it. I turned, and, sure enough, Cashmere had it, holding it by the handle in his mouth.

I groaned. "Cashmere, give me my bucket of staples."

His eyes sparkled with mischievousness as he backed a step away and curled his lips into his teasing grin. Despite my frustration in trying to get my work done, I had to laugh. I had never seen an animal that was such a prankster.

I let go of the wire and started walking slowly to him, knowing he would spill all of the staples if he dropped the bucket. "Okay, Cashmere, give me my bucket of staples."

Cashmere kept backing away. When I was almost up to him, I lunged for the bucket. He spun as he had before and took off across the pasture with the bucket in his mouth. He kept his head turned to the side as he ran so the swinging bucket didn't hit his long legs. I knew very well what was going to happen, and ran after him. Sure enough, after about 75 yards he dropped the bucket as he thundered on his way. When the bucket hit the ground, it bounced a couple of times, spilling staples everywhere.

It wasn't as bad as it could have been, but still I had to dig through dirt and grass to retrieve as many as possible. I didn't want them getting into the horses' hooves. I was still hard at it when Cashmere finished his run and came sauntering up, acting like he should have an apple.

He whinnied to me. "Oh, right," I said. "You think I'm going to give you an apple when you spilled all of my staples?"

Cashmere hung his head briefly, then looked up at me and whinnied. "Oh, no, you're not forgiven that quickly. You've been a naughty, naughty horse."

He walked over to me, head hanging down. He put his head right beside me and looked out the corner of his eyes as if checking to make sure I saw how penitent he was. "Right," I said. "You haven't changed. You'd do it again as soon as I turned my back."

I finally finished picking up what staples I could find, found my pliers and fencing tool, and started back to the fence. Cashmere followed me, head still hanging. When I got to the fence, I put my hammer in the bucket with the other tools and put the bucket between my feet to protect it. Cashmere nudged me, and I laughed. "All right. It's hard to stay mad at you. Go run and I'll give you another apple."

He seemed to understand me more than any animal I had ever been around. As soon as I said it, he was off. He made his run and came panting back to me. I broke the apple and gave him his piece.

I continued to work, to watch him run, to feed him apples, and to talk to him like he was human. There was so much about him that made me feel like he understood more than a person might think he did.

With me protecting my fencing equipment, he quit teasing me – mostly. He did get hold of my pliers once and took off with them. I searched where I thought he had dropped them, but couldn't find them. I told him I was mad and went back to fencing. A few minutes later he came back, head hanging, with the pliers in his mouth. He dropped them by me. I did give him an apple for that, although I didn't know if I was rewarding good behavior or bad.

I had worked almost all morning, and was getting close to being done patching up the worst segment of fence, when he finished another run and begged for some more apple.

"Sorry, boy, I only have one left, and I am saving it for something special."

He begged and nuzzled and whinnied, but I wouldn't give in. There was something I just had to do.

I hadn't dared tell Hannah what I had in mind, because I was sure it would have scared her too much. But every time I watched Cashmere run around that pasture, I felt an urge to be on his back, to feel the wind in my hair, and to be moving with him.

That desire had built in me to the point it was almost uncontrollable. I didn't even really understand it. But, somehow, I just had to ride him.

I finished the last section of fence and walked over to the gate. He followed me, as I was sure he would. I set my tools outside the fence, and then I climbed up on a post. I broke the apple into two pieces and held one out for him.

At first he came straight toward me. I knew I couldn't jump on his head. I moved my arm to the side, and he followed it. He was still a distance away, so I put the apple piece in my other hand and held it out to the other side of me. He turned and walked to my other hand.

I felt he was close enough I could make the jump, as long as he didn't move. I gave him the apple, then reached out and placed my hands on his back. He didn't move. I laid my chest on him. He didn't move, though I could feel him tremble a little. I rested my weight on him, and again he didn't move, though he turned his head to look at me.

I thought about how stupid I was. I wasn't even sure he was broken to ride. But after being around him, I felt he had to be. Finally, I carefully reached my foot out. I could only get up to my calf over him and still hold on to the post. When I let my foot rest on him, he trembled, as if he was excited, not as if he would jump. He had finished the apple, but still he didn't move.

My heart was racing faster than I could ever remember it doing before. It was about to pound its way up my throat. But I knew I had to take a chance. I just had to. I didn't know why, but I did.

I took a huge breath and jumped. I barely had time to grab his mane, and he was off. I wasn't on straight, but I was able to pull myself completely on by the time I saw us approaching the fence on the far side of the pasture.

He was heading straight for it, and I could swear he didn't plan to slow down at all. I had seen him run this before, and knew he turned as if on a banked race track. I clamped my legs tightly and leaned to anchor my body in preparation for the turn.

And turn he did. We turned so quickly I knew I would have gone over the fence if I hadn't been ready.

After we made the turn my feeling of fear subsided, being replaced with pure exhilaration. Looking down I could see the ground flashing by at a horrendous pace. I could feel his muscles expanding and contracting like a giant spring in rhythm with the movement of his legs.

We were approaching the next corner, so I gripped against him with my legs locking myself to him. Again, he hardly slowed as we made the turn.

This side was the longest, as the pasture was not quite square, so I urged him on. "Go, Cashmere, go!"

He didn't need my urging. He leaped forward even faster, stretching his legs out further and further. His head bobbed in time with his legs. I felt like we were in a race, not a race against other horses, but instead it felt like a race against everything earthbound. It felt like we were soaring, free from anything that held us down. It was just Cashmere and me under a clear blue sky in a wide open space.

As we approached the next turn, I once more prepared for it by locking myself to him. As we made the turn, I saw something I didn't expect. A car full of people had stopped on the side of the road, and they were watching us. This really annoyed me. The pasture was on the foothills of the mountain on a seldom traveled road, and I didn't think

34

anyone would bother us. This was supposed to be my moment with Cashmere, free of observers, and free of anyone or anything else in the world.

Then another thought hit me. What if the people got out of their cars and approached the fence? Cashmere might rear as he did when he saw strangers. I was also concerned about what would happen when we reached the gate, because he often slid to a very abrupt stop.

I clamped my legs tighter than I ever had, unsure what would happen. But Cashmere didn't show any signs of slowing.

"Cashmere, what are you doing?" I asked.

But as if to answer my question, his speed only quickened. I knew we were going over the fence, or we were turning, because he didn't plan to stop. And as we approached the corner, he turned.

I was glad that I had prepared as well as I had, because the quick turn still almost unseated me. I figured I would be killed if I fell from the height of his back at the speed we were going.

This was the first time he had not stopped after one lap, and the mares got excited. They started running as if they were racing us. We caught them and quickly passed them. As we made the turn at the first corner I looked to see them turn as well as if they were once more running their smaller track.

After we made the second turn, I looked to the road and saw two cars stopped there with a third pulling in. How could there be so many? There was hardly ever a car on this road. I found myself yelling, "Go away!" but I could hardly hear myself amongst Cashmere's heavy breathing, the pounding of his hooves, and the wind rushing by.

When we made the final turn, Cashmere was breathing so hard I was concerned, but as we approached the gate, he still didn't slow. "Cashmere," I yelled, "you've got to stop, or you will kill yourself."

I let go of his mane briefly and reached both arms down around his neck and pulled back, trying to let him know I wanted him to stop. But if it had any effect, I couldn't tell. He approached the gate, only slowing from tiredness, and I quickly grabbed back onto his mane, knowing whether he suddenly stopped or made the turn, either way, I better be ready.

And he did turn. But he wasn't pushing quite as hard, and his breathing was so loud he sounded like a steam engine snorting air. I grew more and more concerned for him. "Whoa, boy! Just stop!"

But he continued to run, though gradually slower and slower. Finally, we made the last turn on that lap. Four cars were there by then, and some people had stepped out of them. I didn't know what Cashmere would do, but I knew all I could do was prepare and hold on.

As we approached the gate, Cashmere finally slowed to a trot, gasping for air, the people watching started to clap. As he pulled up to a stop, my fears came true as some of the people approached the fence.

Cashmere reared and squealed at them.

I hung on for my life, calling to him to calm him. "Down, Cashmere! It's okay."

He reared three times as the people dashed back behind their cars. Each time he rose, I could feel myself slipping a little more. I knew I didn't want to slide off the very back, or I would likely be trampled. Finally, knowing I couldn't hold on much longer, when his feet hit the ground, I swung my leg over and pushed hard away from him, afraid I might land under his hooves.

I landed on my feet, but I was off balance, and I fell to my backside. With the people now a safe distance away, his attention turned to me, and he seemed concerned that I was hurt. He stepped over to me and nuzzled me. I grabbed his head, and he pulled me clear off the ground before I could let go.

I started rubbing his head. "Good boy!"

One man called out to me, "Are you okay?"

"Yes." But, then, as the people started coming toward us again, I called to them. "Please stay back. He doesn't like strangers."

Cashmere nuzzled me, and I remembered I still had half of an apple. I pulled it out and held it for him. "That was awesome, Buddy. But I'm not sure I should ever do that again."

As I slipped out to get my brush, he whinnied his concern about me leaving. Some of the people climbed back in their cars and left, but the others surrounded me, and that really seemed to frighten Cashmere. He seemed afraid they'd hurt me, and he started rearing and squealing. I called to him, and he eventually calmed down.

As I was grabbing the brush, one man said, "Wow! That was some magnificent riding!"

"I have never seen a horse run like that!" another man chimed in.

"Is he a race horse?" a little girl asked.

I knelt down by her. "I really don't know. I'm just the one that takes care of him."

"Can I go pet him?" she asked.

"I'm afraid not. He doesn't seem to trust most people. You saw how he reared when people approached the fence?" She nodded, so I continued. "He always does that when someone he doesn't know comes near."

"Who owns him?" the girl's father asked.

"The lady I work for," I answered. "She had him shipped here. She said she'd tell me more about him when she comes, but she hasn't been here since then."

"You ought to see if you could enter him in some races," the first man said.

"That wouldn't be up to me," I replied. "That would be up to Brenda. But I doubt he would be allowed to race with the injuries he has had."

"What injuries?" the man inquired.

"It looks to me like his front knees have been broken and haven't healed properly," I told them.

They all strained to see, and one of them said, "Oh, yes, I see what you mean."

We talked a bit more, and then they all started to leave. As a lady moved around to get in her car, Cashmere felt she was too close and reared in agitation. The lady slid along her car and quickly slipped inside.

Soon Cashmere and I were alone again. I retrieved the brush and climbed inside the fence. He still seemed tense from having that many people around. "It's okay," I said, as I started brushing his neck. "They were really nice people. A little annoying, but nice."

He was still breathing hard. "You're a little winded, aren't you, boy?" I said. "I can't believe you can run that far, and especially that fast."

The longer I brushed him the more his breathing slowed. As I reached his shoulder, he turned back and nuzzled my pocket. "Sorry, Buddy. There aren't any more apples. Besides, if I feed you any more, you might end up getting sick. Brenda wouldn't like that."

I brushed him some more and continued talking to him. "Cashmere, why do you like Hannah and me, but no one else?" I asked.

He, of course, didn't answer, but as I continued to brush him, he leaned his head to one side as if he was half asleep, and his eyes drooped. "Tired?" I asked.

His only response was to droop his eyes a little more. When I finished brushing him, I packed up to leave. He grew quite excited.

"Why are you always so concerned about me leaving, Buddy?" I asked. "I promise I'll be back."

But when I drove away, he again raced along the fence, whinnying. As for me, I knew I would never be the same. Having once ridden the wind, it would be impossible to be satisfied having my feet always planted on earth.

And there were so many things about him that I wanted to know. I hoped Brenda would be there the next week, like she said.

# Chapter Five
# Brenda Comes
# Home

**B**renda called and said she would be home on Saturday and would meet me at the horse pasture. I could hardly wait to see her and see what Cashmere's reaction would be to her. But more than anything, I wanted to hear more about him. He fascinated me. He seemed far smarter than any horse I had worked with. But more than that, there was something deep within him that seemed to speak to me.

After I got up that morning, I quickly ate breakfast. I didn't want to be late. In fact, I wanted to be there early, not wanting Brenda to get close to him without me being there. I hurriedly stuffed some apples in my pocket and headed on my way. I stopped and got some grain at the barns, but I was still almost a half hour ahead of the appointed time. Yet, when I pulled onto the road leading to the pasture, I could see Brenda's pickup just pulling up to the pasture.

I increased my speed to faster than I normally felt comfortable driving, especially on a gravel road, but by the time I arrived, Brenda was already approaching the pasture gate. The horses had come running when they saw Brenda's pickup because I drove it on days I had to haul hay, and they thought it must be time for their grain.

I pulled my pickup to a quick stop, but before I could get out, Brenda had reached the fence. Cashmere went crazy, squealing, rearing, and shaking his head. The other horses backed away from him and away from the fence.

Brenda fell back in surprise and retreated behind her pickup. As I came up near her, she turned to me. "I thought you said he was gentle!"

"I said he was gentle with Hannah and me," I replied. "You stay here and watch."

I walked to the fence and called to him. He immediately stopped rearing and nickered softly to me. I pulled an apple from my pocket and split it. He reached across the fence and nuzzled me. I put a piece of the apple in the palm of my hand, and he took it from me with his lips tickling my hand. I scratched his neck as he chewed on the piece I gave him.

"Watch this!" I called to Brenda.

I climbed through the fence and rubbed my hand along his back. He didn't stir, except to put his head against me and push me as if to tell me to do more.

"Here's the best part," I told her. "Watch him run!"

I gave him a little push. "Go, Buddy. Go run, and I'll give you some more."

He didn't need any more encouragement. He turned and headed full speed across the pasture. His head was high and his tail arched upward as he flew along the fence line.

Brenda came back up to the gate. "Wow! He's beautiful!"

I smiled. "I think he is just about the most amazing horse I have ever known."

The other horses ran after him for a short distance, but quickly returned to grazing.

Cashmere barely slowed at the turns. There was now a path around the pasture, the grass worn completely away, and a slight dusting of dirt flew up behind him. As he ran, I felt as if I was again on his back, the wind rushing past me, his speed a feeling of exhilaration to my own soul. I could feel my heart start to pound as the adrenaline poured into my bloodstream.

As he made the last turn, I suggested to Brenda that she go back behind the pickup and let me introduce her.

"Introduce me?" she asked.

"I think I can do something to get him to like you, but I'm not sure," I replied.

She took up her previous position, and Cashmere came flying toward me. As always, he didn't appear to be stopping, and Brenda yelled for me to watch out. But, as usual, he slid to a stop in front of me.

I gave him the other piece of the apple and petted him. "You're a good boy, Cash."

I then climbed out through the fence and turned to talk to him. "Cashmere, I want you to meet someone."

I split another apple, and then walked to where Brenda was. "Here," I said to her. "Take this piece of apple in one hand and link your other arm through mine."

She did as I said, and then we turned to walk toward Cashmere. I talked to him the whole time we approached. "Cashmere, this is Brenda.

She is my friend, and wants to be your friend, too."

As we kept coming, I kept talking. He snorted a little bit, and shook his head up and down, but he didn't rear or squeal. Finally, we got up to the fence, and I suggested Brenda give him the piece of apple.

Brenda had been around horses a lot, and yet she still trembled the slightest bit as she held it out due to his size. He reached out slowly, cautiously, and finally nuzzled the apple from her hand. As he ate it, we both reached up slowly to pet him. He snorted slightly as Brenda's hand came closer, but he didn't move. It took a few more slices of apple and some more petting before he finally seemed comfortable with her.

I stayed beside her a lot longer than I had with Hannah because Brenda made him nervous. And still, when I moved to get the grain and brush, leaving him with Brenda, he started to snort.

When I brought the grain back, I suggested that she feed him some of it. She did, and he calmed back down. I still didn't dare let her climb through the fence by him, so I did, and I poured out the piles the way I always did. The other horses came running to get their share.

I brushed him while he ate. Brenda walked over and flopped the tailgate down on her pickup, and sat down on it.

"He is really a good-looking horse," she said. "A whole lot better-looking than he appeared in that dark stall of his. But what I really can't believe is how gentle he is with you."

"I'll admit he scared me to death when I first saw him," I told her. "And when I was trying to get the gate shut and he slid to a stop that first time like you saw him do, I thought I was dead. But it's like . . ." I paused, not knowing how to put it into words.

"I'll tell you what it's like," Brenda said. "It's like he sees you as his savior from the dark world he was in. But I think there is even more."

That made me curious. I stopped brushing him and climbed through the fence. The horses finished their grain and moved off to graze. Cashmere begged another apple off of me, and then I told him to go graze, so he started eating grass close by, not wanting to be far away.

"What do you mean he sees me as his savior and more? What was his life like? And how can he run so fast? And where did he come from?"

Brenda held up her hand and laughed. "Slow down. One question at a time." She patted the tailgate beside herself. "You better have a seat. It's a long, long story, and I have something to show you, but the story comes first."

I sat down by her, and we watched Cashmere while Brenda told the story.

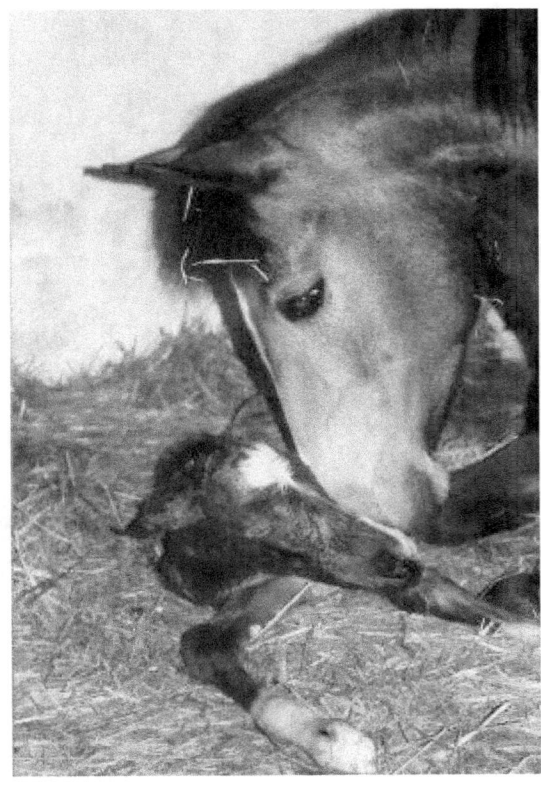

# Chapter Six
# The New Colt

Frans was enjoying the food at the party. Germany has some of the best Christmas celebrations in the world. But as the time for dancing grew closer, his anxiety increased. He felt awkward in the graces of the social elite. In addition, his concern for Midnight was growing. Finally, he slipped away to the front door and asked the butler for his coat. He had just slipped it on and turned to leave when he saw Anna.

"Where are you going, Frans?"

"I'm worried about Midnight. She is overdue and more than ready to foal, and I'm concerned something might go wrong."

Anna smiled her beautiful smile at him, and her blue eyes sparkled brighter than the lights on the Christmas tree. "It's Christmas Eve. You should be more interested in parties, food, and, of course, dancing."

He smiled at her vivaciousness. "I'm not sure there are any girls here who would want to dance with me, as old as I am."

Anna laughed. "I think that Frau Brauer would love to dance with you."

"Frau Brauer is old enough to be my grandmother's grandmother," Frans said. "I may be older than most of the young people here, but I'm not that old."

"But I saw her making eyes at you." Anna snickered.

"Only because her eyesight is so bad she was trying to figure out who I was."

Anna laughed, but quickly grew more serious, though her smile was constant. "I would save a dance for you, Frans, or even quite a few. I did ask you to be my guest this evening."

Frans could feel his face grow warm. "I would like that, Anna, and I have never appreciated an invite more, but I truly am worried about Midnight. She's old to be having a foal, and this one is really important. Besides, I'm not sure your father approves of me spending a lot of time with you since I'm just a horse trainer."

Her smile almost faded as she spoke strongly. "I've heard Father say you're the best horse trainer he has ever seen, despite your young age. Besides, I'd take a horse trainer any day over those highbrow boys that come around."

"I'm sure that those highbrow boys are much more in your league than I am."

Anna frowned. "I ought to slap you for that!"

"I didn't mean it as an insult, Anna. Your family is wealthy. My family is just common laborers."

"I like common people more than the rich and the airs they put on."

"Well, even still," Frans said, "you are young and stunningly beautiful, and I'm much older. I'm sure you could have your pick of any guy you wanted."

Even though Anna smiled at his compliment, the way she rolled her eyes told volumes even before she spoke. "Twenty-four is not that old. You act as if you're ready for a nursing home. And four years isn't that much difference in age between two people. Besides, my father would probably be glad to think I have any prospects at all. When I turned 20 this year and wasn't in a serious relationship, he acted like I was already an old maid."

Frans smiled. "I'm sure it wasn't quite that bad. I've seen the steady stream of richly dressed young men just about banging your door down."

"Yes, all thinking I should be thrilled to have their interest in me, when, in fact, I'm not. You remember, it was you I asked to be my guest."

"And I've enjoyed the evening immensely," Frans said. "But I am still worried about Midnight and her foal."

"Are you sure you aren't just trying to get away from me and the dancing?"

"I must admit," Frans replied, "that I don't feel that comfortable dancing. But that has nothing to do with you. I'm just not that graceful. I would never want to get away from you."

"Well, whatever," Anna said. "If you aren't going to stay for the dance, I'm not going to hang around those stick-in-the-mud guys. I'm coming with you."

Frans shook his head. "I don't think so. Your father will throw a fit if you leave."

"Let him. It will help him wear off some of the strong eggnog he has been drinking."

"But you can't go to the barns dressed in your Christmas dress!"

"Says who?"

"Well, me."

"And when did you become the boss of me?"

Frans could sense the challenge in Anna's voice, and knew he best back off. "I didn't. It's just a beautiful dress, and you could get it dirty."

"So I'll get it cleaned." Anna turned to the Butler. "Emerich, would you get my coat, please?"

"Of course, Frau Anna."

Anna sighed. "Don't be so formal, Emerich. Just Anna will do."

Emerich nodded. "Yes, Anna."

Once she had her coat on, she turned to Frans. "All right. I'm all set."

"All right, Just Anna."

Emerich smiled, and Anna giggled. "Very funny, Frans."

He grinned. "Seriously, though, don't you need to tell someone where you are going? They might worry if you just disappear."

"Let them worry." She looked at him and he frowned, so she rolled her eyes. "All right, I'll have Emerich tell Mother. But I'm not telling Father, because he'll make a big deal of it."

Emerich said he would relay the message, and then Anna grabbed Frans's hand. "Come on!" She almost dragged him out the door as she spoke. "What a relief to have an excuse to get out of here!"

When the door closed behind them, Frans felt he should pull his hand away, but Anna held even tighter when he tried. It wasn't that he didn't want to hold her hand, because he did. It was just that he didn't feel it was really appropriate. Anna might joke about their differences being minor, but he was sure her family wouldn't approve. And, in reality, he couldn't imagine that Anna really did herself, even if she teased him about it.

He glanced over at her. Her blond hair fell in long curls from underneath the hood of her coat, and then she turned and smiled at him, and her smile took his breath away. He quickly turned away, embarrassed to have her see him looking at her.

He had been only 19 when he had started working for Anna's father at Adler Farms, and at first Anna had annoyed him. He didn't feel a girl that was 15 should hang around the barns, the high-spirited horses, and especially the men.

Her father didn't think so, either. But the more Mr. Adler tried to stop her, the more she did it. She especially had hung close to Frans, and he had felt somewhat protective of her, even though her stubbornness had initially agitated him. But the more he got to know her, the more he realized that Anna was very real, and her stubbornness came from a determination not to be locked into the pomp of her family's wealth and position. She was nothing like her siblings. They wouldn't be caught dead hanging around the barns, except for an occasional ride. He liked them, but they just weren't Anna.

Both of Anna's older sisters had married sons of wealthy businessmen. Her younger brother was engaged to a daughter of a corporate CEO. And then there was Anna.

The biggest problem was that the more time she spent with him, the harder it was for him not to have feelings for her. He had seen her grow from a strong, determined young girl into a beautiful, strong, determined young woman. And, while his heart was telling him how nice her hand felt in his, his mind kept telling him it really didn't mean anything, and he couldn't let it.

As he reached for the door of the barn, Anna dropped his hand long enough for him to open it for them. But the minute they stepped into the barn, she grabbed his hand back again before he had a chance to even think about it. He wondered what her father would think if he saw them, alone, together, in the barn, holding hands, especially dressed in their Christmas party clothes.

He flipped the light switch, and the barn was flooded with light. As they walked toward Midnight's stall, he could tell by the way Anna was holding onto his hand that she didn't plan to let go, so he quit trying to pull away and enjoyed the moment.

But as they neared Midnight's stall, he could hear her groans. Anna must have heard it too, because she quickened her pace at exactly the same instant he did. When they reached the stall, he flicked the switch that bathed its occupant with light.

Midnight blinked her eyes, but didn't otherwise stir, other than to strain in birthing. At first glance, and the sight of a hoof, Frans felt happy. But then he realized something was dreadfully wrong. It was a back hoof, and there was only one. The colt was being born breach, and one hoof was still lodged inside.

As he pulled off his suit coat and pulled one arm out of his shirt, he didn't even have to tell Anna what was wrong. She had spent enough time with him and the horses that she already knew what had to be done. He spoke to her as he pulled the tie from around his neck.

"Anna, all of the men are off to Christmas parties. I might need some help. I think Johan is over at Kruger's. Would you please go call and see if you can get hold of him?"

"No, I won't!"

"But, Anna, I'm not sure I can do it alone. I really need . . ."

"What am I, chopped liver? I can help you."

"Anna, you are dressed in your Christmas dress."

"And you are dressed in your Christmas suit. It doesn't appear to be stopping you."

"But you are a . . ."

Frans stopped. He knew better than to finish that sentence, although he knew she was already going to be mad.

"I'm a what? Go ahead and say it. I'm a girl. That's what you were going to say, wasn't it?"

Frans half smiled at her belligerence. "Actually, I was going to say you're a lady."

Anna paused for a moment, the wind taken out of her sails, but only for a moment. "Lady or not, I can do almost anything a man can do, and do it better than most."

Frans had to admit that was true. He also knew better than to argue. Her help could make the difference between the colt living or dying. He finally nodded.

"Okay. I'm going to have to shove that hoof in and reach in and see if I can get the other one out. Even if I can, this won't be easy for Midnight with the colt being breach."

Anna nodded. "What do you want me to do?"

"Take her tail and pull it around as far as you can to give me more room to work."

Frans shivered in the cold December air. He tied twine to the hoof so he wouldn't lose it, and then he started shoving it back, but the minute he did, Midnight pushed against him. He stopped and waited for her to pause, and then he quickly shoved. He almost got it in before she pushed again.

It took a few more attempts before he could get the hoof back in enough he could reach past it. He felt around and felt the back hock of the other leg. He was relieved that it was close, but the hoof was still a long way away. He started to move his hand along the leg when Midnight pushed. Her muscles clamped around his arm, cutting off the blood until he felt his arm would fall off.

Finally she quit, and he pushed his arm in farther, feeling along the leg. He finally found the hoof, but at that angle he couldn't get enough of a grip on it to pull it free. He tried again and again, twisting his arm and body every way he could think of, but all to no avail. Time was passing, and with each minute there was more of a chance the colt would be lost. In addition, the pressure that Midnight's muscles were exerting on him was sapping his strength.

He knew he needed to do something to get a grip on that hoof, and he had to do it soon. He asked Anna to get him another piece of twine. She let go of the tail, and the pressure on his arm increased immensely. She handed him the twine and then, patiently, without a word of complaint, went back to her former position, all the time speaking words of encouragement to him and to Midnight.

Frans had to pull his arm out enough to grab the twine. It took him some time to move his hand back down to the hoof. He created a little loop around his fingers and worked to get it around the hoof. Each attempt met with failure. He kept trying because there were few other options. He was just about ready to give up and try to figure out something else when Midnight strained, and the hoof moved just enough he was able to slip the loop around it.

He pulled the string with his other hand, and it held. Then, pulling ever so gently with the one hand, he worked the hoof carefully up with the other. In just minutes he had the two hooves together and positioned where he needed them. When he pulled his arm out, Midnight strained, and both hooves came out.

He lay there, too tired to do anything for a moment. But feeling progress, Midnight didn't wait. She continued to push, and soon, a small tail emerged. Carefully wiggling the legs, Frans started working the baby out. But once the umbilical cord reached the tight passage, he started to pull more frantically. The blood and oxygen supply would be cut off, and with the head still inside, the baby could suffocate.

But within seconds, the head was coming through, and almost instantly, a huge baby horse slid into the golden straw. As soon as it did, it raised its head and sputtered, blowing bloody mucus everywhere.

Anna laughed, and Frans looked at himself. He was plastered in goo. But in his relief, he just smiled. Then he looked at Anna and laughed himself. "You weren't spared, either."

Anna looked down at her beautiful Christmas dress, and it was splattered, too.

She laughed again. "I never did like this one anyway."

As Frans stood, Anna reached for his hand, then thought better of it. "Perhaps you should wash," she said.

Midnight seemed quite stressed, and unable to stand, so before he washed, Frans pulled the little colt around by her head. As he did, Midnight neighed gently. Once the colt was where she could reach him, she started licking it clean.

Frans went over to the water trough and washed as well as he could. He shivered from the cold water. As soon as he had slipped his arm back in his shirt, Anna took his hand and smiled at him. "That was a beautiful way to spend Christmas Eve – watching new life come into the world."

Suddenly the barn door was jerked open, and there stood Anna's father. The glare on his face said everything. He looked at them holding hands, and Frans felt himself quiver. He tried to pull his hand away from Anna's, but she clenched her fingers around his and turned to face her father.

Mr. Adler took a deep breath as if trying to control his anger. "What are you two doing out here alone?"

"What do you think?" Anna asked.

His voice deepened. "I don't want to think about what two young people would be doing alone in a barn when they should be inside."

"Well, then," Anna said, her own voice trembling in anger, "the problem is with you, not with us. Before you jump to conclusions, you ought to think about it."

"Think about what?" her father replied. "I can see the condition of your clothes."

"And what condition is that?"

"All mussed up."

"With bloody mucus on them," Anna added.

Her father suddenly stopped and looked more closely. "Bloody mucus on them? But what . . ."

Ana spoke stiffly. "If you would quit being so cynical, Father, you would realize we came out here to check on Midnight and ended up needing to help her foal."

Mr. Adler seemed embarrassed by his snap judgement, so Frans tried to ease the tension. "Would you like to see the colt, Sir?"

Mr. Adler nodded. As Frans turned to show him the horse, he felt Anna's grip tighten on his hand, letting him know she didn't plan to let go. Frans wondered if she really wanted to hold his hand, or if she was just defying her father.

Mr. Adler noticed as well, and looked at Anna. She in turn only raised her eyebrows, as if challenging him to say anything about it.

They walked hand in hand to the stall, and Frans felt ever so awkward. He had never held Anna's hand before, and he wasn't comfortable doing so in front of her father.

As they looked into the stall, the little colt struggled to stand but quickly fell down. Frans looked over at Mr. Adler. "It's a colt, Sir. He is a big one, and he was born breach."

"And one hoof was caught," Anna added, "and Frans had to get it worked into position so he could be born. When you came in, I was just telling Frans that seeing a new baby born on Christmas Eve was probably the neatest thing ever."

The tension seemed to lift slightly as Mr. Adler nodded. "How's Midnight?"

"I'm not sure, Sir," Frans replied. "She hasn't tried to get up yet. But I'm sure with as big as he is, and with a breach birth, she is probably quite stressed."

As Midnight continued to lick the colt, he shook his head and struggled to his feet. He fell down and tried again with the same results. After a few more tries, he finally wobbled into a standing position.

Mr. Adler gasped. "My heck, he is tall."

Anna laughed. "Yeah, but he's all legs."

He started rooting against his mother, trying to find milk. In response, Midnight tried to stand, but collapsed. She tried a couple more times, but finally just gave up.

"I don't think she's going to stand for a few days," Frans said, "if she stands at all. I think I had better get some of her milk to feed him."

"Oh, can I feed him?" Anna asked excitedly. "Please!"

Frans nodded. "Of course. But it might be messy."

Anna looked at her dress. "Not like it matters now, anyway."

Mr. Adler frowned. "Perhaps it would still be best if you changed."

Anna sighed. "If it will make you feel better, Father." She then turned to Frans. "Don't feed him without me. I'll be right back." Frans nodded, and Anna said, "Promise?"

Frans nodded again, and Anna dropped her grip on his hand and soon disappeared out the barn door. As soon as she was gone, Mr. Adler turned to Frans.

"Mr. Fuhrmann, you are a good young man, and I want you to know I have nothing against you. But I really feel it is best if you and Anna don't . . . , uh, how should I say . . ."

"We shouldn't have feelings for each other?"

"Yes, that is it."

"I know how you have felt, Sir, and I've tried to keep some distance between us."

"I appreciate that, Mr. Fuhrmann, but maybe it would be best if..."

Suddenly he stopped, and seemed to be staring past Frans. Frans turned to see what he was looking at, and there stood Anna, still in her Christmas dress. She didn't even try to hide her anger.

"Best if what, Father?"

Mr. Adler looked at Frans and then back at Anna. "Anna, perhaps it would be best if you and I spoke privately."

Frans felt uneasy and tried to act like it was no big deal. "I really need to get a bucket I can milk into. I hope you will excuse me."

He walked out of the barn, even though the buckets he needed were inside. He hadn't even stepped into the dark before he heard Anna's voice, loud and angry.

"Father, Frans is a good, honest, hard-working man. And if I decide I like him, that should be the only thing that matters to you."

"But his family is one of the poorest in the district. You have a position to maintain."

"Position? What position? A position of arrogant, pompous, prideful . . ."

"That's quite enough, Anna!"

"No, it's not! If you expect me to marry one of those self-centered young men you keep introducing me to, you have another thing coming!"

"I'll have you know that the young men I have introduced you to are some of the finest young men there are!"

"Fine in what way? Because they were born into wealthy

families? Most of them haven't worked a day in their life. I don't think any one of them is half the man that Frans is."

Frans wandered farther away from the barn, feeling he should not be listening in on their conversation. He appreciated Anna standing up for him, but he hated to feel he was the cause of a rift between her and her father. He also wondered if she really did have feelings for him, or if she was just intrigued by the difference she saw between him and those young men she seemed to despise. Or maybe he was just a chance for her to stand up to her father.

He tried to think of some bucket he could get, but they were all in the barn, and he was worried about the new colt's need for food. He hoped Anna and her father would be done with their discussion, but like it or not, he needed to feed the colt.

He made his way back to the barn, interrupting their heated discussion.

"Perhaps," Mr. Adler said, "it would be best if Frans found other employment."

"He is the best horseman you have ever had," Anna retorted. "You've said so yourself."

"But he really shouldn't be making any kind of advances to you."

"You stop right there, Father. Frans has been nothing but a gentleman and has made no advances. If anyone has flirted, it is me. And I'll flirt with whomever I like."

"You are so much like your mother," Mr. Adler said. "She has the same kind of feelings about our position."

"Our position? We are not better than someone else just because we were born with money and they weren't," Anna fired back.

"Well, I think perhaps it would be best to see if Frans could get another job so that you two . . ."

Anna didn't even let him finish. "If you send him away, I go, too."

"You don't mean that!"

"Try me!"

There was a sudden quiet, and Frans felt this was as good of a time to step back into the barn as any. He entered and quickly grabbed a bucket and made his way toward Anna and Mr. Adler, who still stood by Midnight's stall. Anna and her father were both glaring at each other. Frans glanced at Anna and then at Mr. Adler. Mr. Adler seemed to be sizing up the situation and wondering if Anna would make good on her threat. By the look on Mr. Adler's face, he seemed to think she would.

When Frans looked at Anna and saw the steel resolve that showed in her face, he felt she probably would, too, if just to spite her father. As he neared the pen, he didn't say a word; he didn't dare. He simply went into the pen.

The colt was still nuzzling his mother and whimpering slightly, begging for food. Frans moved up by Midnight and pushed her leg back. He started to milk some milk into the bucket, an arduous task on a mare.

Anna appeared at his side and spoke as calmly as if nothing had ever happened. "How are we going to feed him?"

"If you want, you can go get a bottle. There is one in the cabinet in the tack room. It is just a big pop bottle, and there are some small nipples next to it, along with a funnel. They will need a quick rinse."

She left, and Mr. Adler stepped up beside him. He spoke quietly after Anna left. "I suppose, as loud as we were, you probably heard at least part of our conversation?"

Frans nodded. "Look, Mr. Adler, I know you feel I'm not good enough for Anna. I feel the same way myself. I've tried to be careful and not allow myself to have feelings for her, and I've tried to not do anything that would promote her feelings for me."

Mr. Adler nodded. "I know, Frans."

"I don't want to come between you and your daughter. I think you're right. It would be better if I found another job. You don't have to send me away. I will go on my own."

Mr. Adler shook his head. "That wouldn't work. If you leave now, they will think I sent you away."

"They?" Frans asked.

"Oh, Anna's mother is of the same mind as Anna. They like you more than you have any idea, Frans."

Frans looked down, concentrating on the milking. "I know you feel she can do better. I want you to know that I think the world of Anna, but I think she can do better than me, too. I will talk to her and try to help her understand. I will explain to her why I must leave."

Mr. Adler reached out and put his hand on Frans's shoulder. Frans looked up at him.

"Actually, I think there is no need for that," Mr. Adler said. "Instead, I would like to apologize. I think Anna and her mother are right."

Frans felt didn't understand this sudden change in Mr. Adler. "You do?"

Mr. Adler nodded. "Yes. And I want you to stay. And further, if Anna chooses to like you, I would be okay with you liking her back."

Almost immediately, Anna was there. Frans looked at Mr. Adler, and then at Anna. He wondered how much she had heard, but when she smiled at her father, Frans knew she had heard some.

But what he couldn't understand was why the sudden change? Was it genuine? He felt confused. But he didn't have a lot of time to think about it. The colt needed feeding.

Frans funneled what milk he had into the large pop bottle, and the milk nearly filled it. He slipped the nipple onto the bottle and handed it to Anna. She put the nipple of the bottle next to the colt's mouth. But the colt just pushed past her, trying to reach his mother.

Anna pushed him back a bit, and stepped between him and Midnight. He didn't like this and bunted her with his head. Anna started to fall backward, and Frans quickly reached up and put his arm around her to catch her.

She turned and smiled at him. He smiled back, but then glanced out of the corner of his eye at Mr. Adler. Mr. Adler was smiling, and Frans felt relieved.

Anna tried to give the baby horse his bottle again, but he snorted and shook his head. Frans put his arm around the baby horse's neck to hold him steady. He didn't like it and immediately pulled back, dragging Frans a few steps.

Frans laughed. "Wow! He's strong!"

"Do you think he is going to be the horse we hoped for?" Mr. Adler asked.

"We have bred him to beat Brewster Farms' horses," Frans replied. "I definitely think he has it in him."

"But first we need to get him to eat," Anna reminded them.

Frans got a good grip on the baby horse, and Anna tried again. The baby horse fought to pull away.

"I'll get his mouth open, and you stick the nipple in," Frans said.

He reached around the baby horse's nose and pressed from each side behind the teeth. Its mouth opened, and Anna stuffed the nipple in. It tried to shake the nipple out, but Frans had a good grip, and held it steady.

The baby horse got just a taste of the milk and blinked his eyes, showing he was thinking. Almost immediately he went after the bottle, nearly pulling it from Anna's grasp.

Frans relaxed his grasp a little, and the colt surged forward, pushing Anna backward. Frans stepped up beside her to help her. The baby horse sucked powerfully, even if awkwardly. The bottle drained quickly. When it was empty, he bunted it hard and sent it flying from Anna's hands.

"I had better get him some more," Frans said.

Anna tried to pet the baby horse while Frans started milking, but the colt was nearly taking her down.

Mr. Adler laughed. "Let me give you a hand, Anna."

"But, Daddy, you are in your Christmas suit."

"Being dressed up hasn't stopped the two of you," he replied.

He stepped around Midnight and helped hold the baby horse while Frans continued to milk. Midnight seemed to understand what they were doing and was calm through all of it.

"By the way, Daddy, what is his name going to be?" Anna asked.

"It is partially dictated by convention," Mr. Adler replied. "I planned on Cashmere Napoleon something, something, something."

"'Something, something, something' is a strange name," Anna

giggled.

When Frans felt he had enough to fill the bottle again, he funneled the milk into it and handed the bottle to Anna. Mr. Adler stepped back.

"Here, Frans. You go ahead and help Anna. I'm going to head back in. My wife is probably wondering where I am."

He walked away, with Frans staring after him. Frans was surprised that Mr. Adler would leave them there alone.

"Frans, are you going to help me?" Anna asked.

"Uh, yeah," Frans said, turning his attention back to her.

As they fed the horse, Anna smiled at Frans. "What did you and Father talk about while I was getting the bottle?"

"How much did you hear?" Frans asked.

"I heard him say he wanted you to stay."

"I told him I didn't want to come between him and you and thought perhaps I should leave."

"Don't you dare!" Anna said.

"Well, it was funny. He suddenly changed and apologized for what he had said to you about me. And that was when he asked me to stay."

"I think it helped him understand what a great guy you are."

"What did?"

"The fact that you would be willing to leave so as not to come between us."

"Well, it is true. Nothing is more important than family, and I would feel horrible if I caused any kind of rift between you and your father."

Anna looked Frans right in the eye. "Frans, I love my father. It may not seem so sometimes, but I do. The problem is, Father likes to micro manage everything and has his own ideas on how things should be. I don't always agree with him. But even if he thinks I should marry someone with a lot of money, I can promise you that he has a lot of respect for you."

"I hope I can measure up to that," Frans replied.

Cashmere finished his bottle and wanted more, but Frans felt too much would make him sick. He gathered up the bucket and the bottle, and the two of them headed out of the pen. Cashmere followed them all the way, almost tromping on their heels.

After they shut the gate behind them, he whinnied to them. "He sure is sweet," Anna said.

Frans took the bottle and bucket to the hydrant and washed them, then returned them to the tack room. Anna grabbed his hand. "Are you going to come back to the dance?"

Frans laughed. "My clothes are a mess."

"You could go change."

Frans shook his head. "I don't have anything else nice enough to wear."

"Well, you were my invited guest for the evening. You owe me a dance, so I guess we'll have to dance right here."

She went over to the old radio the men used when they were working in the barn. She turned it on and turned the dial, scrolling through the stations until she found a song she liked. She walked over to Frans and held out her arms. "Well?"

Although he felt awkward, he took her into his arms, and they danced. She laid her head against him, and he could feel his heart start to pound. Would it be okay to fall in love with her? Could he stop himself from it anyway? It felt so wonderful to have her in his arms.

When the song ended, they just stood there in each others arms.

"Frans," Anna said, "I want to help you train Cashmere. May I?"

Frans held her close. "I would like that, Anna."

Everything felt right, and Frans couldn't remember a more wonderful Christmas Eve.

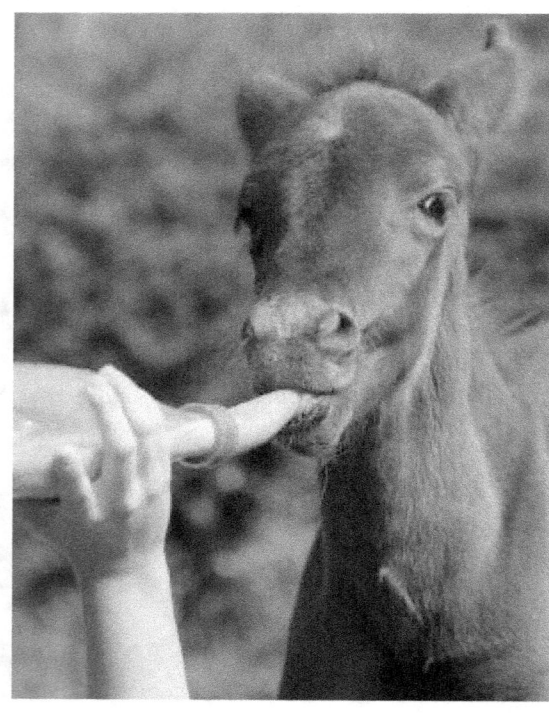

# Chapter Seven
# Christmas

When Frans got up on Christmas morning, he hurried to check on Midnight and Cashmere. Midnight still couldn't stand, so he milked her. He hadn't even gotten enough for a full bottle before Anna appeared. The dress was exchanged for jeans and a riding shirt. Frans thought that even if Anna was somewhat of a tomboy, she was still very much a lady.

"You weren't going to feed him without me, were you?" Anna asked.

Frans laughed. "I figured either you would be tired and asleep, or you would show up here soon, anyway. I would only feed him if you decided to sleep until noon or something."

"I want to help you feed him every time, until Midnight can feed him herself," Anna said. "If you are ready to feed and I'm not here, tell Emerich to call for me."

Frans stood up from milking and bowed impishly. "Yes, Just Fräulein Anna."

"You 'Just Fräulein Anna' me, and I'm likely to punch you," Anna teased back.

"I promise to always have you help me feed him," Frans said more seriously. "Besides, I will enjoy the company."

Anna was satisfied with that. When Frans had the bottle ready, he handed it to her.

"Aren't you going to help me?" Anna asked.

"I would bet he will take it just fine," Frans replied.

"Still, just in case."

Frans stood beside her when she offered the bottle to Cashmere.

Cashmere took it readily without any fuss. But Anna leaned against Frans, and he put his arm around her. He only did it lightly, telling himself he was just helping to steady her, though he really knew otherwise.

As they walked from the stall, Cashmere followed them to the gate and whinnied after them.

Anna took Frans's hand and stood in front of him. "You are coming to Christmas dinner, aren't you?"

"Anna, don't you think it should just be your family?"

"But, Frans, you are very much like family. You've been with us for five years."

"Some of the other workers have been here longer."

"All of the other workers went home for Christmas, leaving you to do all the chores."

"I actually volunteered to be the one to stay because I was afraid Midnight would foal, and it's a good thing I did."

Anna acted hurt. "And I thought you stayed because I asked you to be my guest at the Christmas Eve party."

Frans grinned at her impishness. "I must admit that helped sway my decision."

Anna drew him closer. "Frans, I know you have tried to keep a distance between us all of these years because I was young and because Father didn't approve. But all of that is changing now. I like you, Frans, a lot, and Father seems okay with my feelings, perhaps even deliriously happy that I have found someone I like."

"I wouldn't push it that far," Frans said.

"Well, I can tell you one thing," Anna added. "Mother adores you. She likes my brothers-in-law okay, but she says you are so much easier to get along with. And David's fiancé, Katherin, is almost impossible to please all of the time. Actually, she is almost impossible to please any of the time."

"You talk to your mother about me?" Frans asked.

Anna gave him a sly smile. "All the time. But you should have heard Mother and Father last night. We talked about what happened in the barn, and Mother made it clear to Father that she has no qualms about us."

Frans felt awkward knowing that they had been talking about him, and Anna seemed to sense it. "Frans, you will come to dinner, won't you? Mother is cooking a huge goose."

"Will your sisters and their families be there?"

"Yes."

"What will they think about having a horse trainer there as a family guest?"

"Do I really care what they think? Let them be jealous that I have such a nice guy with me."

"Jealous wasn't quite the emotion I imagined," Frans replied.

Anna squeezed his hand. "Frans, you can't worry about what they think. What matters is that I think you are the greatest guy there is. I hope that is what matters to you."

Frans nodded. "Yes, Anna. That is what matters. However, I am going to have to get used to this a little. Until yesterday, I just thought we were friends and assumed that was where our relationship would stay. I was sure that your father would never approve of anything more. I also thought everyone in your family saw me as just a horse trainer, even you."

"That's because you don't take hints very well. I've tried to flirt with you for, like, forever. I finally decided that I was tired of you not getting it, and I was going to be more blunt this Christmas. That was why I invited you as my guest to the Christmas Eve party. And just so you know, I'm sure my brother and sisters would approve, too. So will you come?"

Frans felt quite assured, even if it might be awkward. "Yes, Anna, I would love to come to dinner with you."

She leaned against him, and the closeness felt so right to Frans. But soon Cashmere whinnied, and it reminded them he needed a second bottle. Frans got the milk ready, and Anna fed Cashmere.

When they finished with that, Frans knelt down and started rubbing Midnight. When Anna asked him what he was doing, he looked up at her as he continued to rub. "I'm hoping to get her muscles working as much as possible. We need to get her on her feet fairly soon, or, just like anything else, her muscles will atrophy, and she won't ever be able to stand again."

Anna joined him in rubbing Midnight, and Cashmere made a point to see if he could coax some more milk out of them, stepping all over them as he nuzzled them. They were still rubbing Midnight when Mr. Adler poked his head above the stall door. "How's she doing?"

"She's showing no sign of wanting to get up," Anna replied. "We are trying to work her muscles to get the blood circulating and help her to stand."

After they had worked on her for a while, Frans nudged her a little, and she tried to stand. She wobbled to her feet, but she wasn't up very long before she started to tremble. Cashmere had already moved up beside her, and Frans moved quickly and pushed the colt out of the way. Midnight collapsed, and, due to Frans's quick thinking, missed falling on Cashmere. But Frans's leg was trapped under her. It took all three of them pushing and shoving on Midnight to free him.

"I think we better move Cashmere to a separate stall until his mother is more stable," Mr. Adler said.

Frans and Anna nodded their agreement, and Frans went to prepare the next stall so he could be by his mother.

Meanwhile, Anna and Mr. Adler played with the colt. "I can't believe how strong he is," Mr. Adler said.

"Do you think he will be the one that will finally help us beat Brewsters?" Anna asked.

Mr. Adler turned to Frans as he came back. "What do you think, Frans? You are the one that talked me into breeding Midnight to the stallion we did. Do you think he is going to be everything you dreamed he'd be?"

Frans nodded. "With the right training and work, I think he will."

Mr. Adler seemed pleased with that.

When they moved Cashmere, Midnight started to whinny. Frans stepped into her pen and started scratching her ears. "It won't be for too long, old girl; just until you are stronger."

When they were all done with Midnight and Cashmere, Frans turned to the task of feeding the other horses. Anna insisted on helping. Mr. Adler headed to the house. "Don't be too long, you two," he said as he disappeared from the barn.

"Anna, why don't you go ahead?" Frans said. "I will take care of things. I'm sure your family will have family things to do."

"I will go when we are done. Besides, you are going to come to church with us, aren't you?"

"I did plan to go to church, but I would think it would be awkward for your family to have me sit with you," he replied.

"No, it wouldn't."

"What will your family think?" Frans asked.

"I thought we agreed to not worry about that, didn't we?" Anna replied.

"With my nice suit still dirty from last night, I will have to wear regular clothes, and I'm sure that will embarrass them."

Anna frowned. "Well, let them be embarrassed. If you would like, I will wear what I have on, too."

"No. I just don't want them to wish I wasn't there."

"Then I'll see if David has an old suit you can wear."

"Do you think David's clothes will fit me?" Frans asked.

"You're right. His pants might, but his shirts and coats won't since he doesn't have your muscles," Anna said, punching Frans playfully in the arm.

"I wasn't saying that," Frans replied. "I was just saying he is smaller."

"Same thing," Anna said.

They visited as they fed the other horses. As they were finishing, Anna slipped into the house to get Frans some clothes. She returned carrying a nice wool suit. "Mother said you should keep this because Father never wears it anymore."

Frans thanked her, and they went their separate ways to get ready for church. When he was ready, he wondered if he should go up to the house or stay at the bunkhouse and wait. He didn't need to worry because, before he knew it, Anna was at the bunkhouse door calling for him. When he joined her, she smiled. It made him feel good, but he had to take a deep breath as he felt his heart jump in his chest.

Anna was always beautiful. He figured she would be, even if she were covered in mud and wearing old overalls. Nothing could hide her beauty. However, Frans knew it wasn't just because she was very pleasant to look at, but because she also radiated goodness and genuineness. But this morning she was even more beautiful, wearing a red and white dress with puffy sleeves that was pulled tight around her waist, highlighting her female figure.

She took his hand as they walked to the house where the car was waiting. Anna climbed in, and Frans slid in beside her. Mrs. Adler greeted him and smiled. "We're so glad you could join us today, Frans."

Frans smiled back. "Thank you, Mrs. Adler."

"Oh, Frans," she said. "You have known us for so long. Mrs. Adler sounds so formal. Please call me Elsa."

"I don't know," Frans said. "It doesn't sound too respectful."

"Frans, I know you are a very good, respectful young man. But you are really like family, and it would make me happy if you would address me by my first name."

Frans agreed, though it still felt quite awkward to him. Mr. Adler just nodded his head through it all, though Frans thought he might have seen the slightest smile. Maybe it was because he was wearing Mr. Adler's suit, or maybe it had to do with the previous night's conversation.

Both Frans and Mr. Adler were mostly silent during the drive while Anna and her mother talked about Christmas and dinner.

When they arrived at the church, the rest of Anna's family joined them there. Frans knew Anna's sisters and their husbands. He also knew her brother, David. But he had only seen David's fiancé from a distance and had never been formally introduced to Katherin. If anyone was shocked at him joining the family, no one said anything. No one, that is, except Katherin. When they turned to walk into the church, she spoke to David, purposefully loud enough to make sure all could hear.

"Isn't he the horse trainer?"

When David answered that he was, she spoke louder still. "I guess all of the decent guys were out of town."

Anna had grabbed Frans's hand, and he could feel her grip tighten when Katherin spoke. He turned to look at Anna, but she was staring at Katherin, and the look on her face said everything. Katherin turned and looked at Anna, and her smile seemed to say that she enjoyed Anna's anger. She then turned back to David.

"And can you believe that suit he's wearing? It must be from the Middle Ages. What decent person would wear a suit like that? Not me. Not even to be buried in."

Anna spoke with a slight, malicious impishness. "Katherin, were you saying you don't like Daddy's suit that Frans is wearing? It has been one of Daddy's favorites."

Katherin looked at Mr. Adler, and then at Anna, and her arrogant grin was gone. She stuttered as she spoke. "Oh, no. I'm sure it was . . . is a nice suit. I was just saying . . . you, know, that the style is kind of out of date. I mean, not that it was ever a bad style. It just . . ."

Anna seemed to revel in Katherin's discomfort at having spoken against a suit that had belonged to Mr. Adler, and she did nothing to help rescue Katherin from sticking her foot deeper and deeper into her mouth.

Mrs. Adler, on the other hand, took pity on Katherin. "Yes, that suit was made of the finest wool. It's too bad they don't make clothes like that anymore," she said.

Frans noticed the look on Anna's face and knew she wished her mother had let Katherin keep talking. But everyone immediately went quiet, and Katherin let out a relieved sigh, happy to have the attention turned from her faux pas.

As Frans thought more about it, he wondered if Mrs. Adler had been trying to help Katherin out, or if she was trying to quell the storm that seemed to be brewing between Katherin and Anna. Or, he wondered, was she trying to spare his feelings? Was his presence causing a division in the family? He had known most of the family for some time. They seemed to accept him and maybe even liked him. But he wasn't sure about Anna's sisters' husbands. And he obviously didn't need to even guess what Katherin thought.

The family filled two large pews. Anna slid in and Frans took his seat beside her at the end. He felt more comfortable only being by Anna, and she seemed to know that would be the case. Before the meeting started, Anna's four-year-old niece came to him.

She looked up at him and her big blue eyes had a look of admiration in them. "Do you really train horses?"

Frans smiled at her. "Yes, I do. Do you like horses?" She nodded.

Anna leaned over to talk to her. "Maddie, did you know that Frans helped a new baby horse be born last night?"

Maddie looked up at Frans like he was something special. "Can I sit with you and Aunt Anna?"

Frans smiled and pulled her up onto his lap. "Can I see the baby horse?" she asked.

Anna nodded. "When we get back to Grandpa and Grandma's house, we'll take you out to see him if it is okay with your parents."

Maddie quickly slid down from Frans's lap and went to ask her parents if she could. When she came back, she brought her two-year-old cousin with her. Maddie climbed back up on Frans's lap, and Anna pulled Sophie onto her own.

Maddie could hardly contain her excitement. "Mamma said I could go with you to see the baby horse!"

Maddie was so excited about the new baby horse she could hardly sit still during the meeting. Sophie didn't seem to understand, but Maddie's excitement made her excited, too.

After church, Maddie asked her mother if she could ride in "Frans's car." Wilma, Anna's oldest sister, laughed and smiled at her little daughter, and at Frans, and told Maddie she could. Where Maddie went, Sophie went, so Maddie asked Sophie's mother, Varena, if she could come with them. Varena smiled at him and told Maddie it would be fine for Sophie to ride with them, too. Frans felt he was accepted, at least by both of Anna's sisters.

As soon as they were home, Maddie was trying to drag them to the barn. The others pulled up, and Wilma called out to them. "I want to come, too!"

The whole family joined them, with Katherin reluctantly bringing up the rear. Anna once more took Frans's hand.

When they opened the door into the barn, Maddie ran in, squealing happily, with Sophie right behind her. Anna opened the door into Cashmere's stall, and he immediately pushed his way out, trying to find a meal. Frans blocked his path, but Mr. Adler put his hand on Frans's shoulder.

"Why don't we go ahead and let him out into the center here? There would be more room for everyone to see him."

Frans wrapped his arms around Cashmere's neck and held onto him while Anna retrieved a small halter and a lead rope. Frans got the halter on, and Cashmere didn't like it. He started trying to back away, so Frans wrapped the rope around Cashmere's backside and held onto it to keep him still.

The two dads held Maddie and Sophie up where they could safely pet Cashmere along with everyone else. Frans held Cashmere steady, even though he seemed to think that if he was going to put up with all of the attention that he should be getting some food out of the deal. Even Katherin reached out her hand and rubbed it gently along Cashmere's neck. Frans saw her smile, but her expression changed to disgust when she saw that Anna was watching her.

While everyone continued to pet him, Anna had to tell the story of Cashmere's birth. She made Frans out to be a hero, embarrassing him.

When Anna finished her story, the adults decided it was time to head to the house. Maddie and Sophie did not want to leave, but the reminder of Christmas presents changed their minds.

As they moved off, Frans touched Anna's arm. "I think that, while everyone is opening presents, I'll stay and feed Cashmere and rub down Midnight."

"Maybe you ought to change first," Ann giggled. "I'll go change and join you in a minute."

"You should spend that time with your family," Frans protested.

"You are like family, Frans," Anna replied.

Nothing would change her mind, so Frans hurried to change. He nearly had enough milk by the time Anna arrived. They fed Cashmere and then rubbed down Midnight. She wobbled to her feet, but couldn't stay up very long.

Anna insisted that Frans join the family for opening presents, too, hinting that she had a present for him. He had something for her, as well. He had whittled a horse and had always meant it for Anna, but he hadn't known how he could ever give it to her until now.

On their way to the house he told Anna he needed to get something and slipped off to the bunkhouse. He wrapped the little wooden horse in a beautiful red cloth and rejoined her.

Frans thoroughly enjoyed watching the family open their presents, especially Maddie and Sophie. They were so excited.

When they were done with the presents, Anna called Maddie over and whispered to her. She hurried out, then came back in with a package and handed it to Frans. He smiled at her. "Is this for me?"

Maddie smiled and nodded. He looked at the tag. It was from Anna and her mother. When he opened it, he found a beautiful shirt and a nice pair of pants.

"Oh, how nice," Katherin said, as if speaking to David. "Anna bought him some decent clothes so she won't have to be as embarrassed when she is with him."

Frans felt Anna stiffen beside him and start to move as if she was going to jump from the couch and tear Katherin apart. But before she could, Mrs. Adler spoke.

"Actually, I helped Anna buy them. What Frans wears is great, but these nice clothes reminded us of his goodness."

Frans knew Mrs. Adler was trying to defuse the situation, but this time, Anna wasn't about to let it drop. "Don't you like Mother's taste in clothes, Katherin?" Then, before Katherin could answer, she added with tone that sounded like a challenge, "And don't you especially like Mother's judgment in the quality of good men?"

Anna glanced at her own father and then at Frans, as if to reiterate her point.

"Oh, absolutely," Katherin said, half choking on the words.

"Now that we are done . . ." Mrs. Adler started to say, and Frans raised his hand.

Mrs. Adler smiled at him. "Yes, Frans?"

"I have something for Anna."

He handed the horse to her, and Maddie and Sophie came up close to see. Anna let them help her unwrap it, and when the cloth fell away, Anna gasped. She turned to Frans. "You carved this, didn't you?"

Frans nodded, and felt quite proud of it. Then Katherin said to David, "Of course he carved it. A horse trainer couldn't afford a real present. And what else would he give but a horse?"

That was the first time that Katherin's words had really hurt Frans, and he looked down, not wanting to meet anyone's gaze. He knew he didn't have much money, and he knew he probably never would, even though the Adlers paid him more than most horse trainers received. He would have loved to do more for Anna, but it was true that he couldn't. He would probably be nothing but a horse trainer all of his life, even though he tried to be the best horse trainer he could be.

But Frans was surprised to hear Mr. Adler speak this time. "Frans, that is about the most beautiful carving I have ever seen. What other hidden talents do you have?"

Frans looked up and tried hard to smile as he shrugged. Katherin was right. Anna probably ought to have someone that was more in her league.

Anna was breathing hard beside him, and Frans could tell she was angry. But, when she spoke, her voice had a forced calmness. "Hey, everyone, how about a little snack? Katherin, how would you like to help me?"

Frans watched a glance pass between Anna and her mother. Mrs. Adler looked as if she was questioning what Anna was up to. Anna tilted her head as if telling her mother to trust her.

Katherin looked around, as if wanting someone to rescue her, but even David turned his eyes from her.

Anna handed the carved horse to Maddie and Sophie to look at and disappeared into the other room. Katherin reluctantly followed.

The house was large, and the kitchen was far in the back, but Frans could still hear Anna's voice slightly, though he couldn't tell what she was saying. They were gone quite a while, and when they returned, they each carried a tray, one of cookies and one of candy.

Anna was smiling, but Katherin looked sullen. Katherin never said another negative word about him, and, in fact, seldom spoke the rest of the day unless she was spoken to.

Maddie wanted Frans to play with her and Sophie, and he climbed down on the floor with them. Anna joined them, and he enjoyed that immensely.

Dinner was really good. The cooked goose was just perfect.

When dinner was over, Frans slipped out to feed Cashmere, and Anna joined him. Maddie wanted to go, too, but her mother sensed they needed some time alone. When they got outside, they walked quietly together. Anna reached over and took his hand, and he gratefully held hers. Finally, he stopped, and pulled her to face him.

"Anna, maybe Katherin is right. Maybe it would be best . . ."

Anna didn't even let him finish. "She is not right. There is no maybe about it. And I explained that to her."

"You explained it? What did you say?"

"I just told her what a great guy you are and that I didn't appreciate her saying anything negative about you."

"You said that?"

"Well, kind of."

"Kind of?"

"I just told her that if she ever said anything again like she had been saying, I would mop the floor with her."

"You didn't!"

"I did," Anna said. "And I meant it."

"But, Anna," Frans said. "I don't want to be a problem for your family. And really, Katherin is right. Compared to your family, I'm . . ."

"Great! Compared to my family, you are great."

"Actually, that's not what I planned to say."

"Well, it's true. You are wonderful."

"Anna, my family is one of the poorest there is. We are immigrants – hard working, but poor. Even my position as a horse trainer is a step up in the world. I have no college degree. I've just learned along the way. I've loved horses since I could walk, and I hung out around the stables and horse races. The men were kind and gave me jobs, and I gradually learned things."

"You can do things with horses no other man can," Anna said.

"But that is just the point. I've watched and learned, but I will never be as educated as your family."

"Not all education comes from school," Anna said. "Look, Frans. I want you to promise me that the difference in our social status or what people say about us won't be the determining factor. If you decide we are not meant for each other because of who we are and not due to financial reasons, I will try to understand. But if you base your decision on our different stations in life, I just feel that is wrong. Promise me you won't let that get in the way of our relationship."

"I'm not sure I can."

"Frans, over the years I've grown to admire and then love you. To me, you are worth enduring what others say so I can be with you. Am I worth it to you?"

"You are definitely worth it to me," Frans said. "What they say about me I have no problem with. But what is hard is when I hear them say something derogatory about you because of me."

"You let me deal with that. You know my family is behind you, even Father."

"Even your father?"

"He is now."

Frans felt strange about how things had changed so much in just a few days. "But what about David?" he asked. "Surely with the way

Katherin talks . . ."

"Don't worry about David," Anna said, stopping him. "He didn't like what Katherin said about you. He told me he is going to have a talk with her and perhaps their engagement needs to be called off. They are both only 18, so it's probably a good thing, anyway."

"I hate to think that I am the cause of their engagement being broken."

"You are not the cause. She is the cause. David is seeing a part of her he is not pleased with."

They stood there quietly, looking at each other for a moment, and then Anna squeezed his hand. "Come on. Let's feed Cashmere."

Frans milked enough milk from Midnight to fill the bottle, and then they fed Cashmere together. Cashmere emptied the bottle quickly, and Frans filled another one. He really enjoyed this time with Anna.

They took some time rubbing Midnight. She again tried to stand, but wobbled and fell down. Frans and Anna sat down on a hay bale, held hands, and talked. Frans realized that he had been falling in love with Anna all along.

# Chapter Eight
# Raising and Training Cashmere

It had been a full week since Cashmere had been born, and still Midnight had not been able to stand for more than a brief instant. Anna always helped Frans feed Cashmere and rub Midnight, and they had lots of great talks together.

Things were definitely changing between them. He was no longer seeing her just as the boss's daughter, and he knew she didn't view him as just a horse trainer. She, of course, claimed she never had, for she said she had always thought of him as more than that.

On January 2nd, the other men came back from their Christmas vacations. Frans was glad to have the help on all of the chores and hoped it would give him more time to work with Cashmere and Midnight. A few days later, when he and Anna tried to get Midnight to her feet, she wouldn't even try. Frans decided they had to do something more.

One of the other men, Fredric, was also a horse trainer. He was old and pretty much retired. When he saw Midnight's situation, he asked Frans what he was going to do.

"The problem, as I see it," Frans said, "is that she has a pinched nerve. But here's the deal. The pinched nerve is making it so she can't stand, and if she can't stand, she can't get over the pinched nerve."

"Do you propose we just put her down?" Frederic asked.

Frans shook his head. "We really can't. I need her milk for Cashmere. Besides, there are two more things in my arsenal that I've previously seen done. Once, at the stables where I worked as a teenager, we rigged a wooden framework that we used to lift a horse, and that eventually got her walking."

"That sounds like a good idea," Frederic said.

"But there is one other thing I would like to try first," Frans told him. "I once met a man who was a horse chiropractor – not a widely known field. I had my doubts, but I watched him work on horses, and I was amazed at what happened. The change in the horses was phenomenal."

"Do you think we could get him to come here?" Anna asked.

"I think he moved to another area," Frans said. "However, I was so intrigued by what he did that I talked him into letting me work for him a couple of days each week. He didn't pay much, but during the two years I worked there, I tried to learn everything I could from him. Though I don't know everything, I want to give it a try."

Word spread quickly, and all of the men gathered around. Anna ran to tell her father, who came out with David at his side.

Frans was embarrassed at the attention. But there wasn't much he could do now. Some of the men joked and teased him, calling him the "horse doctor," and he knew if he failed it would be even worse.

Frans felt along Midnight's spine, feeling for a slight bump in her back. When he found it, he placed his hands flat on her back, one palm on the back of the other.

"If this works," he told everyone, "it might hurt her a bit."

He took a deep breath and pushed his hands downward with all of his weight. There was an audible pop, so much so that the group gasped.

Midnight kicked her foot out at him, but, as soon as she had done so, she started licking her lips and blinking. "That's a good sign," Frans said. "She's thinking about it."

Frans felt along her back and found the spot again. Once more he snapped his weight against her back. This time only a small pop sounded, and, once more, Midnight licked her lips and blinked, but she didn't kick.

Frans tried one last time but didn't sense any change. It was time to try to get her to her feet. He spatted her rump, she rose on her front legs, and then she stood. Frans leaned against her on one side and Frederic leaned against her on the other to steady her.

"I think her legs might take a minute or two to get the blood flowing," Frederic said.

She almost went down but was able to catch herself. Frans and Frederic started rubbing her legs.

After about ten minutes, she stiffly took a step. She wobbled slightly but didn't go down. They continued to rub her legs. After a few more minutes, Frans had them open the gate to her stall, and they walked her slowly out into the open barn.

"When Anna told me what you had in mind," Mr. Adler said, "I thought it was crazy. But I figured it couldn't hurt anything to try. But, if I hadn't seen it myself, I wouldn't have believed it."

"I felt the same way when I first saw it," Frans said. "I just wish I knew more."

"Still, all the same," Mr. Adler said, "I think I would rather not put Cashmere with her until she is steady."

Both Frans and Frederic agreed with that. "I know that when she is better that it will be best for him to be with his mother," Anna said. "But I'm going to miss feeding him his bottle."

Frans walked Midnight outside. With every step she seemed to become more stable. The novelty wore off, and the men went back to their work.

After he had walked her for quite a while, he decided it was time to put her back and teach Cashmere to lead. He knew he had to start young since Cashmere was so big, or it wouldn't be long before Cashmere would think he was the boss. Frans put a halter on the little colt and tried to lead him. Anna opened the gate, and Cashmere followed happily out of his stall and into the yard. When he realized that he was not going to be fed, he planted his little feet and stubbornly refused to budge.

"Do you want me to whack his backside?" Anna asked.

"No. I try not to do any more of that than I have to," Frans replied. He asked Anna to hold the rope while he found a longer one. Suddenly he heard Anna yelling. Frans ran back out of the barn to see Cashmere pulling her across the yard.

"He is really strong!" she said.

Frans tied Cashmere to a hitching post to let him pull for a while. When the little horse finally decided that he couldn't win against it, he stood still.

Frans made a loop with the longer rope and put it around Cashmere's backside, sliding it up under his tail. Cashmere didn't like it. Frans then untied Cashmere and tried to lead him. When he refused to go, Frans pulled on the rope that was under the tail. Cashmere moved forward to try to get away from it. They did this for a couple of hours, and Cashmere began to realize that if he would just go forward, he wouldn't get the tug under his tail.

After he had walked for a while without the tugs, Frans dropped the rope from behind the tail. But the minute the rope was gone, Cashmere wouldn't go.

"He's awfully smart," Frans said.

Frans put the rope back, and Cashmere kicked at him. He barely connected, but the sharp little hoof made Frans hop in pain.

"Stubborn little mule," he said. "It's a good thing we're starting young."

It took the rest of the morning and several times dropping the rope and putting it back before Cashmere began to understand that the hated rope wouldn't be under his tail if he would walk when asked.

When Frans felt Cashmere was leading better, he turned the lead rope over to Anna. It was getting close to lunch time, and Anna suggested they stop and feed Cashmere and also get some lunch for themselves.

"Before we do," Frans said, "we need him to behave. We don't want him thinking we will reward bad behavior."

Frans put the rope around Cashmere again and tucked it under the tail, handing the lead rope to Anna, while he, himself, held onto the one that was under Cashmere's tail. When Cashmere refused to go, Frans would pull the rope. It wasn't too long before Cashmere began to obey Anna. When Frans was satisfied the little horse was doing well, they tied him up, and Anna fed him for the last time, since Cashmere would be safe with Midnight after that. When Anna finished feeding him, he nuzzled her. Frans knew Anna was growing attached to the little horse, just as he was.

While they brushed Cashmere, Mr. Adler came over. "He's quite the little horse. He's got a great build, but do you think he has the spirit to run?"

Frans nodded. "I don't doubt it at all. Once in a while he acts like he can hardly contain himself. I was thinking that if the sun would warm the bit of snow from the ground so the pasture wouldn't be slick, I'd turn him loose in there and just see what he would do."

Mr. Adler liked that idea, and said he wanted to be there to see it.

Most of the men brought their lunches from home, but since Frans lived in the bunkhouse, he usually slipped in there to fix himself something. However, since Christmas, Anna had insisted he come to the house for lunch and dinner.

This hadn't gone unnoticed by the other men, who teased him about it until Old Frederic told them to stop. "Hey! Anna knows a good catch when she sees one." That embarrassed Frans even more, but he was glad Frederic thought highly of him.

By late afternoon, the sun had thawed the pasture enough that Frans felt Cashmere could run. While he led him out, Anna went to get her father. The men also came over to watch. Anna asked if she could be the one to let him go, and Frans nodded.

When Anna unhooked the lead rope, Cashmere just stood there. She tried to shoo him off, but he, instead, reached over and nuzzled her.

"I think he expects some milk," Frans said. "Why don't you step out of the corral?"

She did, and for a moment, Cashmere stood there, looking at them

68

across the fence.  Frans was beginning to feel it was going to be a disappointment when a small breeze flicked the hair on his mane.  As if something magical was touching him, his ears perked up, and he started flaring his nostrils.  A horse out in another pasture whinnied, and, suddenly, without any warning, Cashmere whirled and ran in that direction.

When he reached the fence where the other horses were, they came running to meet the new member of the farm.  They reached out to sniff him.  He backed away slightly, and then took off running along the fence, as if to show off.

One tall mare raced up along side of him, and when she did, he put on a burst of speed to stay ahead of her.  Neck and neck they raced to the next fence line where the mare slid to a stop and Cashmere slid clumsily into the fence.  The mare turned and headed back down the fence line.

The little show-off looked at her for a moment, and then raced to catch up.  As he came alongside of her, the mare increased her speed, stretching out her neck, with the little horse racing awkwardly beside her.

"My heavens!" Mr. Adler exclaimed.  "He's keeping up with old Tilla.  I wonder if she is running at full speed."

"I don't know if she is going full out or not," Frederic said, "but that little horse has the fire of competitiveness."

They watched him run for quite a while.  Tilla got tired and moved off, but Cashmere seemed to just want to go and go.  When they finally coaxed him over so they could put the lead rope on him and take him back to his stall, Mr. Adler reached out and petted the little horse admiringly.  "Yes, sir, this little horse was definitely born to run."

# Chapter Nine
# Preparing For The
# Big Day

Anna glanced around to make sure no one was watching, and then she slipped Cashmere a sugar cube. But Frans had seen her.

"That horse is going to be spoiled rotten, and it will be your fault," he said with a laugh.

His laugh warmed Anna's heart. "Oh yeah?" she said in a falsely haughty tone. "I've seen you feeding him treats, too."

Frans pulled her up close to him. She acted like she would have none of it, pushing against him, but then, smiling, she slid her arms around him, too.

It had been just over two years since Cashmere was born, and they were preparing him for the big race. And this was probably the most exciting day yet. This was the day they were going to take him over to the racetrack to run him through his first timed trials. The timed trials would not only determine his eligibility for the race, but also his position.

"Besides," Anna said to Frans, giving a fake, stern look, "I was just giving him a little boost in preparation for his run today."

Frans grinned. "It's a good thing that sugar isn't considered a race enhancing hormone, or he would have so much in his bloodstream he would be banned from racing."

"Ha, ha, ha," Anna said. "What about all the apples you feed him? I think you have pretty much emptied the apple orchard feeding that horse."

"I believe in a reward system of training," Frans said.

Frans and Anna had been almost as one for more than two years. From the evening Cashmere had been born, and all through his training, they had spent almost every free moment together.

Anna knew that her father frowned at anyone giving his horses sugar cubes. But once Midnight had recovered enough that Cashmere could be put with her, Anna had missed feeding him his bottle. And really, could she help it that he liked to lick sugar from her hands? And licking sugar just led to sugar cubes.

Cashmere finished his sugar and put his lip up and whinnied slightly at them, which looked like he was laughing at their antics.

Anna thought about herself and Frans. She had grown to love him so much. She also knew he loved her. She was ready to marry him any time he asked, and she had been ready for quite a while.

She was grateful that her family had accepted him. Even her father already treated him like a son. In fact, her father had dropped hints to Frans that it was time he asked her to marry him. But Frans still hadn't asked; at least, not yet. But Anna thought she knew what was holding him back.

Frans had encouraged her father to put a lot of stock into Cashmere, and Frans seemed to feel Cashmere's success was also his own. She felt that if Cashmere could just show he was what Frans felt he could be, Frans would have the confidence he needed to ask her and forget about the differences in their backgrounds. So, although this was a big day for everyone on the Adler Farm, she felt it was as big for her and Frans as it was for Cashmere.

Frans had done most of the riding and training of Cashmere. He had let Anna ride a few times. She loved the feel of his speed and strength. But it also made her parents nervous.

They had hired a jockey, who had ridden Cashmere a couple of times to try to get used to him. The jockey seemed awed by Cashmere's speed and power.

But the speed and power were also a great concern. The jockey had done well with him, but Anna knew only too well that in the excitement of a race, Cashmere might not respond to commands as he should. She had too often seen a wonderful horse, refusing to obey the commands of the jockey, burn itself out in the race running too fast at the first or fighting the position the jockey tried to move to on the track. Some had fought with other horses or maimed themselves against the fence.

Another disadvantage would be Cashmere's age. Since all race horses are considered another year older on January first each year, Cashmere was determined to be a year old only a week after he was born. He would be forced to race as a three-year-old even though he was much younger. That would put him against the best and most experienced horses.

However, even though he was young, Cashmere's size wouldn't be a disadvantage. He was more than 17 hands tall, even though he wasn't fully grown.

Perhaps this was the year that Brewster Farms would finally be beat. Their horses had won every year for as long as she could remember, and their latest champion had won four years in a row. In fact, he hadn't lost a single race he had been entered in, and no other horse had been within a length of him when he crossed the finish line.

The "Adler Farms" trailer was brought around. Anna opened the trailer door as Frans brought Cashmere up. He stood so tall that he had to duck his head down to go in. He slipped in as gently as if he was going through a gate. Frans had worked hard to make sure he would.

Anna turned and looked at her father. He stood there, dressed in his finest clothes, as if he was going to the actual race. He seemed proud of Cashmere. As Frans swung the door of the trailer closed, Mr. Adler patted him on the shoulder, and Anna happily realized her father was proud of Frans, too. There was no better horse trainer anywhere.

But what was more important to her was Frans's goodness and loyalty. Word of his good work had spread, including his bit of chiropractor work, and Mr. Brewster had offered Frans a job at twice what Anna's father could pay. Frans had turned it down. Frans didn't know Anna had overheard him tell Mr. Brewster that the Adlers were more than employers. He had said they were like family. She hoped they soon would be family.

Frans climbed into the truck to drive. Anna slid in beside him. She thought her father would join them, but to her surprise, he just shut the door. "I'll ride with David and your mother," he said.

Anna knew that her family was continually trying to give her and Frans time alone, hoping he would take the next step. Even David had expressed his hope that Frans would someday be his brother-in-law. It hadn't actually been too much of a surprise since David had broken off his engagement with Katherin after the way she had treated Frans.

Anna smiled as she thought about Katherin. Since she and David had broken their engagement, Katherin had been spending time with Sven Brewster. If Cashmere won the race and beat Brewster Farms' horse, Anna felt that might be a little payback to Katherin. The thought just felt good.

As they pulled through the gate near the horse track, Anna spotted both of her sisters. Frans had barely brought the truck to a stop when she was out and running toward them. Wilma hugged her tightly.

After a moment, Anna pulled back. "I'm so glad you made it."

"Made it?" Wilma said, "We wouldn't miss it for the world."

Anna felt a little tug on her belt. She looked down into Maddie's sweet face.

"Aunt Anna, is Cashmere going to win?"

"I hope so," Anna said. "He definitely has it in him."

David and their parents joined them. They had visited quite a while when Anna saw that Frans had tied Cashmere near the stables but was nowhere nearby. She excused herself and headed in Cashmere's direction when she heard Frans's voice, clear and commanding.

"Leave her alone. She's with me."

It was coming from the area Frans had warned her about. But since he was already there, she felt it was safe. As she rounded the corner, she was shocked to see Katherin standing behind Frans, her face covered with tears, looking extremely frightened. In front of Frans stood some rough looking men.

"We were just trying to make friends with her," one of them said in a sarcastic tone.

"Well, that's kind of you," Frans said, pretending he didn't understand the insinuation. "But she needs to get to the grandstands for the trials. See you guys around." He then turned to Katherin. "Come on, Katherin. We need to go."

Katherin turned with him, hanging so close to Frans that she was nearly stepping on his feet. Anna joined them. When they turned the corner around the barns, Katherin could control herself no longer and broke into sobs.

Anna's feelings of animosity toward Katherin melted away, and she reached out her arms. Katherin fled into them. Anna comforted her for a time, and when Katherin's sobs subsided, Anna pulled back and looked at her.

"Didn't anyone ever tell you not to go to that area without an escort?"

Katherin nodded. "But I didn't go there alone. Sven was with me. And then, suddenly, he was gone, and I was alone. Then all of those men gathered around me. I was so scared."

Katherin turned to look at Frans. "I'm not sure what would have happened if you hadn't come, Frans. Thank you."

Frans seemed embarrassed. "They are a bit coarse, and it is no place for a lady, but I don't think they would hurt anyone."

As they continued toward the grandstand, suddenly, Katherin stopped. The others turned to where she was looking. There was Sven with his arm around another girl who was dressed in clothes that left very little to the imagination, and the girl was flaunting her good looks. Her flirting was obvious, and Sven's acceptance of it was as well.

Katherin stared for a moment. When Sven saw her, he seemed embarrassed, and quickly took the other girl and disappeared.

"I hope your horse leaves the Brewsters' horse in the dust," Katherin said angrily.

Frans walked with them until they were back with Anna's family. Once he knew they were safe, he turned and headed toward Cashmere. Everyone was busy visiting, but their conversation stopped when they saw Katherin. She looked down timidly as the silence turned awkward. It was even more so when David turned to see why everyone had suddenly become quiet.

Katherin didn't seem to know what to say, so Anna was the one that finally broke the silence. "Sven abandoned Katherin over near the stables. Some men were being quite coarse and rude to her, so Frans rescued her. Is it okay if she joins us?"

Everyone nodded. David even stepped forward and asked her if she would like to sit with him. Katherin nodded, but before she turned to walk with David to the grandstand, she turned back to Anna and spoke as if to everyone, though specifically addressing her. "Anna, I want to apologize for what I said about Frans. If there is anything I have learned the last couple of years, it is that the goodness of a man is not dependent on his position in society."

"That is for sure," Anna said. "Maybe, sometime, you ought to tell that to Frans."

Katherin nodded as they all climbed into the grandstand. Anna watched as David and Katherin started to visit, awkwardly at first, but more openly all the time. Anna felt her dislike for Katherin starting to fade. Perhaps she wasn't so bad after all.

As the time trials approached, more and more people filled the stands. The Brewsters' horse would be last to run, as it was the defending champion. Anna wondered when Cashmere would run.

The first horse up was a beautiful roan, probably a hand and a half shorter than Cashmere. When the gate opened, the crowd in the stadium roared to life. Anna watched her father. He had his stop watch out. Everyone watched as the horse thundered around the track. As he came back around to the finish, her father held his stop watch at the ready. As the horse crossed the line, he snapped it. "Two minutes, forty-six seconds," he said. "Not bad for 2.5 kilometers, but no record."

Anna knew the fastest horse's time on 2.5 kilometers was two minutes and twenty-four seconds. It was run by an American horse named Secretariat on what Americans called 12 furlongs, or a mile and a half. The 2.5 kilometers and the 12 furlongs were almost identical.

Anna didn't know which number Cashmere had drawn, so as each horse lined up at the starting gate, she checked to see if it was Cashmere. They knew how many horses were to run for the day, and when there were only two left, she knew the next one had to be Cashmere. Sure enough, she saw Frans leading him to the starting gate with the jockey sitting astride. Once they were in position, she could hardly breathe. Frans ran to the grandstand where he could have an unobstructed view. He had barely made it when the gate was opened and Cashmere was off. The whole family rose to cheer as he thundered by.

Anna watched Frans as Cashmere flew around the track with his tail up. Frans's whole body seemed to pulse with each movement of the horse, as if it was him in the saddle. As Cashmere turned at the far corner, she heard Frans say to himself, "He's fighting too hard to be free. He's using up all of his energy against the bit."

Anna looked to see what Frans was seeing, and she could see the jockey holding him back, trying to keep Cashmere from burning himself out, but Cashmere just wanted to run free.

As they approached the final turn, she heard Frans say, "Let him go!"

As if in response, the jockey let the reins out. Suddenly, Cashmere surged forward with a speed that brought the whole crowd to their feet. Cashmere stretched out, appearing as if he was about to take flight, the dirt kicking up behind them.

Everyone around the Adler family held his or her breath as Cashmere crossed the finish line, and Mr. Adler clicked his watch. "Two minutes thirty-eight seconds."

People started yelling and cheering. She could hardly contain her excitement. He had run more than six seconds faster than the next fastest horse of the day. But when she turned to share her excitement with Frans, he was not yelling and excited. He was watching Cashmere down on the track.

Anna saw her father turn to Frans, and she saw that he, too, realized Frans was concentrating. "What is it, Frans?" Mr. Adler asked.

Frans pointed down at Cashmere. "Look at the way he is fighting the jockey. He's not ready to quit and wants to keep running." Once the jockey forced him to quit fighting to run, Cashmere's whole demeanor changed. "Look at that," Frans said. "He is trotting with his head and tail in the air, acting cocky, like he isn't even winded."

Mr. Adler nodded. "He does act that way, doesn't he?"

"I was sure his energy would be gone with the way he fought the bit," Frans said.

He started to say more, but he was drowned out by the roar of the crowd. Anna turned and could see Brewster Farms' horse being brought up to the gate. He pranced and danced all the way into position. Anna looked down to where the Brewster family and friends were sitting. She saw Sven with the other girl.

She looked at Katherin and saw her looking over there, too. The expression on Katherin's face made it clear how she felt. And when the gate opened and the Brewster family and friends exploded to their feet, Anna saw Katherin grit her teeth.

The horse, almost the same height as Cashmere, burned up the track. Anna's attention turned to Frans. He was concentrating, watching the run, straining for details on how the jockey was working him. As the horse rounded the final turn, everyone stood and cheered. When the horse crossed the finish line, Mr. Adler snapped his watch. Everyone turned to him, and he called out, "Two minutes, thirty-two seconds."

As the crowd exploded, Anna felt her heart sink. The Brewsters' horse had beaten Cashmere by six seconds. She turned to Frans, thinking he would be disappointed. But he didn't seem fazed at all. In fact, he was concentrating on the horse again, watching him. Anna saw her father also look at Frans and then look out at the horse. He watched it for a minute and then turned back to Frans. "What are you seeing, Frans?"

Frans turned to him then pointed at the Brewsters' horse. "Look at how his tail droops. Look at how his head is down slightly and his chest is heaving. That horse was at the very end of his energy, while Cashmere, when he finished, acted like he was ready to run again."

"What do we do?" Mr. Adler asked.

"If you watched what the Brewsters' jockey did, he let the reins out a quarter of a kilometer before our jockey let Cashmere's free. And with the amount of energy that Cashmere had left, and the amount he lost fighting the bit, I think we should let him out as we come around that first corner to the open stretch."

"Are you sure?" Mr. Adler asked. "That is a good half of a kilometer or more before where you said the Brewsters' horse did, and he was exhausted. Aren't you afraid Cashmere might burn out?"

"I'm sure he has it in him," Frans said. "I almost think he could do it from the opening gate, but I think we need to keep him under control around the first section to try to keep him from being boxed in. He also has a competitive spirit in him like no horse I've ever seen. It is one thing to be out there running and another to have a horse out ahead of him."

"Frans," Mr. Adler said, "I will leave it to you. You have my full trust."

Frans smiled, and Anna reached down and took his hand. "We all do, Frans. Win or lose next week, you are the best."

Frans blushed, but smiled. "There will be no losing next week."

Mr. Brewster approached, looked at Katherin with David, and frowned before turning to Mr. Adler. "Ben, that's a nice horse you've got there. Might amount to something some day. How would you like to sell him?"

Mr. Adler's voice told his surprise. "Sell him? Why would I want to sell him?"

"Well, he did run a distant second to our horse," Mr. Brewster said. "I'm sure you know it was a six second split, and six seconds is a lot to make up."

"I think Cashmere can do it," Mr. Adler said.

"Not likely," Mr. Brewster said. "I'm prepared to offer you a quarter million for him right now. But after he has a loss under his belt, he won't be worth as much."

Anna saw her father flinch at that amount of money, but he still stood strong. "Sorry, Denton, he's not for sale."

"It's your loss," Mr. Brewster said. With another quick scowl at Katherin, he headed back to his group.

Anna could hold in her feelings no longer. "The nerve of him!"

Frans smiled. "Actually, it is a compliment. If he is willing to pay that much for Cashmere, at least he sees something in him."

"Maybe he's scared we'll win," Anna said.

"I doubt it," Mr. Adler said. "He has never lost before."

"Well, he's about to," Anna said. "Isn't he, Frans?"

Frans smiled. "I think Cashmere has barely begun to race."

# Chapter Ten
# Last Minute Preparation

ach qualifying horse had one more week to prepare for the race. This was a critical time for Frans to test his strategy. Their practice track at home was only about 3/4 the length of the one Cashmere would race on, so it took some calculations to determine at what point he wanted the jockey to let the reins loose. When he was ready, he talked to the jockey about it.

The jockey, who was very experienced, was concerned. "I have ridden a lot of horses, but I have never had one that could open up for that kind of distance."

"I know it's unusual," Frans said, "but he is an unusual horse. He can run a race that will almost kill other horses, and he acts like he hasn't run at all."

"Well, I suppose it doesn't hurt to give it a try," the jockey said.

Mr. Adler took his stop watch and positioned himself where the finish line would be. Anna stood at the point where the jockey was to loosen the reins, and Frans climbed a tower that was constructed to give an unobstructed view. The jockey fought Cashmere, who just wanted to be off. Finally, once he was under control, Mr. Adler gave the signal.

Cashmere was off, but this time, due to listening to Frans, Anna was very aware of how much Cashmere was fighting the bit. "Don't fight it, Cashmere," she said, "it costs energy." The jockey let the reins out when they passed her, and she watched Cashmere surge forward with a fire that she had never seen in a horse before. The power and speed at which he moved made her tremble with excitement.

From up on the stand, Frans was calling, "Go, Cashmere! Go!"

And go he did. He didn't slow at all. If anything, Anna thought he just went faster and faster. When he crossed the finish line, everyone held their breath. Mr. Adler stood stoically, not saying a word, and Anna felt a dread come over her. Cashmere must not have done as well.

Suddenly, Mr. Adler laughed, and as he did, everyone knew he was faking it and ran toward him. As she and Frans reached him at almost the same time, Mr. Adler held up the watch. "Two minutes, thirty seconds."

Anna let out a squeal and threw her arms around Frans's neck. He hugged her for a minute, and then pulled back. "Look at Cashmere."

All three of them turned to where the jockey was trying to keep him reined in. "He still wants to run, doesn't he?" Mr. Adler asked.

"He never seems to want to stop," Frans said.

Just as at the time trials, after the jockey was able to calm him down, Cashmere pranced around with his head up and his tail in the air like he hadn't done more than a casual trot around the block.

"Do you think he could beat the world record?" Mr. Adler asked.

Frans nodded. "I have no doubt he could if the conditions were right. There is one thing more I want to try, as well as some other things I feel he needs to practice."

"What is that?" Mr. Adler asked.

"As competitive as Cashmere is, I'd like to see what he does when he is put up against other horses. I'd also like to try to work him in some tight situations with other horses in case he gets boxed in. I'm afraid he might try to fight his way through."

After Cashmere was rested, the other horses were prepared. None were as fast as Cashmere, and Anna knew he would soon leave them in the dust, so she wondered what Frans had planned. He started out by putting the fastest horse inside the rail. One of the other ranch hands rode him, and Frans told him to cut away from the rail to keep ahead of Cashmere.

When they took off, Cashmere moved quickly ahead, even with the jockey holding him back. But then the ranch hand cut his horse across the inside green, so that as they came around the first corner, he was now ahead of Cashmere. Cashmere fought the jockey harder than ever, wanting to catch the other horse, and when they reached the point where the jockey let the reins loose, Cashmere leaped forward with such a surge it was like he was coming out of the gate again.

As they reached the next corner and the other rider turned his horse and cut across the green again, Cashmere was moving so fast his feet were hardly touching the ground. By the time they reached the finish line, Cashmere had passed the other horse and was a full length ahead.

This time he was breathing a little harder, but he still trotted around with his cocky air. He had won, and he wanted everyone to know it.

"Wow!" Anna said. "I wish we'd had a timer on him."

"We'll time him again before the big day," Frans said, "but right now he needs to just get used to what he'll face."

The next training Frans worked on was putting him with horses in tough situations. They had done this before, but it was more critical now. He had two riders on horses about an eighth of a kilometer ahead. When the signal was given, they all took off. Cashmere didn't like having horses ahead of him and really fought the reins. It didn't take long for him to catch the other two. As he approached them, the one farthest from the rail pulled back so the head of his horse was right at the flank of the other.

Cashmere, coming up on the inside, was boxed in by the rail. He hated it, and it was all the jockey could do to keep him from smashing his way through. As they approached the point where the jockey was to give him free rein, his jockey pulled him back. He then pulled Cashmere to the outside.

When the jockey let him go, Cashmere surged past the other horses as if they were standing still, and, even coming around the corner, he passed them quickly. He ended many horse lengths ahead of the others.

Through the week Frans tried many scenarios with Cashmere, trying to get him used to the tight quarters of the track, when the horses would be pressing hard on each other. Soon, each time he was boxed in, Cashmere instinctively worked to the outside.

Frans tried to be careful with him, trying not to overwork or stress him, but Cashmere would always come back as if he hadn't run at all. The other horses, on the other hand, had to be rotated frequently. Even the jockey became tired under the strain, and Frans took some turns riding Cashmere.

Finally came the last test. Mr. Adler stood ready with his watch. The jockey pulled Cashmere up to the starting line. Three other riders were out about an eighth of a kilometer. At the signal, they were off. Cashmere made up the difference quickly. He was fighting his rider just as hard, but was obeying commands better. He caught up to the other horses as they were coming around a corner, and, with very little direction from the jockey, he moved outside so he would not be trapped.

He thundered past the other horses and crossed the finish line many lengths ahead of them. As Cashmere's jockey tried to get him to stop, everyone rushed to Mr. Adler, who just grinned. "Two minutes, twenty eight seconds."

Everyone yelled and cheered. Frans picked Anna clear off the ground and swung her around. When he set her down, they both turned and looked at Cashmere. He was prancing with his head high and tail up. Frans laughed. "You cocky boy, you. I hope you are ready for tomorrow."

# Chapter Eleven
# Race Day

The day of the race dawned clear. The sun was barely peeking over the horizon when Anna made her way to the barn. Frans was already there, brushing Cashmere. He was concentrating so hard he didn't even see her coming. She put her arms around his waist and hugged him from behind.

"You are going to brush that horse until there is nothing left of him but a pile of hair," she teased.

He laughed. "Me? What about you? You brush him a lot, too. Besides, not only is he powerful, he is handsome. And there's no reason he can't show off a little."

"That's true," Anna said. "But we better hurry. Mother wants you to come in and get some breakfast whenever you can take a break."

"I'm so nervous, I'm not sure I can eat," Frans replied.

"Well, you have to eat something," Anna said. "Besides, I haven't eaten yet, so we could at least spend a little quiet time together."

Anna grabbed a brush and started on the other side. They washed and scrubbed Cashmere, and his black coat glistened in the rising sun. He liked the brushing, but he didn't like the water.

Anna set her brush on a stump, grabbed the hose, and washed his front hooves. When she reached for the brush, it wasn't there. She didn't even have to guess where it was because this wasn't the first time it had happened. She looked at Cashmere, and sure enough, he had it between his teeth.

"Cashmere, give me the brush," she said.

He curled his lip up, as if laughing at her. She grabbed and tugged until Cashmere opened his teeth. She lost her balance and fell flat on her backside. Cashmere let out a laughing whinny, and Frans even laughed.

"You think that was funny?" Anna said. She turned the hose on Frans.

He fought his way through the water. Dripping wet, he hugged her, and she, too, became soaked. They continued to laugh and work on Cashmere for some time. The sun shone its full circle above the horizon by the time Frans declared the job done.

"We better get some breakfast and hurry and change," Anna said.

As she turned to leave, Frans grabbed her hand and pulled her into his arms. "Before we do, there is something I want to say." He held her even closer. "Anna, I love you."

He leaned down and kissed her. He had never kissed her before, and Anna felt so happy. Cashmere whinnied and threw his head up and down as if he approved.

Anna grabbed Frans's hand and pulled him toward the house. They hurried and ate. After everyone had dressed in their nice clothes, it was time to get Cashmere loaded. Katherin came to join them for the ride to the track. She and David had been spending a lot of time together again. Anna didn't mind now that Katherin seemed to admire Frans and only had praise for him.

As Anna slid into the truck by Frans, her stomach was doing flip flops from excitement. She was happy Frans had kissed her, and she thought it wouldn't be long before he asked her to marry him. She was slightly worried that if Cashmere lost, he would feel he couldn't. The day just had to go well so that Frans would ask her.

Anna's sisters and their families were already at the track when they arrived. Maddie came rushing over. "Is Cashmere going to win today?" she asked.

"I think so," Anna said, sweeping Maddie into her arms.

Maddie reached out her arms to Frans. He took her from Anna and gave her a big hug.

Everyone else took their seats in the grandstand while Frans and the jockey took Cashmere to the stable and then went to the jockey weigh-in. The group in the grandstand all talked excitedly, watching for the horses to move into the lineup.

Everyone quieted down when the announcer's voice boomed over the speakers. "In first position – Bruin, from Brewster Farms, the undefeated national champion with the fastest qualifying time of two minutes and thirty two seconds, six seconds faster than the next qualifier."

Anna felt proud as she watched Frans lead Cashmere to his

starting gate with the jockey on Cashmere's back. The announcer's voice came again. "In position two – Cashmere from Adler Farms, the youngest horse, with the second best qualifying time of two minutes, thirty eight seconds."

As the horses continued to line up, there was whinnying and squealing as some of the horses expressed their displeasure with the close proximity of the others. When the horses were all in their individual positions, and the trainers moved to their places to watch just outside the track, everything grew quiet as everyone anticipated the start of the race. Anna could feel her heart pounding.

And then the gates opened, and they were off.

The horses shot forward. Bruin and Cashmere raced neck and neck with their jockeys holding them back to prepare for the turn. But the horse in the third position was not being reined in at all and surged forward at full speed. His jockey pulled him just ahead of Cashmere, and then reined back hard. The horse to Cashmere's left had his head alongside Cashmere, and Cashmere's jockey couldn't pull around and could do nothing but rein Cashmere in.

Cashmere was boxed in against the rail with Bruin breaking forward from the others. The cutoff and the boxing in looked deliberate, because no jockey reins a horse in like that in a race. Anna felt anger swell in her as she watched Bruin start to pull away. The crowd felt it was deliberate as well, and an audible rumbling was heard.

But suddenly, Cashmere pulled back, now behind all of the other horses, and cut far to the outside. No one could box him in there, but it was much farther to run. It appeared that Cashmere did it as much on his own as the jockey did.

Now, in the very rear, Cashmere reached the point where Frans had told the jockey to give him free rein. And that was what he did. Suddenly, Cashmere surged forward, as if he was only beginning to race. Even having to swing wide around the turn, he still moved past one, two, three horses. Coming down the straight away, horses number three and four started to burn out and began to fade to the back.

By the time they reached the next turn, Cashmere was ahead of all the horses except Bruin, and it appeared that Cashmere had him in his sights. But Bruin was still three full lengths ahead. Cashmere's jockey cut Cashmere to the rail coming around the turn, and by the time they came out of the turn, Cashmere's had pulled up to Bruin's tail. With the long straight away left, Anna could see Cashmere moving up fast.

The crowd could see it, too, and everyone was on their feet screaming. Bruin's jockey pushed him hard. But Bruin was already at top speed, and Cashmere effortlessly moved past him. When Cashmere's head moved into the lead, the screaming and cheering was deafening.

The speed was beginning to tell on Bruin, and he started slowing, even as Cashmere was still picking up speed. Soon Cashmere was one

length ahead, and then two, and then it was over.

The announcer, screaming over the speaker: "Cashmere wins by three lengths with a time of two minutes and 25 seconds!" He could barely be heard for the cheering and screaming.

The other horses crossed the line with horses three and four far behind.

Anna looked down at the track. Cashmere's jockey was still trying to pull Cashmere in. He wanted to continue running, and the crowd noticed. There was some laughter, but when Cashmere finally slowed down and started his cocky head and tail-high strut, the stadium erupted into both applause and laughter.

As the jockey led Cashmere to the winner's circle, Mr. Adler and Frans joined them. From her vantage point in the stadium, Anna felt proud of all of them. There were tons of pictures and the usual accolades, but all Anna could think about was that they had finally done it. They had finally beaten the unbeatable Brewster Farms.

As the group moved from the winner's circle and headed back to the stables, Anna noticed David pull Katherin close. She also noticed Sven's glare in their direction from the middle of the sullen group from Brewster farms while Mr. Brewster quickly headed toward the stables.

She felt that since Frans and her father were already down there, it would be safe to make her way down there, too. It took a long time to work her way through the crowd. People who knew who she was wanted to stop and congratulate her. She pressed through the crowd as fast as she could. She could hardly wait to see Frans and throw her arms around him and congratulate him. She knew he must be excited.

But the first scene she came upon stopped her. She slid into the shadows of a barn to listen. Mr. Brewster was in a heated discussion with the owners of horses three and four. Though Anna didn't know them well, she knew who they were.

"You promised you would make sure he couldn't win!" Mr. Brewster yelled. "That's what I paid you for!"

"We had our jockeys box him in," the one owner said. "We could not keep him from dropping back."

"Besides," the other owner said. "No horse has ever been able to drop back like that and come around the outside. That is an incredible horse."

"Well," Mr. Brewster said, "I paid you to guarantee my win. And I didn't win, so I don't owe you anything."

"Perhaps we should inform the Horse Racing Association of what you did," one owner said.

"You would be as guilty as I would," Mr. Brewster said. "If they banned me, they would ban you, too."

At that point Anna stepped out of the shadows and looked directly at the men. They instantly went quiet, but they knew she had heard them. They stared at her for a moment, and she glared back. But then she heard Frans's voice, loud and angry. Frans was almost never angry, so it surprised her. She moved quickly in the direction of his voice.

The scene she came upon was not the one she expected. There with her father, Frans, and the jockey was a group of men she didn't recognize. Frans was visibly upset, and when he spoke to her father, his voice betrayed bitter disappointment.

"Well, then, I guess you don't need me anymore!" And with that, he turned and headed away.

Anna ran to them. She stopped and looked at her father, but he turned his eyes from her. She ran after Frans, grabbing his arm and pulling him to a stop. "Frans, what is it?"

Frans turned to her but wouldn't look her in the eye. He took some short breaths as if trying to control his emotions. And when he finally did speak, the words cut deep into her heart.

"Your father sold Cashmere."

# Chapter Twelve
# Winning And Losing

Frans started to pull away from Anna, but she tightened her grip on his arm. "No, Frans," she said. "I won't let you go."

Frans turned back to her. "Anna, with Cashmere gone, Adler Farms doesn't need me anymore."

"But I need you," Anna said. "I will always need you." She stepped around in front of him, though he wouldn't raise his eyes to look at her. "Please, Frans," she continued. "Please don't go."

Frans relaxed slightly, but Anna couldn't help but sense the pain he felt. Suddenly, her father was by them. "Frans," he said, "I'm sorry. I didn't mean to."

"How could you sell a horse and not mean to?" Anna asked.

"When that man asked to buy Cashmere," Mr. Adler said, "I told him no. But then he said, 'Everyone has a price.' I thought of the most ridiculous price I could think of, and said, 'I wouldn't sell him for a penny less than five million.' I didn't in my life think he'd say yes."

Anna gasped. "Five million? Mr. Brewster agreed to pay you five million?"

"Not Brewster," Mr. Adler said, pointing to a man in the group of men around Cashmere. "Him. The one right next to Cashmere."

Anna looked at the man who was rubbing his hand along Cashmere's side. He looked slightly familiar, but she couldn't place how she knew him.

"Who is he?" Anna asked.

"He's a movie star from America," Frans said with disgust. "The others call him Mr. Donaldson, or Sir, depending on their position."

"I really didn't mean to sell him at any price," Mr. Adler said. "But I can't back out now, or I would lose my honor."

"What now?" Anna asked.

"Maybe we can try to breed another race horse," Mr. Adler said.

"Midnight is too old," Frans said. "I don't think there will ever be another Cashmere."

"We have other mares," Mr. Adler said.

Anna replied before Frans did. "But none are as fast as Midnight, at least as fast as she used to be when she was younger."

As they were talking, the man who bought Cashmere came over. He smiled flirtily at Anna. "I'm Phil. And who might you be?"

Anna didn't answer his question, nor did she even try to hide her disgust as she spoke. "What do you want with a horse like Cashmere?"

"Young lady," he said, speaking in a demeaning tone, "do you realize that this horse was only a second off of a world record and just beat what many considered an unbeatable horse? Just owning a horse like that is prestigious."

"He's not a trophy," Anna said. "He's a race horse."

"He'll be whatever I decide he'll be," Mr. Donaldson retorted.

Suddenly Cashmere started to rear. They all turned to see one of the men that was with the movie star holding the lead rope. He must have done something to startle Cashmere. The men fled from the huge horse, and even the jockey moved away. Frans ran to Cashmere, speaking gently to him. "It's okay, boy. It's okay."

Cashmere settled down, and Frans grabbed the lead rope. Cashmere was breathing hard, his nostrils flaring, and Frans gently stroked him, continuing to talk to him. Once Cashmere calmed down, Mr. Donaldson came over.

"You're his trainer, aren't you?" he asked Frans. Frans nodded, so Mr. Donaldson continued. "I'm sure he is used to you. I will need someone who knows him. Would you like a job?" Frans paused, so Mr. Donaldson continued. "It would pay $7,000 per month."

Anna gasped, and even Frans's eyes widened briefly. Frans spoke quietly. "The money is not as important as the horse."

"I'm glad to know you feel that way about him," Mr. Donaldson said. "Are you interested in the job?"

Frans slowly nodded, speaking even slower. "For Cashmere."

Suddenly, Anna felt fear fill her heart. Would Frans leave? She grabbed his arm and looked him in the eye. Frans took her hand in his and squeezed it, helping calm her pounding heart. But Anna could see by the look in his eyes that he felt unsure what he would do if Cashmere was gone.

Mr. Donaldson turned to Mr. Adler. "I need a place to keep him until I can have my people arrange to have him shipped to America. I'd be willing to pay $100 per day for his boarding."

Mr. Adler simply nodded. Suddenly a reporter was there. He stepped in front of Mr. Donaldson. "Mr. Donaldson, I understand you just bought the winning horse."

Mr. Donaldson smiled as he spoke, turning so the reporter's assistant could take a picture. "Yes. I figured it would be good for a horse of this type to be owned by a man of my renown."

Anna thought she was about to be sick. A few of the reporters had questions for Mr. Adler, and a few for Frans and the jockey. One reporter even asked her what she thought of the win. But most of the reporters gathered around Mr. Donaldson, as Anna thought, like dung flies around a manure pile. She could tell that Frans just wanted to leave, and she felt sorry for him. The day that was supposed to be a day of celebration for all of them had suddenly become a tragic nightmare.

She looked at her father. Reporters asked him about the five million dollars, and he glanced at Frans and tried to change the subject. Even with all of that money, he didn't want to celebrate. She almost felt worst of all for him. He knew the loss of Cashmere was his fault.

Cashmere became anxious about all of the attention, and Frans suggested they should take him home. Mr. Donaldson refused, at least until there were lots of pictures taken. But once Cashmere started rearing because of all of the flashes, even he agreed it might be best.

Frans was quiet as he loaded the beautiful horse into the trailer. When he climbed into the truck, Anna climbed in beside him. Still, Frans never said a word.

Finally Anna spoke. "So, now what, Frans?"

Frans breathed a huge sigh and shook his head. "I don't know, Anna. All my years of work at Adler Farms was to create and train a horse that could win. And that's all gone."

"But he did win. And we could try again," Anna said.

"With what?" Frans asked. "We might be able to get a mare bred to Cashmere's father, but we don't have another one like Midnight, and she's too old."

"With the money Father made, he could buy the best mare."

Frans was quiet for a moment, and when he spoke he spoke quietly, and the hurt he felt was evident. "To what? To just sell the horse again if he wins?"

Anna hurt for Frans, but she felt defensive of her father. "Frans, you heard Father say he didn't mean to sell him."

"You can't set a price and not mean to sell him," Frans said, "because there's always a chance the offer will be accepted."

They rode in silence the rest of the way. Frans stared straight ahead. When they arrived home, Frans quickly took Cashmere from the trailer. He tied him up and brushed him. Anna helped him, but they worked in silence. Frans didn't seem to want to talk, and Anna felt that if she did, she would cry.

When they finished, Frans turned Cashmere out to pasture. Cashmere ran and pranced around the pasture as if he knew he was the champion. Frans watched him, and Anna watched Frans. She could see that he was hardly able to control his emotions. When she reached out and touched his arm, he just turned and walked away.

Anna watched Cashmere for a brief moment, and then she followed Frans to the bunk house. When she reached the door, she knocked, but he didn't answer. When she knocked again and still received no answer, she went in.

What she saw made her heart ache. Frans was packing his belongings into a duffle bag. Unable to keep the hurt from her own voice, she asked, "Frans, what are you doing?" He didn't answer, so she placed her hand on his duffle bag to stop him from putting anything more into it. "Frans, what about us? I thought you loved me. I thought you were going to ask me to marry you. You were, weren't you?"

Frans didn't answer her question and still wouldn't look at her. "I think it's time for me to leave."

She couldn't stop the tears now. "I'm coming with you."

Frans shook his head. "No, Anna. You belong here. I don't. Just like Cashmere was born to run, I was born to work with horses like him. I've done my job here, and there is really no job left for me to do. It's time to move on. When I leave here in a couple of days to go with Cashmere to the United States, I don't know what will happen, or when or even if I will ever be back."

"I'll come with you," Anna said. "I belong with you."

"No," Frans said. "This is your home. You belong here."

Anna didn't know what to say. Her own feelings were in a quandary, and she was sure Frans's were even more so. Could he be blaming her for what her father had done, just because he was her father? Did his anger at her father make it so he could no longer love her? Was he saying he would leave and never come back? Was it because, without Cashmere, he no longer felt he was on the same level as she was, and that her family might feel the same way?

Frans spoke quietly, interrupting her thoughts. "I'm sure they will be expecting you at the victory celebration."

Anna turned and walked from the bunk house. She hadn't made it very far when she could no longer control her emotions. Instead of going to the house she went to the pasture to watch Cashmere, and she sobbed. The more she watched him run, knowing he would be gone, the harder she cried. When her tears started to subside, she suddenly realized she was not alone – her father was standing there.

She turned away from him as he walked up beside her. He touched her shoulder, but she pulled away from him. He spoke quietly. "Anna, I'm sorry. I really didn't mean to sell him. But once I had said it, I would have lost my honor to back out."

"Honor?" Anna said, turning to him. "What about the honor to your family? What about your honor to Frans who has worked so hard? What about your honor to Cashmere, who has just won the race for you, and now you are going to honor him by selling him and shipping him to the United States to become a trophy?"

Mr. Adler looked down. "I don't know what I can do. The deal is already done."

"Well, I hope your honor was worth it," Anna said. "Frans is packing to leave. He doesn't feel he is needed here anymore. And he feels he has nothing to offer, and that our relationship should end."

"I'm sorry, Anna," Mr. Adler said. "I don't know what else to say."

"There's only one more thing to say," Anna said. "When Frans leaves, I will not stay here."

With that, she turned and left. When she stepped through the door to the house, she found a mixed mood. There was the joy of the win, but it was tempered by the fact that Cashmere would be gone. She visited briefly with her sisters, but when Maddie asked, "Is Grandpa really going to sell Cashmere?" her heart ached so much that she decided it was time to leave.

As she turned to go to her room, her mother stopped her. "We'll be having dinner soon. Do you want to make sure Frans knows?"

Anna shook her head. "You might need to eat without us. Neither of us feels like celebrating."

Anna went up to her room and cried again. She couldn't get herself to join the party even though her mother and sisters each came up to invite her. When her father came, she wouldn't even open the door.

The party, which normally would have lasted into the early hours of the morning, faded away by 11:00 that evening. There seemed to be dismal pall hanging over everyone, and it even affected the guests.

The next couple of days passed slowly, but as a big blur. Her emotions were overwhelming her ability to think clearly. She and Frans hardly said a word to each other. He never joined them for any meals, though she knew her mother had invited him. Her father more than once tried to apologize to her. But an apology that fixes nothing seems so empty.

When the dreaded day arrived, her whole family gathered. They all planned to go to the airport for the farewell. Anna didn't go down to breakfast. When her mother came up to check on her and found her packing, the anguished look on her face told her feelings.

"Anna, what are you doing?"

"I'm leaving, Mother."

"Why?"

Anna continued to pack as she talked. "Why don't you ask Father?"

"He told me what you said, but I didn't think you meant it."

"When Cashmere leaves, Frans feels he is no longer needed or wanted here. And when Frans is gone, I will feel the same way about myself."

"Anna," her mother said, the tears now streaming down her face, "please don't do this. Your father didn't mean to sell him."

"Mother, Frans and I trained Cashmere. That is what we lived for during the last couple of years, that and the love that we shared as we worked together. And now Cashmere will be gone. I think Father could have stopped the deal, but the money was too tempting. Well, he can keep his money. I want no part of it!"

Anna heard a sound and turned to see her father standing in the doorway. He had obviously heard the whole thing.

"Anna, I would undo it if I could," he said, even as the tears started to flow down his face.

"Really?" Anna replied. "You could have still told him no, even after he agreed to the five million. But your honor to a stranger was more important than your honor to your family."

"Where will you go? What will you do?" her mother asked.

Anna snapped her suitcase shut. "I guess that doesn't matter, as long as it is away from here."

She picked up her suitcase and brushed past her father on the way out the door. She walked outside and put the suitcase on the porch. She went to the pasture where Frans was riding Cashmere. He seemed reluctant for the ride to end. When he finally brought him in, Anna was there to meet him.

"I want a turn," Anna said.

When Frans climbed off, they were suddenly standing face to face. Frans looked down as he spoke. "Anna, I . . ." He paused. When he continued, he simply said, "Let me help you up."

Having him help her felt good. They hadn't been that close, nor had he touched her in days. As she rode, she looked over at Frans. Her father came and talked to Frans for a while, then Frans disappeared into the bunkhouse for some time. When he finally emerged, he was carrying his duffle bag and a manila envelope. He took them to the truck and stuck them inside, then came back to the fence and watched.

Anna could see Frans smile at her, though she could sense his pain. Way too soon, it was time to prepare Cashmere for his journey. She brought him in, and Frans unsaddled him. Together they brushed him, just as they had so many times before, only this time they again never said a word.

Frans loaded Cashmere in the trailer. She wondered if she should climb in the truck with Frans. Or would it be too uncomfortable for them? She finally decided to ride in the car with her sister's family, and Frans drove alone.

Maddie climbed on Anna's lap and leaned against her. She started crying as she asked, "Aunt Anna, will we ever see Cashmere and Frans again?"

"I don't know, Maddie," Anna said. "I hope so."

At the airport, Frans pulled up to the gate. After a moment it was opened, and he drove through. They stopped all of their cars outside the gate, and then walked out onto the tarmac. Frans loaded Cashmere onto the chartered plane, then retrieved his belongings.

He walked over to where they were all standing and set the duffle bag down. He looked up at them and forced a smile. "Well, I guess this is it. I want to thank you all for everything."

Maddie broke away from her mother and ran and threw her arms around Frans's waist. "I love you, Frans."

Tears showed in Frans's eyes as he hugged her in return. "I love you, too, Maddie."

"Frans," Anna's mother said, "we want you to know you are family to us. We hope you aren't gone too long, and you will come back to us." Frans only looked down.

Frans went down the line to say goodbye. Anna's sisters, mother, and the children hugged him, as did Katherin. Anna noted how much Katherin's feelings about Frans had changed.

David and Anna's brothers-in-law shook Frans's hand, as did her father. When her father did, he held Frans's hand and didn't let go. "Frans, I was stupid, and would do anything to undo what I have done. I even contacted Mr. Donaldson and tried to get Cashmere back, but he refused. I'm hoping to buy the best mare I can find and try to raise a new colt. If you will ever forgive me, I would really love to have you come back." Again, Frans said nothing.

Anna was last. As Frans stopped in front of her, he could no longer hold back his tears, and she couldn't either. "Anna," he said. He couldn't seem to say any more for some time. Finally he held out the manila envelope. "This is for you."

He reached out his hand, and she shook it. He then picked up his duffle bag, turned, and started to walk away. When he reached the airplane stairs, he stopped. He stood there for a moment, then he suddenly dropped his duffle bag, turned around, and ran back to her and pulled her into his arms. He kissed her and held her tightly for a long time. She could feel his tears against her face. Instantly her anger and hurt from the last few days were swept away. He did love her. So why had he acted as he had? Why was he leaving?

When he finally let go of her, he turned and ran to the plane, grabbing his duffle bag as he went. He bounded up the stairs, stopping at the top. He slowly turned and waved. Everyone waved back. He then entered the plane, and the stairs were pulled away. The engines fired, and gradually the plane started to pull away.

"Look," Maddie said. "It's Frans."

Anna could see him waving through the small window. The plane started to move away, and soon he was out of sight. Anna picked Maddie up so she could see better as the plane turned. It started coming back, going faster and faster. Just when it was almost straight across from them, it lifted off of the runway and climbed into the sky.

Everyone waved. Anna and Maddie waved until it was completely out of sight. "I wish he didn't have to go," Maddie said.

That was when Anna remembered the manila envelope. Everyone gathered around as she opened it. Out fell a little box and a letter. She opened the box and found a beautiful diamond ring. She gasped, knowing Frans must have spent a huge amount of his wages on it. She then opened the letter and started to read.

*My Dearest Anna,*

*I must apologize for these last few days. Katherin tried to convince me to stay and told me that you felt like I didn't love you. Nothing could be further from the truth. I love you more than I have ever loved anyone, and I view you as my very best friend. But just as Cashmere was born to run, I was born to work with horses like him.*

*When he belonged to your father, and I worked there, I felt like, maybe, I was somebody, something more than just a horse trainer, and I had something to offer you. But now that he is gone, I really don't feel I do anymore. You deserve so much more than just a horse trainer.*

*And without Cashmere, I feel it is time to move on, and I cannot take you away from your family. Your father told me you planned to leave. Please don't leave on my account. They are your family, and they love you.*

*I want you to know that no matter where I go, I will always love you and will never forget you. The ring is for you. I purchased it, hoping that after the race, if Cashmere won, I could ask you to marry me. I felt like then I would have shown that I was somebody. I could never sell it or give it to anyone else because it represents my love for you, and that love can never belong to another. I hope the ring will always remind you of that, and help you remember me and the good times we shared.*

*With All My Love,*
*Frans*

Anna handed the letter to her mother to let her read it, then turned to Katherin. "Katherin, you really tried to help save our relationship?"

Katherin nodded. "I felt things were just wrong, and after my experience with Sven, I realized what a wonderful relationship you two had. I knew Frans truly loved you, and you loved him, but the events of the past days were getting in the way. But no matter how much I tried to convince him, he now feels he will never be worthy of you."

When Anna's mother finished reading the letter, she looked up. "So, Anna, what now?"

Anna felt a steely determination come over her. "I know we can't bring Cashmere back. But knowing Frans still loves me, I will go to the ends of the earth to be with him."

Anna's father stepped up and put his arm around her shoulder. "Anna, I can't totally make up for the harm that I have caused, but I will do whatever I can to make things as right as possible."

Anna took a deep breath. "I'm going after Frans. I will bring him home, or I will stay with him. Either way, even if we lose Cashmere, I'm not going to lose Frans."

Anna's mother smiled. "If you end up staying in the United States, don't forget to invite us to the wedding."

# Chapter Thirteen
# Some Things Never Should Be

F rans waved out the window for as long as he could see everyone below. When they faded from view, he sat back in his chair and closed his eyes, trying to make the pain in his heart go away. He loved Anna so very much, but she deserved so much more.

The noise, the movement, and the angle of the plane frightened Cashmere, and he started to snort in his enclosure in the back of the plane. Frans could see him from his position and called to him, but he could not go to him while the plane was still climbing.

Once they reached cruising altitude, the captain turned off the seat belt lights, and Frans was able to go to Cashmere. He talked to him, calming him. When they reached America, they had to land and refuel. The landing was even more frightening to Cashmere, and it took a while to calm him down again.

One more takeoff and one more landing, and then they were in California. The two men that had been with Mr. Donaldson at the race were there to meet Frans. This time they introduced themselves. The biggest man was named John, and the smaller man was named Hank. They were driving a big new pickup with an equally new horse trailer. Frans loaded Cashmere into the trailer, threw his duffle bag into the back of the pickup, and then climbed in with them.

They snaked their way through more traffic than Frans had ever seen before. He wondered if every person in the state of California had a car and was driving it there. When they arrived at their destination, Frans could not see any race track, only lots of stables with a few small riding arenas.

"Where's the race track?" he asked.

They laughed. "You ain't going to see no track around here. These are just riding stables."

"But Cashmere is a race horse, not a riding horse," Frans said.

"Not anymore," John said. "He's a show horse now."

Frans had to bite his lip. The thought of Cashmere being purchased just to show him off irritated him. In fact, it made him angry.

They pulled in and parked. A small crowd gathered over to see what new horse was there. When Frans led Cashmere from the trailer, the people in the crowd gasped at his size. He towered over every horse there.

A little girl tugged on Frans's shirt. "That is sure a big horse, Mister."

Frans nodded. "He is a champion race horse from Germany."

People started asking questions about where he raced. One big man, who seemed to be somewhat in charge of things, asked about the length of the race and Cashmere's time. Frans only knew it in meters and not in miles so the man didn't understand. Frans then compared it as equal to the Kentucky Derby. When he told the time again, the man gasped. "That's almost as fast as Secretariat!"

"And," Frans bragged, "Cashmere was hardly winded."

Frans found his strong German accent also drew people around. The attention Frans was getting seemed to annoy John and Hank. When someone asked why Cashmere was there, John jumped in to answer. "Phil Donaldson, the famous movie star, bought him for five million dollars." Everyone gasped. Then, speaking in a derogatory tone, John added, pointing to Frans, "This man is just the trainer."

Cashmere was prancing, and Frans thought that after the long flight the horse needed to release some energy. "Is there a place I could let him run?" he asked of the group.

The big man, who also spoke with an accent different from the others, said, "Not really for a race horse. All we have are little riding corrals, nothing long enough for a race horse to run."

Frans decided that was better than nothing and saddled him. He wished everyone would leave, but most of the crowd hung around. Just as he finished saddling Cashmere and untied him, there was a big commotion. His eyes followed the crowd's, and he saw a caravan with a limousine followed by various cars.

The cars pulled up near them and parked. The chauffeur got out of the limo, opened the door, and Mr. Donaldson stepped out. The occupants of the other cars joined him to walk over to Cashmere.

"Ladies and gentlemen," Mr. Donaldson said, addressing the group that came with him, "this is the horse."

One lady, dressed in a beautiful gown, which Frans thought looked ridiculous at a riding stable, said, "My, he's huge. Is he dangerous?"

"Oh, no, he's well trained and gentle as a lamb," Mr. Donaldson said, turning to Frans. "Isn't that right, Frans?"

"He is well trained, Sir," Frans replied. "But he is a race horse, and every race horse has lots of power and energy and can be somewhat unpredictable. It is best to keep a distance."

He had barely said it when a man dressed in a tux reached up and touched Cashmere right near his flank. Cashmere jumped forward, knocking Mr. Donaldson and a couple of others down. By the time Frans was able to bring Cashmere to a stop and calm him down, many of the group were moving to the safety of their cars.

Mr. Donaldson was only slightly hurt, but he was immensely embarrassed. "You lock that horse in his stall!" he yelled.

"But he has been flying all day and needs a chance to release his energy," Frans said.

Mr. Donaldson only became angrier that Frans would dare question him. "Do you think I care about that? Do what I tell you, or I will find someone who will."

Frans nodded and turned to John. "Where do I put him?"

John led the way to a stall in the stable. "This is his stall. The one next to it is for our use as well, for feed and other things."

Frans nodded. He decided not to unsaddle Cashmere, thinking he would be able to ride him later.

Once he was in the stall, Mr. Donaldson was able to convince the group to come back. They all walked cautiously so they would not step in anything. They all tried to converse intellectually about race horses, but Frans thought they sounded foolish. As he listened to them and looked at the ladies dressed in elegant clothes, Frans's thoughts suddenly turned to Anna. How he missed her. She didn't pretend to be anything she wasn't. He knew the guy that she married would be lucky.

"Don't you usually take the saddle off before you put him in his stall?" one man asked, acting all knowledgeable.

"Of course we do," Mr. Donaldson said. He then turned to Frans. "Frans, why is he still saddled?"

"I was thinking I might ride him a little when we are done here," Frans said.

"I think from what I've seen that he is too dangerous to ride at a place like this," one lady said.

Mr. Donaldson, seeming to want to appease her, agreed. He turned to Frans. "That is true. Frans, you should unsaddle him."

"But, Sir," Frans said. "He needs a chance to . . ."

Mr. Donaldson interrupted him. "That will be all, Frans. I won't have a horse of mine hurting anyone. You can put him on the walker."

Frans gasped. The thought of a race horse's only exercise being a walker seemed ridiculous. "But, Sir, a walker? He is a race horse, and he

. . ."

Again Mr. Donaldson interrupted him. "He is not a race horse now. He is my horse. And we will do with him what I say. And I say he will not be ridden here since it is too dangerous."

Frans bit his tongue and breathed hard before he spoke. "Is there any place where we could take him to ride him sometimes?"

"I'm not really worried about that," Mr. Donaldson said. "That is not his purpose anymore. You can just unsaddle him and keep him here so that he and everyone around him is safe."

Frans nodded. Mr. Donaldson and his group started to leave. As they did, John and Hank smirked at Frans. John said, "Yeah, that's not his purpose anymore."

Frans was so angry he could hardly speak. But who was he angry at? Was it John and Hank? Was it Mr. Donaldson? Was it Mr. Adler for selling Cashmere?

He just wished he could take Cashmere away from there. A race horse should not be stuck in a small stall only to be put on a walker.

Frans led Cashmere from the stall and started to unsaddle him. As he did, the big man with the accent came and stuck out his hand. "Hi, people here call me Hernandez."

Frans let go of the saddle strap and took Hernandez's hand. "I'm Frans."

Hernandez nodded. "Yes, I heard. I'm sorry about your horse. He is way too much horse for a place like this."

Frans finished unstrapping Cashmere's saddle as he spoke. "Mr. Donaldson only bought him to be a trophy."

"That is a terrible thing for a horse like him," Hernandez said. "It is nothing but a prison sentence. I think that is like torture for him."

Frans nodded. "Well, at least I'll take him and put him on the walker."

They walked together to the walking machine. It had a center pole that went down to a gearbox. On the top of the pole, long, thick, metal pipes stuck out much like the spokes of a wagon wheel. From these hung some chains with a loop where a horse could be tethered. Frans clipped one to Cashmere's halter, and with a click of his tongue, signaled for Cashmere to move forward. Cashmere took off running, pulling hard. The heavy gear in the center box started to turn. Faster and faster Cashmere trotted, and then ran until the gear box started to smoke. Cashmere was pulling so hard against it that the thick metal pipe he was connected to started to bend. By the time Frans was able to work Cashmere to a stop, the pipe was shaped slightly like a large C.

"Perhaps we need to just release the resistance and let him go," Hernandez said.

"Maybe we ought to turn him around and see if he will bend it the other way first," Frans said.

They let him run in the other direction, and indeed, he did bend it back. Frans stopped Cashmere to examine the pipe. It was better, but it was in an S shape now. Hernandez shifted the gear to the lowest resistance, and Frans let Cashmere go and urged him forward. Again, Cashmere took off. With the resistance on the lowest setting, Cashmere circled the walker as fast as he could with the hindrance of the tether. His hooves kicked up a slight sand storm.

Frans and Hernandez told the gathering crowd to keep back. Cashmere continued to run and run. After a time, Hernandez asked, "Does he ever get tired?"

Frans shook his head. "Hardly seems to. After a race, he acts like he has just had a walk in the park."

After a while, some other people wanted to put their horses on the walker. Both Frans and Hernandez knew they couldn't put other horses with Cashmere or he would likely drag them around, so Frans brought him to a stop. Cashmere didn't like being stopped, and snorted his disapproval.

Frans took Cashmere back, brushed him, and put him in his stall. Cashmere whinnied and pawed at the door, begging to run.

Hernandez smiled. "I haven't ever seen a horse like him. He acts like he could run forever."

"I have been around a lot of race horses," Frans said, "but I have never seen one that has his unbounded energy and speed."

"How did a man like Donaldson end up buying him?" Hernandez asked.

Frans told the story, and then Hernandez said, "It is wrong for a horse like him to be owned by a man like Donaldson just to show him off to his friends."

When Frans finished his work, he went and watched people riding. The sign by the gate of the riding rings said, "No racing."

Frans began to wonder why he was here. It was becoming clear that Mr. Donaldson didn't plan to ever race Cashmere. Frans remembered telling Anna that, just as Cashmere was born to run, he was born to work with such horses. So if Cashmere was not able to run, he was not able to train him. He had heard Mr. Donaldson imply that he just wanted Cashmere so he could brag about him, but somehow Frans hadn't believed it. Maybe he just felt badly enough that he came to do for Cashmere what he could. But he was beginning to realize that he could do very little.

As it started to get dark, Hernandez came and found him. "Do you have a place to stay?"

"I thought I would just sleep in the stall next to Cashmere for the night to help him feel more secure," Frans replied.

"Okay. But I have an extra couch you could sleep on until you can find yourself a real apartment."

"Thanks," Frans said, "but I think I'll pass."

"Hey," Hernandez said. "At least come to dinner. You've still got to eat."

Frans nodded and accepted. When everything was closed up for the night, they walked to Hernandez's home. They passed lots of big homes and continued to walk to a part of town where the homes were smaller. Eventually they stopped at little adobe house.

It was well cared for, with vine flowers growing over trellises that led up to the door. Hernandez opened the door and called out. "Daddy's home!"

Immediately he was surrounded by six beautiful children, ranging in age from about four to about seventeen. His wife came in and smiled as Hernandez kissed her. "This is Mariana," Hernandez said, obviously proud of her. He then introduced each of the children.

Hernandez then turned to his wife. "Frans is new here from Germany. He came with the horse Mr. Donaldson bought that I told you was coming. I invited him to eat with us."

Mariana smiled. "You are most welcome, Mr. Frans."

Frans smiled. "Thank you."

They had a wonderful dinner like nothing Frans had ever eaten. It was chicken and beans in taco shells. It was very good.

As they gathered around after, Hernandez asked Frans to tell his children the story about Cashmere. They listened with fascination. When he finished, Mariana asked, "So, Mr. Frans, do you have a wife and family?"

Frans shook his head. "I have a wonderful lady that I was ready to ask to marry me."

"Is she pretty?" one of the younger girls asked.

"Yes," Frans said. He pulled out Anna's picture and showed them.

Mariana nodded. "She is very pretty. So when are you going to ask her?"

"I can't," Frans said. "She can do so much better than me."

"What do you mean?" the oldest girl, Leanna, asked.

"It was her family that owned Cashmere," Frans replied. "They are very wealthy, and I am just from a poor immigrant family."

"Do you think it is money that defines what a man is?" Hernandez asked.

Frans had never really thought of it in those terms, but he realized he did. "It obviously determines your place in society," he answered.

Hernandez seemed to bristle at this. "Let me tell you something, Mister. Money does not determine a man's worth. When I lived in South America, I was a gaucho, a South American cowboy. I worked hard and was one of the best. I saved every penny I could from what I earned and purchased a small ranch. I started raising my own cattle while still working for the other ranch. I increased my land and grew in wealth and prestige.

"Then came the narcos – the drug traffickers. They had lots of money, ill gotten, dirty money. They bought up houses and land. But even worse, they bought up people. Those who had seemed to be good citizens, for pay, would kill and plunder those who refused to join them. I had the choice to join them or have them destroy me and my family. I knew I couldn't join them and still look myself in the mirror, so I sold my land for a fraction of its value and used the money to move here.

"I have worked many years to earn my family citizenship and to provide for them. I may not be rich in money, but I can hold my head high for what I am. The narcos were wealthy, but they were men of murder, theft, and unspeakable crimes. If you think money is what makes a person, you are wrong, very, very wrong. And if that young lady thinks that way, you are better off without her."

Suddenly Frans felt ashamed of himself. He knew Anna didn't feel that way and never had. The thoughts of a person's value being based on wealth were only in his own heart. "She doesn't feel that way at all," he said. "She is good and kind and has loved me for who I am."

"Then I see no problem," Hernandez said, "except for the fact that you are here and she is there."

"I doubt she would still want me after the way I've acted," Frans said.

"Well, I hope she wouldn't want a man like Donaldson," Hernandez said. He then laughed, as if it was a big joke. Everyone else also laughed, Frans included, though he didn't see what was so funny. Hernandez's boisterous laugh just made him laugh, too.

Frans thought about how disgusted Anna had been with Mr. Donaldson, even if he was rich, famous, and handsome. Frans realized the problem truly was with him, not with Anna. How he wished he could be with her again. But he wouldn't even know what to do, how to apologize, or how to try to make things right.

Hernandez showed Frans his gaucho outfit. It was colorful. The children and Mariana also showed him things from their country and asked Frans about Germany. Frans enjoyed the evening, and again, Hernandez offered him a place to sleep. But Frans felt it would be best to be with Cashmere. Hernandez walked part of the way back with him. Frans thought very few people would bother Hernandez. He was a very big man. As they parted, Hernandez handed him a blanket and a pillow. "This will make your night more comfortable."

Frans thanked him and made his way back to the stall by Cashmere to make his bed. Cashmere whinnied, happy to see him. Frans slept very little. The thought of Hernandez leaving his wealth to stay true to what he believed played over and over in Frans's mind.

The next day, Frans was bored out of his mind. Without having a horse to really train, he had very little to do. He put Cashmere on the walker first thing in the morning, and Cashmere loved it. He left him on it as long as possible, but when others wanted to use it, he took Cashmere back to his stall. Frans had hoped to put him on the walker again later in the day, but it was always busy.

He helped Hernandez with chores around the stables all day, just to have something to do. Frans found out that Hernandez was paid by some of the horse owners to take care of their horses, though most owners took care of their own. Frans learned that Hernandez also received a management fee from the owners of the stables. It wasn't a lot, and if he didn't have the extra work taking care of some people's horses, it would be hard to even feed his family.

"I'm not sure what I will do when it is time for Leanna to go to college next year," Hernandez said. "I want my children to have a better life, and college is the only way."

That night, Hernandez invited Frans over for dinner again. "You can't afford to keep feeding me," Frans replied.

Hernandez laughed. "What's a few more beans?"

Frans accepted and enjoyed it, but decided it was time to find himself an apartment and take care of himself.

The next morning he put Cashmere on the walker early to give him as much time as possible before someone else came. When another person needed the walker, he put Cashmere back in his stall and went searching for a newspaper to see if he could find an apartment. He purchased a paper at a small store and was walking back when he heard the angry snorting of a horse. He was sure it was Cashmere and took off running for the stables.

What he found enraged him. John and Hank had Cashmere out in the open area. Hank was holding a rope that was attached to Cashmere's halter. John had a huge bull whip. Cashmere would snort and rear, and when he did, John would lash out viciously with the whip.

Frans ran up and jerked the rope from Hank. He worked to calm Cashmere down, then turned angrily to face the two men. "What the devil do you think you are doing?"

"Mr. Donaldson told us to get him ready to show," John said. "Now, get out of the way."

"If you think I am going to let you use a whip on him, you are wrong," Frans said.

"I'm warning you," John said. "Get out of the way."

"No," Frans replied.

Instantly the end of the whip reached out, hitting Frans's arm. He felt a searing pain, and the blood flowed from his arm.

"I said move!" John said.

"No," Frans repeated.

"Who do you think you are?" Hank asked. "Mr. Donaldson told us to get the horse ready, and you work for him. You should do what he says."

"He hired me to take care of this horse," Frans replied. "And I am not going to let you abuse him."

"Then you'll take his punishment," John said.

John slashed out with the whip, and Frans felt a pain in his chest as his shirt was ripped open by the rough leather strands. John pulled back again, and Frans covered his face with his hands, barely in time, feeling the biting pain in his arm, the force knocking him to his back on the ground.

Cashmere jerked his rope free from Frans's grasp and bolted toward John, seemingly to defend Frans. As John stumbled back, he fell to the ground. Cashmere rose to strike, and John moved just in time before the hooves hit the ground. John scrambled to his feet and lashed out with the whip as Cashmere rose again.

Frans tried to get to his feet to get to John when Hank jumped on him and hit him in the face. The anger surged through Frans, and he flipped over and was on top of Hank. Hank started begging, "Don't hit me! Don't hit me!"

Frans saw John pulling the whip back as Cashmere rose again, and he ran toward John. John saw him coming and lashed the whip out at Frans. It caught him in his knee, dropping him to his face in the dirt.

As Frans tried to struggle to his feet, he felt the sting of the whip biting into his shoulder, knocking him back to the ground. He lay there for a moment, the pain making it impossible to rise, when he realized it was suddenly very quiet. He looked up and could see Hank running away as fast as he could. Frans turned and saw Hernandez had the whip wrapped around John and was picking him clear off the ground with it.

John's eyes were large with fear. "Please. I didn't mean to hurt anyone."

"You liar," Hernandez growled. "You don't strike at a man or a horse with a whip like this unless you plan to hurt them. Perhaps you would like to feel it yourself."

"No, please," John begged. "I was only doing what Mr. Donaldson told me to do."

Hernandez tightened the whip as he spoke. "If I ever see you use a whip like this on a man or a horse again, I will let you taste of it yourself. Is that understood?"

John, unable to speak and choking for air, nodded. Hernandez gave John an angry shove, and he fell to the ground. He struggled his way out of the whip cords and fled away.

Hernandez came over to Frans and reached his hand out to him. "Are you all right?"

Frans nodded. "I think so." But as he went to stand, his leg collapsed under him.

Hernandez caught him. "Let me help you."

He carefully pulled Frans to his feet and put Frans's arm around his own shoulders to help him walk. Frans turned to Hernandez. "Thanks for coming to my rescue."

"It is not me you should thank, but her, for coming for me," Hernandez said, pointing.

Frans turned, and there was Anna, calmly holding Cashmere's lead rope as Cashmere gently nuzzled her, begging for treats. At the sight of her, shock and shame swept over him, and he lowered his eyes as he spoke. "Anna, I . . ." He couldn't say more. The emotions and pain were too much.

He leaned heavily on Hernandez, and Hernandez said, "We had better get you to some place where you can sit down before you pass out."

He helped Frans to a bucket and flipped it over for him to sit on. Hernandez looked at Anna, who stood there, staring at Frans, and he smiled. "Let me take Cashmere."

He took the rope from Anna and led Cashmere a distance away. Anna came over and knelt by Frans. He looked into her eyes, then looked down again. "Anna, why did you come?"

She spoke firmly. "Frans, Katherin told me about what you said. Do you think I'm so shallow that I am only concerned with how much money you have, or what your social status is?"

Frans shook his head. "No. But you are the most wonderful woman I know, and I don't feel I will ever be good enough for you."

"Well, that's just too bad," Anna said. "Because I feel you are the greatest guy I know, and you are just going to have to get used to the fact that I don't plan to leave you."

"But, Anna . . ."

"Don't you 'But Anna' me," she said saucily. "I have come to stay for as long as you do."

Frans could feel his heart burning in himself as he fought back the tears. Anna reached up and lifted his chin so he had to look at her. "I love you, Frans."

She leaned over and kissed him. He tried to reach up and pull her to him, but the pain surged through his shoulder, and he let out a gasp. All he could do was take her hand and pull her close. "I love you, too," he said.

Suddenly, John and Hank were back, and this time they had Mr. Donaldson with them. He was livid. "What do you mean, interfering with what I told my men to do?"

Anna stood and turned to face him. "What about their interference with what you told Frans to do?"

Mr. Donaldson smiled. "Oh, it's you. What are you doing here?"

"The question," Anna said, not changing her expression in the slightest, "is what were your men doing abusing this horse?"

"Abusing my horse?" Mr. Donaldson asked, turning to look at

them.

"We weren't abusing him," John said, Hank nodding his agreement. "We were just teaching him some manners."

"You don't teach a horse manners with a bull whip," Anna retorted.

Mr. Donaldson turned back to Anna. "The fact is, they were . . ."

Anna cut him off. "The fact is, they were abusing him, and they whipped Frans when he tried to stop them."

Mr. Donaldson rolled his eyes, and laughed an obnoxiously smirky laugh. "John is a famous animal trainer. He knows what he's doing."

John and Hank laughed at her as if she was stupid. But the smile disappeared from all of their faces when Anna spoke again. "Is that so?" She motioned to Hernandez, who led Cashmere back over. "Look at the bleeding cuts on Cashmere and also on Frans where the whip ripped into them."

Mr. Donaldson rolled his eyes. "I'm sure a few small cuts can't be a big deal for a . . ."

Anna didn't even let him finish. "I sure the newspaper reporters would disagree. I bet they would feast on a story about how your men abused both a famous race horse and his trainer."

At Anna's threat, Mr. Donaldson's eyes showed a fear that would have made Frans laugh if he hadn't been hurting so badly. Mr. Donaldson suddenly put on a fake air of concern and looked at Cashmere. "Oh, my goodness, he is bleeding." He then turned to Frans. "And you are, too?" Then, acting furious, he angrily turned to John and Hank. "What have you been doing to my horse and my horse trainer?"

"But, Boss," Hank said, "you told us to . . ."

Mr. Donaldson cut him off. "Just shut up and get out of here! And don't ever touch my horse again."

John and Hank beat a hasty retreat as Mr. Donaldson turned and smiled at Anna. "I'm grateful you were here to protect my horse."

Anna didn't return his smile. Frans knew that she could see through his facade, as they all could. She spoke sternly. "It wasn't me; it was Frans."

He turned to Frans. "I can't express my gratitude enough. I guarantee there will be a bonus in your paycheck."

The thought that money could make everything right disgusted Frans. But he just said, "If it hadn't been for Hernandez, it would have been worse."

Mr. Donaldson turned to Hernandez. "Then I owe you my thanks, too."

Hernandez just nodded, and as he did, Frans had an idea. He knew he didn't belong here. If he couldn't really train Cashmere, he could do nothing for him, and perhaps there was someone who could do more to protect him from men like John and Hank.

"You know, sir," Frans said, "perhaps I'm not the one that you need to take care of Cashmere."

"But you are his trainer," Mr. Donaldson replied.

"I'm a race horse trainer," Frans answered. "But you don't plan to race him. But did you know that Hernandez, here, was one of the best gauchos of South America?"

Mr. Donaldson turned and looked at Hernandez. "Is that so?"

Hernandez nodded, but turned to Frans with a questioning look.

"Since you want to show Cashmere, Hernandez would be the perfect horseman, and he would always be here to watch over him." Mr. Donaldson paused and looked at Hernandez, as if he was thinking about it. Frans continued. "Besides, you ought to see his gaucho outfit. It is impressive."

That seemed to clinch it. Mr. Donaldson turned to Hernandez. "Would you be interested?"

Hernandez nodded. "I would, sir."

"Would you be willing to wear your gaucho outfit when I bring people?" Mr. Donaldson asked.

"If you would like me to."

"Okay," Mr. Donaldson said. "I have some friends coming to see the horse in about two hours. I will give you a try. I will need the blood washed off of him and have him made presentable. And can you wear your costume?"

Hernandez nodded.

"Oh, and the pay," Mr. Donaldson said. "Since you already work here and don't work for me full time, I won't pay you as much as I would a trainer, but I will add some extra if you dress up, look impressive, and act the part."

Once more Hernandez nodded.

"So, the wages would be $4,000 per month, plus an extra $1,000 per month for the costume," Mr. Donaldson said.

Frans smiled as Hernandez's eyes widened just briefly. But Hernandez quickly regained his composure.

"Is that agreeable?" Mr. Donaldson asked.

"Yes, sir," Hernandez said.

"Okay, then we'll see you in a couple of hours and see how it goes," Mr. Donaldson said.

"I will get busy, sir," Hernandez said.

He turned to take Cashmere to prepare him, and Mr. Donaldson nodded to Frans and Anna and strode away.

Frans tried to stand, but the pain burned in his leg, causing him to grimace and grit his teeth.

Anna held onto him. "You shouldn't stand, Frans."

"I'll be okay," Frans said. "Nothing is broken, just torn."

With Anna's help, he limped his way over to where Hernandez was preparing to wash Cashmere.

Hernandez smiled at him. "Did you know how much he would pay me?"

Frans nodded. "Basically. I knew how much he said he'd pay me, and figured it would be similar to that."

Big, strong Hernandez choked back his tears. "Leanna would be able to go to college."

"Hernandez," Frans said, "you go get your gaucho clothes on and let us work on Cashmere. We are going to help you get this job."

Hernandez nodded, unable to speak. He hurried home to get his clothes. Frans and Anna started brushing Cashmere. He liked the brushing, as always, but still wasn't too fond of the washing. No one said anything for a while, but Frans felt he just had to apologize to Anna. He moved around to her side.

He touched her arm. "Anna?" She stopped and looked at him, and he continued. "Anna, I'm sorry for the way I acted. I just felt . . ."

She reached up and put her finger to his lips, stopping him. "It's okay, Frans. I understand. We were both hurting, but you were probably even more than I was." She pulled the ring from her pocket. "I've never put it on, Frans." She took his hand and put the ring in it. "I will accept it back only when you put it on my finger."

Frans held the ring and looked at it. Anna smiled at him. "I hope it doesn't take too long."

Frans smiled back and nodded. "But when I ask you, I want to ask you properly."

Two hours wasn't time to get Cashmere looking perfect, but they worked fast. It wasn't long before Hernandez was back. His whole family came with him, and they were all dressed in fine clothes. As he stepped up to Frans, he laughed. "I must have gained a little weight. I can hardly breathe. I hope Mariana can let these out a bit."

It was almost noon by then, and quite a few people were there riding, grooming horses, or doing a multitude of things. Frans and Hernandez worked side by side so Cashmere would equate the two of them together. Frans had bought an apple when he was purchasing the paper. He cut it into pieces and had Hernandez use it to sweeten Cashmere more.

Mr. Donaldson was a couple of hours late, which gave them time to get Cashmere's coat glistening. He truly was an impressive horse.

When the limo pulled up, people started to gather. Five well-dressed men and five women in gowns stepped out and followed Mr. Donaldson over to the horse.

Everything worked beautifully. Hernandez kept Cashmere calm. When requested, he trotted Cashmere in a circle and Cashmere showed off with his head held high and his tail arched. As the group turned to leave,

Mr. Donaldson looked at Hernandez's beautiful family, dressed in their South American costumes, and then turned to Hernandez. "The job is yours."

"Thank you, Sir," Hernandez replied.

Everyone kept their composure until the limo pulled away, and then Mariana let out a squeal and threw her arms around her husband. After she let go, she turned to Frans. "Thank you, Mr. Frans," she said, and she kissed him on the cheek.

"Yes," Hernandez said. "Thank you, my friend."

"You deserve it," Frans said.

"How could you give up such a great job?" Mariana asked.

Frans smiled and held out his hand to Anna. She took it, and he pulled her close and then turned back to Mariana. "I have more important things I need to do."

That night, Frans and Anna ate dinner with Hernandez's family. Mariana made a special celebration dinner, and Frans and Anna enjoyed the time with the family, but as the evening grew late, Frans led Anna out into the cool evening.

"Anna," he said. "I love you more than anyone in the world. And I may not be able to promise riches, but I can promise I will do everything in my power to make you happy and to be there for you."

With the smell of the ocean floating across the breeze, he knelt down on one knee as best he could with his injuries. "Anna, will you marry me?"

The tears started to flow down Anna's face as she nodded. He stood, slid the ring onto her finger, and pulled her into his arms. He kissed her and held her for a long time to make up for how much he had missed her.

Anna stayed the night with Hernandez's family, and Frans went back to the stall beside Cashmere. The next morning, Frans had already let Cashmere run on the walker and was brushing him by the time Anna and Hernandez came. Mariana was with them. It was Saturday, so Leanna was home from school and could watch the children. Frans and Anna spent the day with Hernandez, Mariana, and Cashmere.

Sunday morning, Anna joined Frans to brush Cashmere one last time. When Hernandez came to tell them that their taxi was there, Frans cut an apple in pieces, and he and Anna fed them to Cashmere. Frans then reluctantly put Cashmere back into his stall. "I'm glad you will have Hernandez to watch over you," he said as he patted Cashmere's soft nose.

Anna patted Cashmere, too. "Goodbye, boy, we'll miss you."

Tears were streaming down both of their faces as they turned to leave. Cashmere seemed to sense something was wrong and whinnied softly after them as they walked to the taxi with their luggage.

After final hugs from Hernandez and Mariana, Frans turned for one last look and raised his hand in goodbye. Cashmere whinnied in response. Then Frans and Anna climbed into the taxi, and they drove away, heading home to Germany.

## Chapter Fourteen
## Nowhere To Run

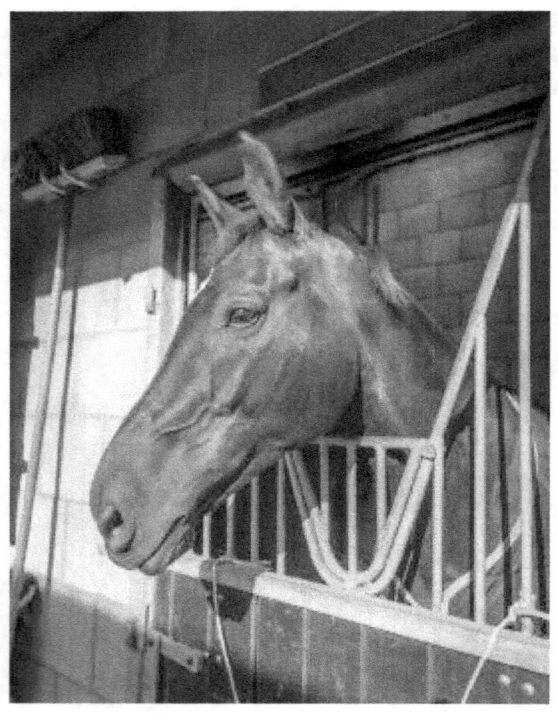

Cashmere whinnied through the bars on his stall. The sun was coming up, and he knew that meant Hernandez would be there soon. He knew the routine, but he didn't like it. Every day Hernandez came just as the sun was rising so that he could put Cashmere on the walker. It was Cashmere's favorite part of the day. He would fly around the circle as fast as he could with the tether rope holding him back.

Once in a while, Hernandez would take him for a walk out in the riding arenas. Sometimes Leanna would walk him. He didn't understand why he wasn't allowed to run. That's all he ever dreamed of doing, but no one ever let him.

He liked it when Leanna came. She came quite a bit during the first year. But after that she only came now and then.

When she would come again, it would give him hope that maybe Frans or Anna would also come again and take him away, back to the pastures where he could run free. In many ways, Frans and Anna seemed like a dream. He was sure they would totally seem that way if it wasn't for the picture that Hernandez had put on the outside of his stall.

It had only been a few months after he had come to this place when Hernandez came and held it up where Cashmere could see it. "Look, my friend," he had said. "Frans and Anna sent you a wedding picture."

Cashmere looked at it, and it looked like Frans and Anna, but it was so small. He sniffed it, and it didn't smell like them at all. But yet, it made him remember – remember them, remember running through the meadows, remember racing around a track, remember being free. He had quivered with excitement, wondering if they were coming back, coming to take him away from this place, coming to open the door on his stall and let him run. But they never came.

Whenever he was outside his stall, tied up, he would look at the picture. It triggered a memory that brought back smells, sounds, and feelings he hadn't experienced in a long time.

Sometimes he would hear a woman's voice and he would think it was Anna. He would put his nose up and sniff, but the scent wasn't her. Sometimes he would hear a man's voice and think it was Frans, but that was always wrong, too.

At times Hernandez would bring things that reminded him of home. One time he brought more pictures. One was of Anna and Frans, and they were holding a baby.

"Look at this," Hernandez said. "Frans and Anna have had a baby girl. And guess what else. Frans is in school to be a horse vet."

Cashmere looked and looked at the picture. He nuzzled it, but it wasn't soft like Anna and Frans – just stiff and cold.

A couple of years later there was one last picture. It was of Anna and Frans, a baby, and another girl about two years old.

"Look, Cashmere," Hernandez said. "Anna and Frans have another baby girl, and he just graduated from college. They also sent me some money to buy you some apples for Christmas. Would you like some apples?"

Cashmere knew that word. He had heard it before. He nuzzled Hernandez, and Hernandez laughed. "I don't have them yet. I still have to buy them, but we should be able to afford one a day for quite a while."

The next day, all of Hernandez's family came, and another man was with Leanna. Almost no one else came by the stables, and Hernandez had to feed almost all of the horses, even the ones people usually took care of themselves. Before he did, he put Cashmere on the walker and said, "Merry Christmas, Cashmere. You can run as long as you want."

Cashmere trembled with excitement. He remembered this day each year, the only one when no one else came to make him stop until he was ready to. Cashmere ran and ran and ran until he was too tired to run and had to walk. The only thing that would have been better is if he hadn't been tethered and could have run at full speed. He found himself tiring sooner and having to walk more. But after he had walked for a while and felt rested, he would run again.

He ran for hours while the others helped Hernandez with the chores. By the time they finished, Cashmere was so tired he was ready to stop. Well, almost, anyway. He would never be really ready. They then tied him up and brushed him and brushed him while he stood with his eyes half closed, enjoying it.

"I swear, some day you and the kids are going to brush that horse until there is nothing left," Mariana said. She laughed, but Cashmere could have had them brush him forever. When they finished, Hernandez cut a few apples into pieces and let each of the children feed him some.

"You're going to make him sick, too," Mariana warned.

"It's Christmas," Hernandez said. "And he never has too much to look forward to."

When Leanna fed him, she stroked his nose. "I sure have missed you while I've been off to school. But I want you to meet David."

The new man stepped up and gingerly put his hand out with an apple. "He won't bite me, will he?"

Leanna shook her head. "He's as gentle as a lamb."

Cashmere used his lips and gently reached to take the piece of apple. Just as he reached it, David dropped it and jerked back in fear. Cashmere snorted his disgust at his apple being dropped in the dirt. Leanna just laughed and picked the apple up and fed it to him.

Far too soon, the family had to leave. Cashmere whinnied after them until they were far out of sight and he couldn't catch their scent on the breeze anymore.

The days passed slowly. Every morning as the sun rose, he prepared himself and waited impatiently for Hernandez to put him on the walker. Hardly anything else happened. Once in a while Mr. Donaldson would bring people, and Hernandez would be dressed in funny clothes.

Cashmere would show off. He was good at that. But that was getting boring, too, and happening less and less. One day, a bird started building a nest at the roof ridge in Cashmere's stall. Cashmere watched it with great interest.

The birds flitted back and forth, gathering mud and horse hairs. There was plenty of horse hair. He had lost quite a few off of his own tail, getting them caught on the metal panels of his stall. The little birds would tug and tug at them until they came out or broke off. They lined their nest with them.

Pretty soon the birds were staying in the nest a lot. Cashmere would reach up and sniff at it, curious about the new smells. Then, one day, he heard a new sound. It was a little cheeping sound. Soon there was more and more of that sound until it sounded like a whole chorus. Cashmere sniffed and listened.

The papa bird tweeted a warning about him nosing too close, so Cashmere sniffed from a distance and leaned his head to one side and listened.

One day, a big tom cat came into the pen. He came through the bars and snuck along the edge. Cashmere didn't like the cat. The cat went freely wherever he wanted, and that made Cashmere jealous. But more than that, the cat flaunted it. If Cashmere ever became annoyed with the cat in his pen, the cat would jump up between the bars, flip his tail in the air, and give an air of a laugh as he jumped out, as if mocking Cashmere for not being able to follow.

Cashmere would watch the cat running back and forth, free to go wherever he pleased, and that annoyed him more. But he loved to watch the birds soar up and down and speed by his pen in flight. It was as if they understood the joy of being able to move fast and feel the wind lift and carry them.

Sometimes, as he watched them, he would find himself thinking of running with the wind blowing his mane and tail. He could feel the grass under his feet and a rider on his back. He was home with Frans and Anna.

But the cat running about didn't give him the same pleasure. It was as if it only used its freedom to annoy others. Each night, after everyone was gone, he would watch it stalk some helpless creature, and that annoyed him, too. Still, he tolerated the cat, feeling it had a right to do what it did.

But as he saw it sneaking along the edge of his pen, he felt something was not right. When it jumped up on the bars near the nest, the father bird started squawking, and Cashmere knew the birds were in danger. Cashmere ran toward the cat, so the cat jumped up into the rafters out of reach. The mother bird raced back to her nest, and the father flew around, darting at the cat, trying to drive him away.

The cat swung at the bird, missing, but kept creeping closer to the nest. As tall as Cashmere was, he couldn't reach the cat. Cashmere squealed and rose onto his back legs, but could not get past the rafters to get the cat. In anger, Cashmere smashed into the wall. The building shuddered, and the cat lost his balance on the rafters, falling and barely catching himself with his front paws. The cat's tail was hanging down and Cashmere grabbed it in his teeth and pulled. The cat started yowling and hung tight, but Cashmere bit harder and pulled more until the cat's paws ripped away from the wood.

The cat tumbled into the straw, and Cashmere struck at him with his hooves. The cat hissed and spit, dodging the hooves, and jumped to the bars on the gate.

All of the noise brought people running, with Hernandez at the front. He got there just as the cat jumped out. The cat dodged through the legs of the people.

The little birds were safe for now, but Cashmere kept an eye out for the cat and made sure the cat knew he was not welcome anywhere near that stall.

He watched the baby birds grow. They became louder and squawkier, and soon they were too big to fit into the nest. It wasn't long until they flew away. The parent birds left, too, and Cashmere missed all of them. His days seemed even quieter.

He often sniffed the breeze. There was a smell of water on the breeze, but it smelled different from what he had known before. It had a smell of salt with it, as well as other things he didn't know. To him it was a smell of freedom, but he didn't even know why. That smell made him tremble with excitement, with an added desire to be free, to run as fast as he could with no tether rope to hold him back.

The next year the birds came back again. They raised another batch of babies. He chased the cat away from them, too. This time, the minute the cat came into his stall, he was after it and didn't even let it get close.

The birds grew and left again, but the parents were back the next year. Cashmere watched them and protected them as he always did. But then, one day, it happened. It was early in the morning, and Hernandez had put him on the walker. He was enjoying his run when he heard it. It was the sound of the birds squawking.

He stopped running and started whinnying, squealing, and rearing. Hernandez came running to see what the problem was. Cashmere was trying to pull in the direction of his stall, but the cursed walker held him. Pulling hard with his size and strength, he started to bend the walker center pole. Hernandez couldn't get him undone with him pulling like that, so he cut the rope.

Before Hernandez could grab his halter, Cashmere raced for his stall. When he dashed into his stall, he found the cat there with the bird nest it had knocked to the ground. Feathers were everywhere. Cashmere struck at the cat. It darted past him through the open gate. He turned to chase it, but Hernandez was there. Cashmere smashed into him, knocking him down as he raced after the cat.

Cashmere raced around the grounds after the cat, determined to stomp him. People fled in every direction. Finally the cat went through a hole in a wall, and Cashmere could follow him no longer. Hernandez was immediately there, trying to calm him.

Cashmere was breathing hard, both from running and from anger. He could see that Hernandez was favoring his one arm, and he sensed he had hurt him. Finally, Hernandez snapped a rope on Cashmere's halter.

"What's wrong with you, Old Boy?" Hernandez asked. "I've never seen you act like this."

As Hernandez led him back to his stall, Cashmere snorted one last time back in the direction the cat had gone. Then Hernandez tugged on the rope to lead him back to his stall.

Once he was back in his stall, he sniffed what was left of the nest. It was shattered across his stall. He sniffed the feathers. He knew that he wouldn't get to see the little birds fly away this year.

Hernandez stopped by a few extra times that day to check on him. "I wish I knew what upset you, Old Boy," he said.

That night, after Hernandez had left for home, and after the sun had faded from the sky, while Cashmere was standing there listening to the sounds of the evening, the cat suddenly jumped up between the bars on the gate to his stall.

Cashmere didn't let the cat go any farther. He reared and struck at the cat. The cat fled away, but Cashmere's leg lodged between the bars. He fought to get it out, and jammed the other one as well. He squealed and pulled and fought to be free. The gate ripped from its hinges, the tearing steel screeching through the still evening air.

With his weight on the gate, he fell forward with his legs still trapped through the bars. Cashmere felt a searing pain in his legs as he crashed to the ground with his legs still trapped under the gate and his weight on top. He tried to stand, but the pain caused him to collapse. He tried again with the same results. For quite some time he struggled, but eventually, he just lay still, waiting for dawn when Hernandez would come.

When Hernandez came, he gasped. "Oh, my heavens, Old Boy, what have you done?"

Cashmere tried to stand again, but once more he collapsed on top of the gate that held him trapped. Hernandez found a hacksaw and carefully cut the bars that held Cashmere trapped. Once in a while he would have to retreat when Cashmere would thrash about. Once the bars were cut, Hernandez used a crow bar to pry them away from Cashmere's legs. Feeling less pressure on his legs, Cashmere reared back. And even though he left some skin on the bars, he was free, and the panel fell to the ground. But as Cashmere's hooves touched the ground, he felt that horrible pain again, and he collapsed.

Hernandez shook his head. "You aren't going anywhere, Old Boy. It looks like your knees are broken, but how do I get you back in your stall?"

Cashmere kept trying to get up, but he would just fall down again. Hernandez stacked some bales in front of him so that he couldn't move any farther away from his pen. As Cashmere struggled and fell farther back into his stall, Hernandez scooted the bales closer. Eventually, Cashmere was in his stall. Hernandez then took the gate off of the adjoining stall where Cashmere's feed was stored, and he put it in place of the one Cashmere had broken.

"It's good you're not a race horse anymore," Hernandez said, "or you probably would have signed your death warrant. But I don't know what Mr. Donaldson will do."

Hernandez left, and an hour or so later he returned with Mariana. She looked at Cashmere. "He's in horrible shape, isn't he?"

Hernandez nodded, "Yes, but Mr. Donaldson doesn't want anyone else to know his horse has been hurt, not even a vet. I am supposed to just do the best I can. But without medicine to knock him out, I don't think I can get them set anywhere near straight."

Hernandez built some wooden boxes that were just big enough to fit around Cashmere's legs. He tied Cashmere's head up tight to the wall.

He tried to straighten one of Cashmere's legs as best he could, but Cashmere thrashed around at the pain. Finally, Hernandez slid the box onto Cashmere's leg. Hernandez then repeated the procedure for the other leg. But by the time the second box was on, the first was nearly off.

Hernandez tied the second box up and over Cashmere's shoulders to keep it on. He then put the first box back on and did the same. He built some straps that harnessed the two boxes over Cashmere's back.

As soon as they were on, Cashmere struggled to his feet. It was painful, but with the boxes supporting his legs and his weight, he could stand. It wasn't long after he was standing that Mr. Donaldson came. He brought no one with him besides his chauffeur this time. When Hernandez showed Mr. Donaldson what he had done, Mr. Donaldson nodded his approval.

"If I ever bring anyone to see him," Mr. Donaldson said, "we will just leave him in his stall where his legs will not be as noticeable, and they can look at him through the gate."

Hernandez nodded, and Mr. Donaldson left.

For Cashmere, the days passed even more slowly. Now there were no birds to watch. They never came back. And with Cashmere's legs hurt, Hernandez didn't take him out to put him on the walker. Without being able to get out at all, Cashmere became angry. He would snort at anyone that came near, even Hernandez, though not so much. At times he would kick his stall. Eventually there were huge dents in the gate, and there were boards missing. Hernandez always tried to patch them up as best as he could and calm Cashmere down.

After about six months of having the boards on his legs, Hernandez came to Cashmere to take them off. But Cashmere was so angry that Hernandez wouldn't climb in the stall with him. He coaxed Cashmere to the gate, and slit the straps holding the board boxes on. Cashmere shook the boxes free, and, for the first time in a long time, felt his legs out of them. The first thing he did was to rub his head up and down his legs, scratching them. That felt so good.

His legs were skinny, and his knees were knobby and crooked. Hernandez looked at them. "Well, they aren't beautiful, Old Boy, but at least you should be able to walk. I wish I could put you on the walker again, but I'm not sure I can trust you, and I'm afraid you might break your legs again."

Cashmere never was out again. Sometimes Hernandez would clear the stuff from the adjoining stall and open the gate between. Once Cashmere went in there, he'd shut the gate between, and that would become Cashmere's new stall for a while so Hernandez could clean the other.

Mr. Donaldson almost never came any more, and if he did, it was no more than once per year. Cashmere stayed in his stall, growing angrier and angrier, and hating people more and more as the years went by.

## Chapter Fifteen
## A Legend Is Real

**B**renda was tired after a long day of meetings and reviewing paperwork. She had had meetings with the directors of four companies. They were all working together trying to win the government contract for the International Space Station. But they hardly listened to her suggestions on changes that needed to be made on the proposal. Their engineering language may have been correct, but to the Washington bureaucrats it would be gibberish. She was looking forward to going to the hotel and taking a much-needed soak in the hot tub.

Just as she was leaving, the secretary stopped her. "You are coming to the dinner tonight, aren't you?"

"What dinner?" Brenda asked.

"With all of the company CEO's coming in tonight for the last two days of meetings, we are sponsoring a banquet in their honor. It's a good way to try to build alliances."

Brenda shook her head. "I think I will sit this one out. I am so exhausted from the day that I think I need to take a break to be ready for tomorrow."

The secretary smiled. "Are you sure? There will be some big name celebrities there."

"Like who?" Brenda asked.

"Like Phil Donaldson, for one," the secretary answered.

"Who is he?" Brenda asked.

The secretary looked astonished. "Who is he? Why, only one of the most famous movie stars there is."

"I hardly ever watch movies," Brenda said. "But his name does sound familiar, for some reason. Let me go back to my hotel and get a little rest and think about it."

Brenda caught a taxi to the hotel, and the whole time she mulled over in her mind where she had heard the name of Phil Donaldson. Was it because he was a movie star? Could it be she had seen his name in a paper or something? She wasn't impressed by celebrities, so that seemed unlikely, and yet it ate at her a lot. She made up her mind that she would go to the dinner, thinking that, maybe, if she saw him, she would remember.

The banquet was typical – everyone trying to impress each other on who they were and who they knew. It was enough to drive her crazy. When she was introduced to Phil Donaldson, seeing him didn't help the memory at all.

"I've heard your name somewhere before," she told him.

He laughed. "Of course you have. Everyone has."

"But it isn't from movies," she said. "I don't go to movies. I think they are a big waste of time."

The smile mostly disappeared from his face. "You are joking, right?"

Brenda shook her head. "No, I'm not. I barely have enough time to live reality without going into make believe. But since I heard your name, it has been eating on me all evening as to where I have heard it before."

This seemed to intrigue him, and his curiosity seemed as great as hers. "How about a magazine?" he asked.

They visited about all of his magazines appearances, but they still could not make a connection. They talked about their college education experiences. They visited about events they had attended. They talked about relatives and friends, but still they could find nothing in common.

When it was time to be seated, he was to be with the VIP people, and she was to be seated with the secretaries and engineers. But Mr. Donaldson asked if she could be as close as possible, in case something came to her mind. It seemed to Brenda that he felt a need to know the answer just as much as she did. The hosts granted his request by putting him at the end of the VIP table and her at the start of the other table. They were almost right across from each other.

After they started eating, they were making conversation in the group when the man sitting next to Brenda asked her about herself.

"I am a contract writing specialist," Brenda replied.

"Where are you from?" the man asked.

"Logan, Utah," she answered.

"I went horse riding there once," the man said.

"I love horses," Brenda replied. "I have a half dozen of my own."

"Horses?" Mr. Donaldson asked. "I'm a bit of a horseman myself," he said, sounding quite full of himself.

Suddenly, it hit Brenda where she had heard his name. "That's it!" Brenda exclaimed, so loudly that everyone around them stopped talking and stared at her. She then spoke in a quieter voice. "That's where I heard your name."

"Where?" Mr. Donaldson asked.

"I was working in Germany on a contract," Brenda said, "when a horse vet named Frans told me the story of a super, incredible horse. That was when I heard your name. Frans said you bought him."

"That I did," Mr. Donaldson said. "One of the fastest race horses in the world."

"Where do you race him?" Brenda asked.

By this time, everyone in the near proximity had stopped talking and was listening to their conversation. Mr. Donaldson seemed embarrassed by the question. He simply said, "We'll talk later." He then turned the conversation to something else. Brenda could hardly think of anything else, but she was polite enough not to broach the subject when she could tell he didn't want to. Her heart raced with anticipation to learn more, and the banquet seemed to go on forever.

When it finally ended, and everyone was getting up to leave, Mr. Donaldson went with her to a private corner and told her about the horse.

"You mean you don't race him?" Brenda asked.

Mr. Donaldson shook his head. "He's too dangerous to race."

"Can I see him?" Brenda asked.

"Oh, you don't want to see him," Mr. Donaldson answered. "He is getting quite old, and he broke his knees when he trapped them in some bars, and, well, he's just plain ugly now."

"Please," Brenda begged. "I can't get this close to a legendary horse and then not see him."

Mr. Donaldson stood there for a moment and then finally nodded. "When would you like to go?"

"I'll be done with work tomorrow at 5:00," Brenda replied. "Could we go then?"

Mr. Donaldson nodded. "I'll pick you up here at 5:30."

Brenda could think of nothing else. The next day she couldn't concentrate on her work and found herself trying to hurry things along a little faster than she should have. The clock on the wall of the conference room seemed to be frozen. But finally 5:00 came, and she was done. The secretary asked her if she had a place to eat, and she told her that Mr. Donaldson was picking her up.

"Wow! Lucky you!"

"We're going to go look at a horse," Brenda replied.

The secretary wrinkled her nose. "That's weird."

Brenda paced around outside the building. She was so afraid that he wouldn't really come, and she would never get to see the horse, but right at 5:30, Mr. Donaldson's big limo pulled in. The chauffeur stepped out, but before he could open the door for her, she climbed in. Mr. Donaldson smiled when she said, "Wow! This is exciting!"

The chauffeur wound the car through the traffic. It was rush hour, and things came to a standstill. Brenda found herself squeezing her hands with impatience until she was making herself tired. She wondered if they would ever get there. Eventually, the traffic started moving again, and when they started driving into an area with horse barns, Brenda knew it was the place.

There to greet them was a big man who introduced himself as Hernandez, Cashmere's caretaker. He walked with them to a horse stall. Brenda gasped at the size of the horse that stood inside. He was huge and black. He snorted angrily at them, threateningly, and stomped and lashed out with his hind feet at the wall of his pen. His anger made them all step back.

"You see," Mr. Donaldson said, "he's far too wild to try to race. We don't even dare let him out."

Brenda could feel something in her heart, something that she couldn't explain. It was a longing of some kind, a yearning deep inside of her that she couldn't fully comprehend.

"I don't even know what to do with him anymore," Mr. Donaldson said.

Brenda turned to him. "Would you sell him to me?"

The shock was evident in Mr. Donaldson. "What would you do with him?" he asked.

"I don't know," Brenda answered. "Probably just let him run in a pasture."

Mr. Donaldson stood there quietly for a moment. When he spoke, he spoke thoughtfully. "Well, I can do nothing with him. He's nothing but a liability for me now." He slowly nodded. "I'll tell you what, for $1500 he's yours, but the minute you buy him, he is your responsibility to move him or whatever."

Brenda nodded. "Deal."

She pulled out her checkbook and wrote a check on the spot. Mr. Donaldson asked Hernandez to get a piece of paper from the chauffeur, and Mr. Donaldson wrote a simple bill of sale on it. Once the transaction was complete, Mr. Donaldson suggested he take her back to her hotel, but she declined. "I think I better stay here and visit with Hernandez to try to figure out how I can take care of him. I'll just call a cab when I'm ready."

Mr. Donaldson nodded and returned to his limo. As soon as he was gone, she turned to Hernandez and asked him to tell her all he knew about the horse. Since the evening was growing late, he invited her to his home for dinner, where he shared Cashmere's long story. Hernandez only had one child left at home, but pictures indicated there were more, and Hernandez and his wife shared their pride in each one.

As the evening was winding down, Brenda asked Hernandez what he thought she could do to get the horse loaded. He said that he felt Cashmere was so wild that the only way to load him would be with lots of men on ropes to drag him to the trailer.

"Can you get me lots of men?" Brenda asked.

Hernandez nodded. "There is a place where lots of migrant workers gather and wait for someone to come hire them."

"Hire all you feel we can use," Brenda said. "Twenty or thirty, if you think it necessary, and get sufficient ropes. I will hire a trailer. I finish my work here tomorrow evening, so let's plan on 9:00 the morning after."

Hernandez nodded, and they shook hands. "I'll miss having the money that taking care of him has brought to me, but I am grateful you plan to give him some freedom to run."

In between sessions of work the next day, Brenda scheduled a horse trailer and someone to haul it to Utah. She was concerned whether Hernandez would have everything ready on his end. She needn't have worried. When she stepped out of her cab at the horse barns that next morning, there stood dozens of big men with ropes.

When the trailer came, Hernandez directed them to back as close to Cashmere's stall as possible. It took a while to get ten ropes on him, and with three men on each rope, and some ropes hooked through the bars on the trailer, they nearly dragged him the fifteen feet to it. Even with more than thirty men, it was a fight as he reared and snorted.

Finally, they had him in and were able to work the inner gate closed, locking him into a smaller area. Brenda had to promise some extra pay to the haulers for possible damage to the trailer as he thrashed about. But, finally, the horse trailer pulled away with Cashmere inside.

Brenda paid all of the men, and as she was ready to leave, Hernandez pulled some pictures from the wall of Cashmere's pen and handed them to her. "These belong to him," he said, and explained about them.

She took them and thanked him. And then she went to do one last thing. She slipped over to a phone booth to make a phone call.

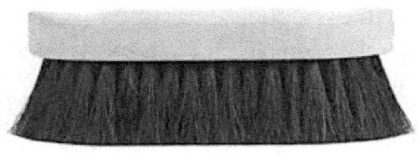

# Chapter Sixteen
# A New Beginning And A
# Longing

As Brenda finished the story, she looked over at me. "And that was when I first tried to call you. No one was home at your house, and that was why the men were almost there before I had a chance to talk to you."

"How long was Cashmere locked up?" I asked.

"From what Mr. Donaldson said, he'd had him for more than 15 years."

"That's horrible for any horse to be locked up that long, but especially one like Cashmere!"

"Yes," Brenda said. "It is."

"But, Brenda, when he came here, he wasn't mean at all like you described. I mean, he acts that way to some people, but not to me, nor to Hannah."

"Is there anyone else he is gentle with?" she asked.

We were still sitting on the tailgate of her pickup, and as I thought, I hopped off to get the blood flowing in my legs again. Finally, I turned around. "No, I guess not. He does act angry to everyone else unless I let him know they're okay."

"I think I know why," she said. She went to the cab of her pickup and reached inside. Soon she returned and handed me some pictures. "Do these people look familiar?" she asked.

I shook my head. "I've never seen them before."

"You won't know them," she replied, "but do they look similar to someone you do know?"

I couldn't figure out what she was driving at, and I couldn't think of anyone they looked like, so I just shook my head. Brenda laughed. "Look deeper. Doesn't the man look like you, and the lady look like Hannah?"

I looked again and could see the slightest resemblance. "I suppose," I said. "But they are not us."

"No," Brenda replied. "They are Frans and Anna. These are the pictures Hernandez gave me. I think Frans looks much like you, and Anna, with her blond hair, resembles Hannah. And even the children in the pictures look like your little girls."

I looked at the pictures once more and agreed that there might be some resemblance, though I didn't feel as much so as Brenda seemed to.

"But," I said, "if that was more than 15 years ago, that would mean Frans and Anna would now be in their late 30's to early 40's, nothing like Hannah and me."

Brenda laughed. "I'm sure Cashmere wouldn't know that. I really feel he thinks you two are them. Besides, there is one other thing that makes me feel he thinks that way."

"What's that?" I asked.

"You are the one that opened the gate of the trailer and set him free to run," she replied. "I'm sure he views you as his liberator. I think he views you and Hannah as if Frans and Anna have come back to save him and let him go free. I think that is also why he is so protective of you."

As I watched Cashmere turn and start running, I laughed. "Did you see that? He does that all of the time. He will be grazing, and then out of the clear blue, he just takes off around the pasture."

Brenda laughed, too. "I can't blame him. I bet he just gets that sudden urge, and with the thrill of being free, he just can't help himself."

As he approached the gate where we were, I stepped up to the fence. He came thundering up and slid to a stop. I took an apple from my pocket, cut it, and held a piece out to him. He took it and chewed happily. When he finished, he reached down and nuzzled me for the other half. I gave it to him and then turned to Brenda.

"So what are your plans for him?"

Brenda shrugged. "I don't know. I don't really have any. I bought him because I couldn't stand to see him trapped in that small pen anymore."

"I doubt he would be allowed to race again, at least with the way his knees are," I said.

Brenda nodded her agreement. "But at least we will get to see him run. And I want Hernandez and Mr. Donaldson to see what he is like now. I could hardly believe what you told me about him, but I brought my camera just in case so I could send a picture to them. I want one with you standing by him so they can see how he acts toward you."

"Well, then, I better brush him up and make him look nice," I said.

I grabbed my big brush that I used for his coat, plus a hair brush Brenda had in her truck that was for manes and tails. I climbed through the fence and set the soft brush down and started working on his mane.

Brenda stood by the fence, and though Cashmere seemed alert at first with her there, he soon relaxed. When his mane was soft and silky, I moved to his tail. When I finished it, I moved to pick up the other brush. Cashmere saw me heading for it, and he grabbed it in his teeth before I could.

"Give me the brush, Cashmere," I said.

In reply, he backed a few steps from me and curled his lips in his teasing grin.

"Cashmere," I said, "give me the brush."

As I stepped toward him, he backed another step away. I lunged for the brush, but hit the dirt as he spun and took off across the field. About 50 yards away, he dropped it, as usual, and continued his run. Brenda laughed as I picked myself up and went to retrieve the brush. Cashmere arrived back at the gate before I did.

"By the way," I said as I returned, "did I ever mention that he is also a prankster and a tease?"

Brenda laughed again. "No, but I can see that."

He nuzzled me for an apple. "I don't reward naughtiness," I said. He nuzzled me harder, knowing I wasn't really mad. "You stand still and let me finish the brushing for the picture, and I'll give you one," I told him.

He seemed to understand and stood still. I stuck the mane and tail brush in my back pocket, though it hardly fit. I didn't want him running off with it. I brushed him until his coat shimmered, and as I did, I told Brenda about the hammer and tool bucket episode. "But," I said, finishing the story, "it sure makes it hard to get anything done."

When I finished with his coat, I tossed that brush over the fence to keep him from running off with it. I then brushed his wind-blown tail and mane smooth. Then I tossed it over the fence, too. Cashmere wanted the apple, but I said, "Picture first."

I stood beside him and reached up and put my hand on his shoulders to show his friendliness with me. Brenda snapped some pictures. Cashmere stood proudly, and looked at the camera as if he was posing, but the minute the pictures were done, he immediately demanded his reward.

As I fed him his apple, Brenda laughed again, and said, "I swear he understands everything you say to him."

I nodded. "I kind of think he does. I wish he could talk so I would know what he was thinking."

I climbed back through the fence, and Brenda listed out the things she wanted me to do. She wanted me to finish the fences and haul some hay.

"I'm also shipping Jackie to California," Brenda said. "I have a friend that is taking his horses down to a pasture he is renting there, and he had room for one more horse in his trailer. I will pay one horse rent on the pasture, and that will be cheaper than the hay we feed her now."

"When will she be going?" I asked.

"Next Saturday. He will meet you at the corrals at 8:00 A.M.."

"I'll be there," I said.

When I went to work on the fences, Brenda left to take care of other things. I worked carefully, watching my tools. Cashmere stayed close the whole time, except, once in a while, he would go for a run. I did make the mistake of setting my hammer on the ground once, and

Cashmere took off with it. Having to run after it helped me remember to be more vigilant. By the time the day ended, I pretty well had all of the fences patched up.

The next Saturday, I met the man that was going to take Jackie. He arrived at the corral about a half hour later than Brenda had said, but I had plenty to do there to keep me busy. Cyrus came over to watch me load her, and we were joined by another old, retired neighbor who said his name was Ernest.

The horses that were already in the trailer whinnied to Jackie and Patches. As I led Jackie from the corral, Patches started to run around, snorting and whinnying, seemingly panicked about what was happening to her friend.

"Make sure you give Jackie a good drink of water before you load her," Cyrus said.

"That's about the dumbest thing I ever heard," Ernest countered. "A horse travels better if they have a light drink and little food."

"Excuse me," Cyrus said, "but she is going to California. The trip will grow hot and tiring, and she needs a goodly amount of water."

"All that will do is make her sick from the motion of traveling," Ernest said.

As they continued to argue, I gave Jackie a drink of water and some hay. Brenda had had both Patches and Jackie bred, and even though I didn't think a horse could get fatter than Jackie already was, she grew fatter as her pregnancy progressed. The driver and I loaded her, but when we tried to shut the gate, her fat belly stuck way out. We had to push her fat in the door to get it shut without pinching her in it. But soon she was on her way.

\*\*\*\*\*\*\*\*\*\*\*\*\*\*\*\*\*\*\*\*\*\*\*

As the year progressed, I had my challenges of school work and earning a living, but I always looked forward to working with the horses. When it was just feeding, I almost always took Kaylynn with me. Sometimes Hannah would bring Linny and join us, and then we would go to the zoo when we finished and have a picnic.

We always depended heavily on what full time work I could find in the summers when I wasn't in school, but all I could find was a night shift driving a forklift in a bean factory. I often worked from 5:00 P.M. to 5:00 A.M., so I fed the horses before and after work.

I didn't sleep well during the day, and it seemed like I was awake when my family was asleep, and then they were awake when I needed to sleep. I seemed so drawn to Cashmere and watching him run. For some reason, the harder things were, and the more work I had to do, the more I wanted to just watch him. I couldn't understand the feeling, but there was something that stirred in me while watching him that I couldn't even explain. I wanted nothing more than to climb on his back and run with him. But there was never time.

# Chapter Seventeen
# Saying Goodbye And
# Baby Horses

As the summer progressed, hay prices doubled, and Brenda became concerned about the cost of feeding all of her horses through the winter. As fall was approaching, the pasture was turning brown, and we needed to supplement their feed.

Brenda reluctantly started hunting around for a place for Tor and the three old mares. She was not about to sell them to just anyone. She wanted them to go to a place where they would be loved and taken care of, even if she had to give them away.

She finally found a dude ranch that could use some older, gentle horses. There they would be ridden and loved by lots of people. She took a lower price than she might have at an auction, but she couldn't stand the thought of where they might have gone if they had been sold there.

She scheduled for them to be loaded and moved while she was away so she wouldn't have to see them go. The weekend prior, she came to say goodbye to them. I picked up some grain from the barn and met her at the pasture. I put Cashmere's out separately, as I always did, and then spread the rest in a line on the ground.

As soon as they were all eating, Brenda came over. Cashmere was used to Brenda now, though he still kept an eye on her as she stepped into the pasture. After he checked to make sure that I was there and safe, he ignored her and went back to eating.

Brenda went to each of the horses, calling them by name and petting them for a short time before moving on to the next one. One old mare, Calypso, whom Brenda had owned since the mare was a foal, was especially hard for her to say goodbye to. Calypso leaned her ears down and Brenda scratched them. I could see the tears flowing down Brenda's face as she spoke.

"You're going to a good home, old girl. There will be lots of kids to pet you, ride you, and love you."

Brenda's tears caused me to choke up, too. I had grown fond of the horses and knew all of their personalities.

"Brenda, why do you keep any horses?" I asked. "I don't think I have ever seen you ride. And I know that they cost you a fair amount of money, both in feed and in my wages."

Brenda stared off into space for a short time and then finally answered. "I don't know. I've asked myself that now and then, but I can't come up with an answer, either."

The next week I had to load the horses. I knew that was going to be hard for me. When the trailer came, I was waiting. I had apples for each one and petted them for a minute or two.

Cashmere looked at me questioningly, as if asking me what was going on. "They're going to a nice home, Old Boy," I said. "You're staying here."

When I loaded Calypso, she nuzzled me for more apple. I gave her another piece. "Goodbye, Old Girl," I said. "I'll miss you."

As I haltered each horse, Cashmere would come up face to face with them. Then he would step up and lean his head against them. They would lean back against him, and it was as if they were hugging each other goodbye.

Tor was last. When I put on his halter to lead him away, Cashmere moved to block the gate for a moment. It was as if he was saying, "You can't leave until I say goodbye to you, too."

He nuzzled Tor, and they leaned their heads against each other. These two horses, who had started their first meeting by fighting, were now good friends. Watching Cashmere say goodbye to each of them was hard for me. Obviously, animals have feelings for each other just as we do, and they miss their friends. But I was happy that Cashmere would still be free to run, and the others would all be together in a good home.

As the truck pulled away, Cashmere whinnied to them, and they whinnied back. It was as if they were calling out one final goodbye to each other.

Brenda wanted Cashmere to be able to stay in the pasture as long as possible, both to allow him room to run and to try to reduce her feed bill. She said she wanted me to pull the old tin off of the roof of the pasture shed, put down some tar paper, and then put the tin back on. "That will keep the moisture off of the wood and keep him dry," she said.

She had purchased the tar paper for me, and that day, after the horses left, I decided I needed to get it done. The weather was already turning cold, and I was concerned for Cashmere because this would be his first winter since leaving California.

I drove to the hay shed to retrieve a ladder that was always leaning against the hay stack there, loaded it into my pickup, and tied it down. I then headed back to the pasture.

Cashmere seemed especially glad to see that I had come back. I'm sure it was because he already missed his friends, or maybe he was afraid I had left, too. I petted him and gave him some apple, and then carried the ladder out to the shed. I figured I'd take that first because it was too big for him to carry off in his teeth. I leaned it against the building and headed back for the tools and the tar paper.

I tucked the tar paper under one arm, picked up the tools, and carried it all out to the shed. Cashmere followed me so closely that he almost stepped right on my heels. I couldn't carry it all up since I needed one hand to hold on to the ladder, so I set down the tar paper. Just as I turned back to the ladder, Cashmere gave the ladder a shove, and it toppled over.

I made the mistake of setting my tools down to set the ladder back up. When I turned to pick up my tools, Cashmere had the hammer in his mouth.

"Cashmere," I said, "give me my hammer."

He opened his lips in his smirky grin and snorted. I could swear he was saying he would trade it for an apple.

"I'm not going to reward naughtiness, you big blackmailer," I said. "Give me my hammer." I took a step toward him, and he backed up a step. I had played this game before, and I wasn't about to do it again. "Give it!" I said without moving.

In response, he took off running and dropped the hammer out about 50 yards away. I knew better than to leave my bucket of tools. I picked it up and walked out to where he had dropped the hammer, then turned and headed back to the shed. He finished his lap before I got back, and just before I reached the shed, he shoved the ladder over again.

This time I didn't set my tools down. It was very awkward, with one arm through the tool bucket's handle, but I eventually had the ladder back against the shed. I climbed up and set the tools on the top, happily knowing he couldn't reach them there.

When I turned to climb down, Cashmere had the loose end of the tar paper in his mouth. I hadn't worried about it, thinking it was too big for him to mess with, but I suddenly realized I could have a very big problem.

"Cashmere," I yelled. "Don't touch that!"

In response, he started backing up with the piece of tar paper still in his mouth. It only had a little bit of tape around the roll to keep it from unrolling, and I hoped for a little luck that it would hold. But, as the old saying goes, if I didn't have bad luck, I wouldn't have any luck at all.

The piece of tape popped loose, and the tar paper started to unroll. I rushed down the ladder while Cashmere continued backing away, unrolling the tar paper as he went. I ran toward him, so he turned and took off running, still holding on to it, until the whole roll was strung out in a big line across his field. Once it was, he dropped it and continued running a lap.

I reached the tar paper and started rolling it, quickly and sloppily, into a roll. I hoped to get it rolled back up before he came back, but my luck stayed about the same. He came back and grabbed the other end in his teeth, and started pulling like we were playing tug-of-war.

"Cashmere," I yelled, "stop it! I'll never get this job done."

He shook his head up and down, as if teasing me to give him the apple if I wanted him to quit.

"Hey," I said. "Give it up, or I may never give you another apple. Ever."

That was a lie and I knew it, and he seemed to know as well. I kept rolling it toward him, making some progress, as I could roll faster than he could back up. I just hoped he wouldn't turn and take off running with it. The thought of him running gave me an idea. I took an apple from my pocket and tossed it so it landed about 10 feet from him, knowing he couldn't chew it and hold onto the tar paper at the same time.

He looked at it and then down at the tar paper, seemingly undecided whether he wanted to annoy me or to get the apple. Finally, he let go of the tar paper and trotted to the apple. I continued rolling as fast as I could.

I finished just about the same time he did. I carried the tar paper triumphantly over to the shed. But he reached the shed just before I did and shoved the ladder over.

I sighed and struggled to set up the ladder and keep the tar paper safe. Once I got the tar paper on top of the shed, I swung my leg over the edge and climbed on top of the roof. I stood up on the roof feeling triumphant, but, as I did, I watched the ladder sliding over to the ground. I turned to see Cashmere grinning at me.

I realized how stupid it was of me not to realize he would do that once I was on the roof. I should have tied the ladder to the shed so he couldn't push it over.

I decided I might as well work on the roof. I could figure out how to get down later. I started pulling the nails from the tin, placing them in the bucket. It took quite a while, and the sun reflecting off of the tin was very hot, but, eventually, I had the tin stacked on one edge of the shed. I rolled out the tar paper, then started nailing the tin back down. By this time, the sweat was pouring down my face, and I wished I had remembered to bring my water from my pickup. I couldn't get down to get it, and I wanted to get the job done, so I worked as fast as possible.

When I had finally nailed down the last piece of tin, I gathered my tools together, along with the last bit of tar paper, and tried to figure out how to get down. It was a fairly high shed, and I didn't want to jump from the top, so I decided I would have to hang down and then drop to the ground, still a fair distance.

I carefully climbed over the edge, doing my best to hang on to the hot, sharp tin. As I started to let myself down over the edge, Cashmere was suddenly there. I don't know if he knew my predicament, wanted me to ride him, or was just curious, but I suddenly realized he might be able to help me.

I reached out my foot to him, and he moved closer, as if wanting me to climb on. I let myself down to the full length of my arms, and was almost right over him. I didn't know what would happen when I hit his back, so I held my breath for a second, and then let go.

The instant I hit his back, he leaped forward, and I nearly went off the back end. I was barely able to grab his mane to pull myself back on. I had only had time to sit square on him for a second before we were reaching the first fence. I braced myself for the turn.

Once we came out of the turn, I was feeling more secure, and started to relax. We thundered around the pasture, and, with the trust I had built in him over the last months, I enjoyed the ride even more than I had the first time I rode him.

Just as he had the first time, when we finished the lap, he headed around again. He ran three laps and was breathing hard but didn't stop. His gait turned into a trot. His head was high and his tail was up. He pranced like he was in a parade, trotting another full lap. "You big showoff," I laughed.

I wondered if he was remembering back to when he won that big race Brenda told me about. Was he remembering the cheering and the proud feeling of being a champion? It was sad that it only happened once, because I was sure he could have been a champion many times over.

When I slid off of his back, he nuzzled me, and I gave him his apple for a reward. I went back to the shed, set the ladder up, and retrieved my tools.

\*\*\*\*\*\*\*\*\*\*\*\*\*\*\*\*\*\*\*\*\*\*\*\*\*\*\*\*\*\*

Cashmere continued to live in the pasture for another month, but then, the last week of October, we had our first snowfall. It melted, but his feed was basically gone, and the water in the small stream was slowing. It was taking a lot of time to haul hay to him, and I didn't know how long the water would last. Brenda decided it was time to move him to a corral.

She had me fix up Dader's corral, as it was biggest. She had me remove the fence between it and Jackie's old corral so it would be bigger still. I finished the work on it in one weekend, so the next weekend, when Brenda came, we moved him. I had never put a halter on him, so I didn't know how he would take it. But when I reached up to put one on, he put his head down so I could reach him. I fastened it and snapped on the lead rope. He walked as gently as any horse I had ever worked with. Brenda marveled. "I still can't believe the way he behaves for you."

"Yeah, he's great," I said, "At least, he is if I'm not trying to get some work done and he's playing pranks on me."

We couldn't use Brenda's trailer because it needed some repair, so I climbed in the back of her pickup, and she drove slowly while I held Cashmere's lead rope. He trotted willingly behind us. When we reached the barns, Patches whinnied to him. She was hugely pregnant now.

I put Cashmere in his corral and was pleased to see that he still had room to run a little bit. At least it was a bigger area than just around a horse walker, and he wasn't tethered, either.

The next Saturday, when I came to take care of the horses, something interesting happened. An orange and white cat came wandering into the horse yard. The neighborhood was full of cats – some wild, some tame. This cat had been there before. It wasn't really wild, but it had no use for me. It always acted like it owned the place.

It jumped up on the pole fence on one side of Cashmere's pen. A sudden change came over Cashmere. He ran at the pole fence, slamming into it. The cat lost its balance and fell into the pen. Cashmere struck at the cat with his front hooves. The cat was stunned by the sudden change of events and barely missed the blow. But Cashmere caught the cat's tail and stomped it.

The cat let out a yowl and came to life quickly as Cashmere continued striking. The cat dodged back and forth between Cashmere's flying hooves. I tried to distract Cashmere, but no amount of hollering or waving my arms seemed to attract his attention in the slightest.

I was calling to the cat to try to get it to go through the fence, but he seemed too confused. Instead, he ran in circles under Cashmere's continually stomping feet. Finally the cat slid under the fence. Cashmere, concentrating on following it, smashed into the fence so hard he knocked the top pole down.

As the cat ran down the road, yowling his complaints to everyone whether they wanted to hear them or not, I tried to calm Cashmere. He was breathing hard and snorting. "What is it, boy?" I asked. I held up an apple, but he didn't pay any attention to me. His eyes were locked onto the road in the direction the cat had gone. I had never seen him uninterested in apples before, nor so concerned about something. He finally started to calm down, and he eventually took the apple, but he kept an eye on the road.

I went to my pickup to get my tools so I could nail the top pole back in place. While I was getting them, Cyrus came over to visit and plopped himself on a straw bale. He sometimes brought his little fluffy dog, and this was one of those times. The dog had already gone into the corral with Cashmere by the time I returned. I gasped, thinking Cashmere would attack the dog, but he didn't. He was as unconcerned as I had ever seen him. He even nuzzled the little dog. The dog sniffed around the corral for a while, and only came out when he was ready. Cashmere didn't bother him at all.

I was lost as to what had set him off before. I didn't know if the cat had done something Cashmere didn't like, or if it had the smell of another stallion, or what.

As the dog came over where Cyrus and I were, I turned to Cyrus. "Cashmere doesn't seem to mind your little dog."

"Nah," Cyrus said. "Neither mine nor Ernest's, nor anyone else's. Our dogs can wander in and out and he pays them no never mind. But let a cat go in there, and you'd think a tornado touched down."

"I saw him like that just a minute ago with a cat," I said. "Does he always do that with cats?"

Cyrus nodded. "Every time I've seen a cat go into his corral, he attacks it like he's trying to stomp it into its grave."

"He doesn't do that to anything else besides cats?" I asked.

"Nothin' I've seen," Cyrus replied. "Sometimes he gets his dander up with people he's not too sure about. But nothing compares to how he goes after a cat."

I started nailing up the pole as I spoke. "I wonder why he does that."

Cyrus shrugged. "Some just aren't cat people."

"Yeah," I replied. "But Cashmere isn't a person. He's a horse."

"From what I've seen in just this week since you moved him here," Cyrus said, "I think he's smarter than some people I know. Of course, with some people, that might not be saying much."

I had to admit that was true.

It was near time for Patches to have her baby, so I kept a good eye on her. Cyrus said he'd let me know if he saw any new developments. It was only a couple of weeks after we moved Cashmere, when I came to feed at the end of the day, that Patches had a new little baby standing beside her.

No matter how many times I see a new life come into the world, it still amazes me. The baby was a beautiful little filly. There appeared to have been no complications, and it was healthy. It had a thick, fuzzy coat to keep it warm, and was already nursing by the time I arrived. Things couldn't have been better.

After making sure all was well, I hurried home to get my family. I had barely mentioned the new baby horse before Kaylynn was pulling on my pant leg. "Daddy, please, me go see?"

I knelt down and put my arm around her. "Of course, Sweetheart. I came to get all of you."

Hannah bundled up Linny while I helped Kaylynn put her coat on, and soon we were on our way. Kaylynn smiled when she saw the little horse. "Baby Patches pretty."

I fed the horses, increasing Patches's grain supplement to help her recover from the birth and have the milk she needed for her foal.

I let Kaylynn feed Patches an apple, and the baby horse came and curiously sniffed us. I held Kaylynn up and helped her reach out her hand to pet the baby horse, carefully watching in case it tried to bite, as little horses often will.

Hannah petted her, too. "She sure is beautiful."

I nodded my agreement. "I don't think I have ever seen a prettier little paint horse."

Cashmere whinnied and snorted and was getting a little miffed that he wasn't getting any apple, so we took one over to him.

For the next two weeks, every evening when I went to feed, I took my family with me. When Brenda came, she was really pleased with the little horse. When I had called to tell her about the new filly, I had asked what she would name her. But Brenda wanted to see her before she decided on a name.

"So, do you have a name for her?" I asked, as we looked at the little filly the next Saturday.

Brenda nodded. "I'm going to call her Splash, like a splash of paint."

"That sounds good to me," I said. "We sure enjoy her."

Brenda turned to me. "Then you're going to hate what I have to say. I am having Patches and Splash shipped to California."

I felt disappointed, and I knew Hannah and Kaylynn would be as well.

"To try to save on feed?" I asked.

"That's only half of it," Brenda replied. "Jackie is showing signs of stress, and I'm afraid she is going to have problems. I want her to be here where you can keep an eye on her. So I'm sending Patches down there and bringing Jackie back up here."

"Aren't you afraid the trip will stress her more?" I asked.

Brenda nodded. "I'm nervous about that. But I can't find anyone down there I trust to keep an eye on her like I know you will."

The next Tuesday at noon, I left school early and picked up my family. We arrived at the horse barns only minutes before the trailer showed up with Jackie in it. She was huge, looking like she was carrying twin draft horses in her belly. She could barely walk. I tied her to the fence, and then led Patches out of the corral with Splash behind her. Kaylynn started to cry when I loaded Patches.

I couldn't get Splash to go in the trailer. Instead, she stood just outside and called to her mother. Patches panicked, thinking we were separating them. Finally, I had to put a small halter on Splash, a task that was no small feat. I tied a rope to it, tied the other end up near her mother, and then I got behind her and pushed. She kicked at me and caught me in the shin with one of her sharp hooves.

Cyrus had come over to watch, and he laughed. "Feisty little thing."

I hopped around for a minute with Kaylynn giggling at me and Hannah trying to stifle a laugh of her own. I tried again, being more careful, and finally got her loaded. I locked the gate, and we sadly watched as they headed on their way. Kaylynn buried her head in my neck and cried. When she finished, I pointed to Jackie. "Jackie is going to have a baby, too, and you can help me take care of it."

That seemed to help, and she calmed down. I took Jackie to the corral gate, but it was only a walkthrough gate, and her belly was far too wide. I thought of trying to squeeze her through it, but decided against it. Instead, I took down part of the fence.

As soon as I took the rope off, she walked into the barn and plopped down in the new straw I had put out for her. I put up the fence and searched for a horse blanket, because Jackie's coat was not filled out for winter. I didn't realize that a horse's coat would adapt to the climate, but it must. Since she had been in California, it hadn't grown to the length she needed in the cold winters of the north. I wrapped the blanket around her and buckled it into place. She was already shivering and nuzzled me, grateful for it.

Once I had her as comfortable as possible, I asked Cyrus if he would keep an eye on her and let me know if he saw any problems. I told him I, too, would check on her every chance I could. I checked her the next morning, and though she didn't seem to want to eat, she didn't appear to be in labor.

I finished an exam at 6:00 that evening and went to my office to call Hannah, as I did at the end of each work day. She was very anxious. "Hurry and get over to the barns," she said. "Cyrus called and said Jackie is having her baby, but she's having trouble."

I rushed to the barns. Cyrus was standing by the corral. He hurried to meet me. "She's been at it quite a while, and I think something is wrong. I only see one hoof."

I was still in my nice clothes, and I knew they would be ruined, but I couldn't worry about that now. Cyrus was right. There was only one hoof; the other was nowhere to be seen. I reached in up to my wrist, but could not feel the other hoof. I was sure I would have to go in after it.

I took off my coat and stripped one arm out of the sleeve of my shirt. The cold winter wind hit me when I did, and I had to close my teeth to keep them from chattering.

I lay down in the straw and reached my arm in. I could feel a little nose – that meant it was head first. I was grateful for that. As I felt around, my fingers went in the baby horse's mouth, and it chomped down.

"Ow," I said. "The little beggar bit me!"

Cyrus laughed. "Maybe it's hungry. But it's good to know it's still alive."

My hands and wrists are large, but my forearms are especially large from years of milking cows. I struggled to get them past the hip bones. They were barely in the opening when Jackie decided to push. It crushed my arm like it was in a vise, and I groaned in pain.

"It's good she has the strength to still push," Cyrus said.

I had helped many cows give birth, but this seemed much tighter. I knew I couldn't get in far enough with the baby horse's leg in the opening, but I didn't want to lose it back in and have to go after it, too. So I did what I had done many times before.

I asked Cyrus to get me a piece of twine. I tied it securely to the baby horse's leg, and then pushed it back in. As I did, Jackie didn't like it and pushed against me. For a brief time we struggled against each other, but, eventually, I was able to push the leg in and down out of the road.

As I worked my arm in, Jackie's natural urge to push worked against me. I would have to grit my teeth to the pressure when she pushed, and, in between, I would push in further. I finally had my arm in to the shoulder, and felt all around. I could feel the little horse's shoulder and followed it downward, but I could only reach to the knee. The hoof was much too far down. I tried for nearly a half hour to work the leg upward, but every time I would pull the knee toward the opening, I would eventually lose my grip and the little horse would move it back down where it was.

I was getting tired, and my progress was decreasing, not increasing. I had to try something else.

"Cyrus, would you be able to hold the tail for me so I can get at a different angle?" I asked.

Cyrus nodded. I knew he couldn't stand for a long time, so I pulled my arm out and found a straw bale for him to sit on.

I prepared a fair length of twine. Usually I would push twine in with one hand, looping it around the end of the hoof, but since I couldn't get to the hoof, I couldn't do a loop. My goal was to put the string down behind the knee, then reach around and pull it on around from the other side of the knee and back out. I hoped that once I had both ends I could pull the leg up enough I could get a loop around the hoof.

Once everything was ready, I lay down on the straw and made the attempt. With Jackie fighting me, it took a long time to get my arm in. I moved the string down and around the knee, but I couldn't grab it from around the other side of the leg. I tried again and again. Just about the time I was ready to give up and try to figure out something else, I hooked it with one finger. I pulled it around, grasped it firmly, and pulled it out. I now had both ends of the twine that was wrapped around the leg.

I held firmly to them and then reached my arm in again with another piece of twine. With my outside hand I pulled on the two ends of twine that wrapped around the leg and carefully pulled it toward the opening. Finally, I was able to feel the hoof with my hand, and I worked the loop of the twine around it. I had to do it three times to make it hold, but once it did, I knew a baby horse would soon be born.

With my free hand, I pulled the hoof toward the opening, carefully working it upward with my hand that was inside. Once it was in place, I pulled the other hoof up and into place.

When everything was ready, I pulled my arm out and took hold of the two strings. "All right, girl," I said to Jackie, "whenever you are ready, let's do it."

Jackie had grown tired and had quit fighting so much. But, eventually, she did a halfhearted push, and when she did, I pulled. The legs came out, and a little nose appeared at the opening. With the feeling of something happening, Jackie really pushed. I pulled, and the whole head emerged. The next push brought the shoulders almost out, and one more push put a little horse at my feet in the straw.

This whole time Cyrus had been giving me suggestions and telling me stories of his work with horses and cattle. I was grateful for his help, but was concentrating so hard I didn't really hear most of what he said. With his excitement as the baby was coming out, a person would have thought he was giving birth to it himself.

Once the baby horse was there, he let out a gasp. "My heck, it's as bald as a bowling ball!"

"It's not bald," I said. "It's just got very short hair, and being wet it makes it look bald."

"Well I ain't never seen any horse born with hair that short," Cyrus replied. "Especially not around here, and especially not in winter. What are you going to do?"

"I'll have to get a blanket wrapped around it," I answered.

"I've never seen a horse blanket that small," Cyrus said.

"I haven't either," I replied. "I guess I'll just have to make one."

I knew I would have to hurry; the baby was already shivering. I looked at my watch and gasped. "Is it really almost midnight?"

Cyrus nodded. "You've been at it a long time."

Jackie seemed too tired to get up, so I pulled the baby horse around in front of her so she could lick it off and get it dried. I found an old gunny sack and rubbed the baby horse with it to give Jackie a head start.

When I finished, I turned to Cyrus. "I'm going home to get an old blanket I can wrap it in. I'll be right back."

As I stepped out of the dim light of the barn into the night, the wind whipped snow into my face. I hadn't even known it had started to snow. At least the three-sided barn gave some protection from the wind and snow.

I hurried home. Hannah was anxiously waiting for me and wanted to hear all about what was happening. She met me just as I came in the door. "So, how did it go?"

"The baby horse is born," I replied. "But it has very little hair and will freeze to death if I don't do something."

I grabbed our oldest baby blanket. It was quite worn, but it was warm. It had all sorts of Teddy bears on it. Just as I was ready to leave, Kaylynn came out of the bedroom. She hadn't been able to sleep knowing a new baby horse was coming.

"Daddy, is hosey born?" she asked.

I knelt down and pulled her to me. "Yes, Sweetheart. But it doesn't have much hair, so Daddy needs to go take care of it."

"Me go with you?" she asked.

I shook my head. "Not this time. But maybe tomorrow I can take you to see it."

Hannah laughed. "Don't you mean today since it is already past midnight?"

I nodded and smiled. "Yes, something like that."

I hurried back to the corral. Cyrus had gone home, but when he saw the lights of my pickup, he immediately came back. Jackie had finished licking off her baby. It was struggling to get to its feet. It finally made it, and, wobbling, stood. It nuzzled its mother, begging for food. Jackie groaned, but stood.

The baby horse was shivering, which was actually a good sign that its little body was trying to warm itself. I moved it into position to eat and then set about tying the blanket around it while it nursed. I rolled the corners of the blanket into little ears and then tied strings on them. I wrapped the blanket around the baby horse, tying it snugly. I also tied it around in front of its chest and ran a twine around each back leg, trying to mimic what the horse blanket did.

When I finished, Cyrus nodded his approval. "You're pretty innovative."

There was one last thing I wanted to do. I started hauling straw in, stacking it up on the third side of the barn, leaving only a small doorway opening. That would help protect the horses more from the wind and blowing snow. Cyrus decided it was time for him to go home, so he left while I stacked the straw.

When I finished, I suddenly realized I hadn't fed the horses. I made sure Jackie had plenty, with a little bit extra. When I went to Cashmere, he whinnied at me.

When he leaned his head down, I scratched his ears. "So, Old Boy, what do you think of your new little neighbor?"

He shook his head up and down as if he was okay with it. I finally finished and headed for home. By this time, I was shivering from the cold. I could hardly wait to shower away the slime and drop into bed.

When I came through the door, I looked at the clock: 2:14 in the morning. The thought of getting up and going to school was almost unbearable. As I sat down on the bed to take off my shoes, Hannah woke and spoke sleepily. "So, you never told me whether the baby horse is a boy or a girl."

I stopped, looked at her, and laughed. "I forgot to check!"

# Chapter Eighteen
## An Old Miser

arly the next morning, I heard banging on our door along with someone shouting. At first it seemed to be part of my dream, but as it continued, and I started to come out of the deep sleep, I realized it was real. I looked at the clock. It wasn't even 5:00 A.M. yet. Who would be pounding on our door at that time of the morning? I got up and went to answer it as the pounding and shouting continued. When I finally swung it open, there stood Harold.

\*\*\*\*\*\*\*\*\*\*\*\*\*\*\*\*\*\*

I heard someone once say that misers make lousy friends, neighbors, and relatives, but they make great ancestors. Whether the second part is true, I'm sure I will never know. But Harold helped me experience the first part up close and personal.

Harold had moved into our apartment complex during the first part of September when the smallest apartment in the complex had come up for rent. In fact, it was so small it was probably just a remodeled closet. Well, maybe it was a little bigger than that, but not much. The rent was very low, but even still, Harold bargained for an even cheaper price.

Harold was a multimillionaire and liked to make sure everyone knew it. Because he had lots of money, he expected everyone to bow to his wishes. He often went to bed at 6:00 in the evening and got up at 4:00 in the morning. He expected it to be quiet after 6:00 P.M., and he had yelled at more than one neighbor because of what he called late night noise. Many, myself included, upset him when we told him we still planned to live our lives no matter what he thought.

This belligerence on the part of his neighbors made him mad. One day, when I was out playing tag with my little daughters at about 6:30 in the evening, they were laughing and squealing, but not all that loudly. Suddenly, Harold came flying out of the building, telling us to be quiet.

I told him we weren't that loud, and we would have fun and play if we felt like it.

"I'll have you know that I am a multimillionaire," he declared.

"What of it?" I asked. "Is that supposed to give you extra privileges?"

"Well," he stuttered, "yes. Yes, it should."

"Why?" I asked.

"It just does," he said.

"Not in my book," I answered.

I told him we would try to be quieter, but we had as many rights as he did, and all of his money would not stop us from exercising them. He left, angry with me, and I was no happier with him.

Often, when I played outside with my family, Harold would peek through his curtains and watch us. I had glanced up once, and he had jerked back to hide. After that, I saw him there watching us every time we were outside.

I would be careful not to glance up at him, but I would catch a view of him out of the corner of my eye. I often wondered why he would spend so much time just watching us. I wondered if he just wanted to spy on us because he didn't like me or was looking for something to hold against me.

One time, before it got too cold, he was coming into the building when we were outside having a picnic. Kaylynn said hi to him, and he stopped and talked to her and even smiled. Hannah invited him to join us to eat, but he said, "I don't want to owe anybody," and turned and headed on his way.

But our worst experience came on Halloween. We had dressed our two sweet little daughters up as Ketchup and Mustard. They were so cute. I had taken them all over the neighborhood, with everyone laughing at their costumes and being so kind to them. When we arrived home, we went to every apartment in our building – everyone, that is, except Harold's. His apartment was dark. That was not unusual. I knew that even when he was home it was usually dark. I didn't plan to make any attempt to visit him because I was sure he didn't care for us, for our children, or for anyone else. But Hannah felt he might feel left out if he didn't get to see the little girls in their costumes.

"He'll think we are coming to ask for candy," I said. "He won't like that, I'm sure."

"When he opens the door, just tell him you thought he might like to see the little girls' costumes," she replied.

I reluctantly agreed to take them to visit him. I had them leave their Halloween buckets at our apartment so we wouldn't have any appearance of asking for anything. We made our way up the stairs, and I knocked on his door. There was no answer. I knocked one more time and felt relieved when he didn't answer, feeling I had fulfilled my obligation.

We had just started to leave when he suddenly jerked the door open and came rushing out of the door toward us. I didn't even get a word out before he started yelling. "Can't you see my apartment is dark? I don't believe in giving to beggars! I don't waste my money on them, and I don't want anyone coming around here begging!"

My frightened little girls hid behind me and started crying. He continued yelling, getting right up almost nose to nose with me, expecting me to back away. Instead, because he had frightened my daughters, the anger surged through me. When he realized I was not going to back away from him, and he saw the look on my face, he suddenly stopped. He began to tremble. He started backing away, and I took a step toward him.

His voice quivered. "Look, I don't want any trouble. I just . . ."

I didn't even let him finish. "You arrogant old man! We didn't come here asking for anything because we know how you are. We would never ask you to spend any of your precious money on us. We just thought you might like to see the little girls' costumes."

I turned and picked up my two little girls into my arms, cussing under my breath. They buried their heads into my neck and continued to cry. When I got back to our apartment, I was fuming. "Why that dirty, rotten, skin flint, old . . ."

I was so mad that I was breathing hard. Hannah tried to calm me down and asked what happened. I told her, and she shook her head in disbelief.

While my own anger pulsed through me, I tried to still my little girls' sobs. I retrieved their candy buckets and talked quietly to them. With a little candy and a lot of hugs, their tears turned to sniffles.

They were finally calming down when there was a knock at the door. The anger in my heart surged again when I opened the door and saw a very subdued Harold standing there. I had to breathe hard to not slam the door in his face.

He spoke very quietly. "I acted poorly. I was thinking that maybe your girls would like these for Halloween." He held out two quarters.

I wanted to tell him to keep his stupid money, but Hannah, sensing my feelings, touched my arm and nodded. I turned to get the little girls, leaving Hannah to visit with Harold. I took each one by a hand and led them to the door. When they saw who it was, they hid behind me. He talked to them kindly, and, with their mother's encouragement, they finally stepped out. He kindly handed them each a quarter.

I hadn't said anything to this point, afraid of what I might say. But I swallowed my anger and said, "Can you girls say thank you?"

Kaylynn said thank you, and Harold smiled. That was only the second time I had seen him smile. As Harold turned to leave, the girls quickly hid behind me again. Once he left, Hannah shut the door and turned to me. "Thanks for not yelling at him."

"I wanted to," I said. "But maybe there is some good in him after all. Or maybe just some shame."

Another episode with Harold came a short time later. There were no designated parking spots, but Harold decided the best one should be his. I just took whatever was available, though I knew he liked that one and tried to leave it for him. But one day, all of the others were full, so I just naturally parked there. I had parked there many times before Harold had moved in, so I didn't even think about it.

I had only been in my apartment a few minutes when he pounded on our door.

"You parked in my parking spot!" he yelled.

"And what makes it yours?" I asked.

"I always park there," he replied. "I claimed it first."

"Actually, I parked there before you came, so if we are going to claim it by firsts, I guess it's mine."

"But I told everyone it was mine," Harold said, quieter, but with frustration sounding in his voice.

"So what gave you the right to just decide it was yours?" I asked.

"Well, I'll have you know that I'm a multimillionaire, and . . ."

He paused. I don't know if the disgusted look on my face reminded him he had already tried that one on me with no success. He took a deep breath and started over.

"I'm an old man," he said, speaking in a pathetic voice. "It would be really nice if I could have that spot."

I was surprised. I had never heard Harold ask. He always just demanded. He wasn't really asking outright, but he wasn't demanding.

"I'll tell you what," I said. "As long as there is another spot, I will try to park somewhere else."

\*\*\*\*\*\*\*\*\*\*\*\*\*\*\*\*\*\*\*\*\*\*

So, now, here it was before 5:00 in the morning after spending the night helping Jackie birth her foal and not getting to bed until nearly 3:00, and I wasn't feeling very charitable.

"Is there something I can help you with, Harold?" I asked.

He pointed out the glass front doors of the apartment. "The walks are covered with snow."

I nodded. "Yes, I can see that."

"Well, aren't you supposed to shovel them?" he asked.

"My assignment to shovel them is not until after 6:00 in the morning," I replied.

"How am I supposed to get to my car?" he asked.

"Where do you go this early every morning?" I asked.

"I go down to the coffee shop."

"Why do you have to go so early?"

"Because they open at 5:00," he answered.

"Why do you have to be there when they open?"

He looked at me with disgust. "Because I want to be the first person to get the newspaper. I hate reading a newspaper when someone has already messed it up."

I understood that. I liked newspapers, too. I liked knowing what was going on in the world. And I also hated to have it messed up, so, even with our limited budget, one of the few splurges we allowed ourselves was a newspaper subscription.

"Why don't you just subscribe to the paper?" I asked.

He sighed and rolled his eyes like I was dumb. "Instead of paying for the paper, I pay for my coffee, and it's like I get the paper for free."

It was my turn to sigh and feel disgusted. "I'm already awake, so I'll shovel today," I said. "But remember that I'm not obligated before 6:00 and need what little sleep I can get."

"Can you hurry?" he asked. "With all this talkin' someone else has probably already gotten the paper."

I dressed as quickly as I could and shoveled a single path to his car. He followed me all the way there, hurriedly climbed into his car, and sped into the darkness.

My real reason for deciding to get going was so I could check on the new baby horse. I ate as quickly as I could, left my family sleeping, and headed to the barns.

I was glad for the snow since it meant there were clouds and it would stay warmer. I thought about how, when I told my friends from the south that I was glad for the snow because of that, they would laugh and think I was crazy. But it is true. The clouds hold in the warmer air.

When I reached the barns, I made my way to Jackie's corral. When I stepped into the barn, it took my eyes a moment to accustom to the dim light, but it wasn't too long before I could tell that the baby horse was doing well. It was nursing, and it still had the blanket wrapped around it, though it had rolled sideways a little. I checked and found out the little horse was a filly, and I took the time while she was occupied to straighten her blanket and tighten it up a little.

Once I was satisfied all was well, I fed Jackie and Cashmere, realizing I had only fed them a few hours before. When I finished, I headed to the university to put some time into studying before my classes started.

# Chapter Nineteen
## Can Labels And Christmas Wagons

I had a hard time staying awake at school, but, finally, it was time to go home. I couldn't wait to pick up my family and take them to see the new baby horse. As soon as I walked in, Kaylynn was begging to go.

I smiled. "Well, then, don't you think you should put your shoes on?"

She grabbed her shoes, and, in her anxiousness, stuffed them on the wrong feet. I relocated the shoes onto the correct feet while Hannah bundled Linny up nice and warm. I took Kaylynn by her mittened hand, and we headed out the door. As we stepped out into the cool air, the little neighbor boy came past, dragging his little red wagon full of snow, heading toward a snow fort he was building.

I watched Kaylynn's eyes follow him until he disappeared around the corner of the house. She wanted a wagon more than about anything. She watched every day as the little neighbor boy played with his. He did everything with it. He hauled rocks in it. He hauled home stray animals. He would sit in it and roll down the slanted driveway by the apartment building. He took it everywhere.

Kaylynn had asked him if she could play with him and his wagon, but he wouldn't let her anywhere near it. She had asked me if we could get one, and the answer was always the same: "We don't have the money."

This time, as she turned to me, I was sure she was going to ask again, and I prepared to give the answer I knew I had to give. But she didn't ask. Instead, she said, "You don't haf a worry about getting me a wagon anymore, Daddy."

"Why?" I asked.

"'Cause I asked Santa for one last night."

That caused a mix of emotions. It reminded me that, while I was helping Jackie with her baby, my family had gone to see Santa at a community Christmas dinner, and I had missed it. I had not only missed the dinner, but I had missed my daughter's first time sitting on Santa's knee, at least her first since she had begun to understand the concept of

Santa.

But an even harder emotion was the feelings of inadequacy as I knew how hard it would be for Santa to fill this wish. It took much of the joy of the event of the new baby horse from me as I could think of nothing else but a wagon for my little girl.

As we drove to the horse barns, Hannah asked me why I was so quiet. "Kaylynn told me she asked Santa for a red wagon last night."

Hannah nodded. I didn't need to say more. She understood what I was feeling, and she knew our financial situation as well as I did. With the hospital bills from Linny's birth, as well as the cost of my schooling, there just wasn't anything left over.

Cyrus and Ernest were there, along with their wives. They had brought another man with them, whom they introduced as Max. His wife was there, as well. They were all retired and lived in the neighborhood. A new baby horse was a whole lot of excitement, and everyone had come to see it.

"Hope you don't mind us bringing our wives," Cyrus said.

I laughed. "Of course not. I brought my family, too."

Everyone loved the new foal, and their happiness raised my spirits and made me feel better about myself.

Hannah and the other men's wives laughed at the baby blanket wrapped around the little horse.

Cyrus's wife said, "Cyrus told me about the birth and how ingenious you were in keeping the little horse warm. It's fun to see it."

"The Teddy bears on the blanket definitely add something," Ernest said.

After everyone else left, we petted the horses, fed them, and made sure Cashmere and Jackie received an apple. We then went to a store. My socks were so worn through that my feet would freeze as I worked outside. Hannah insisted that I had to have new ones. I had a hard time thinking about spending money on myself, but I had to admit that I needed them. When I came home at night after working outside, my feet would be so cold they would take a long time to get warm.

As we walked into the store, I was still deep in thought about not being able to afford the wagon for Christmas when we walked past the shoe section of the store. There, prominently displayed, was the cutest pair of cowgirl boots I had ever seen. I stopped and looked at them. They were only $4, but even that was a lot on our budget. Hannah touched my arm and shook her head.

"It wouldn't hurt to just try them on her," I said.

Hannah didn't look so sure, but I set Kaylynn on the chair and pulled her shoes off and put the boots on her feet. We had her walk in them, and she seemed so proud. Both Cyrus and Ernest wore cowboy boots when they came over to watch me work with the horses. Kaylynn had seen them and had said she wanted some.

When I set her on the chair to take them off to put them back in the box, she started to cry. My heart already ached about the wagon, so I stood and turned to Hannah. "What if we bought her the boots, and I just kept wearing the socks I have?"

"Your socks are so full of holes they are like they aren't even there."

"I'll be okay," I answered.

"Okay? You come home with your feet almost blue and as cold as an ice-block," Hannah said.

"I'll just wear two pair instead of one."

"Twice nothing is still nothing," she replied.

I laughed. "I thought I was the math major."

She only slightly smiled, so I told her I would try to find some at a second hand store. "I've already tried that," she said.

But I wanted those boots for Kaylynn more than I wanted warm socks, and Hannah knew it.

"I think my feet would feel warmer just seeing my little daughter with those nice boots," I said.

Hannah could see I had my mind made up, so she reluctantly agreed. When we told Kaylynn we needed to put the boots back in the box so we could buy them, she didn't understand and thought she wasn't going to get them, and she started to cry again. We finally put her old shoes into the shoe box and let her carry it. She marched so proudly up to the checkout.

When we got there, I lifted her up so the clerk could check the price tag we had left attached.

The next day I went to every thrift shop I could find, trying to find some socks, but to no avail. People don't give away socks; they just wear them out. But it did give me a chance to do what I really wanted to do: to look for a wagon. There was one that was just junk, but nothing else.

The more I searched, the more discouraged I felt. In some ways, I felt like a failure as a father. I loved my sweet little family and wanted to make Christmas nice, but it seemed like all I could do was barely pay for my schooling, our apartment rent, and have food for us to eat.

As I left the very last of all of the thrift stores that I knew about, I drove slowly over to the horses. I fed them, making sure the little filly's blanket was still in place. After I finished, for some reason I felt drawn to watch Cashmere. He ran around his corral space, and I could tell he really wanted to have the more open space of the pasture to run.

When he came over, he nuzzled me for an apple. "Sorry, Buddy," I said. "I forgot to bring any."

I petted his nose. He trotted around his enclosure, getting as much speed as he could. After a few rounds, he came back and nuzzled me again. "That was a nice run," I said. "But I still don't have any apples."

He leaned his head against me as if to say he understood.

"I guess we all feel trapped at times, don't we?" I said.

"What do you mean?" I heard someone say.

I spun around to see Cyrus standing there with Max beside him. I laughed. "You gave me a start."

"You sitting here talking to yourself?" Cyrus asked.

"No, I was talking to Cashmere. I swear he understands everything I say."

"So, what were you meaning about feeling trapped?" he asked.

"Well, Cashmere feels trapped because he can't run, and, to be honest, sometimes I feel the same way. With school and work, and hardly any money, I often feel that way, too."

"You know, I used to feel that way," Cyrus said. "I could think of all the things I wanted to do when I retired. Then I would be free. But you know what? It isn't that way at all. Now that I am retired, I feel trapped by boredom and my inability to do things I want to do. I find myself wishing I could be back working. But I've begun to realize that it's not what life does with me, but what I do with life, that matters. That's a lot of the reason I like to come over here."

"I'll have to remember that," I said. "It's not what life does with me, but what I do with life, that matters."

"Besides," Cyrus said, "would you give up what you have – your family, your life, and all, to be free of the responsibilities?"

"Of course not," I replied, thinking of Hannah and my sweet little girls.

"Then, in all reality, you're not trapped," he said. "You are freely choosing to be and do what you are, even though that requires some unpleasant responsibilities and hard choices."

I smiled. "That's pretty smart, Cyrus."

"You'll find that the best and most valuable parts of life are not the easiest," he said. "You'll do well to remember something else that I learned almost too late in my life. You need to see challenges not as burdens, but as opportunities. If you do that, the future will never be anything but bright."

As I contemplated what Cyrus had said, Max, who had been silent to that point, spoke. "You probably didn't know that I was a prisoner at Auschwitz during World War II when I was a young teenage boy, did you?"

I shook my head, so he continued. "Most of my family died there, and I found myself feeling bitter and resentful, with my only thoughts being thoughts of vengeance. But then something happened to me. I noticed that there were prisoners there who were happy. I realized they were the ones who were able to make themselves free."

"Did they escape?" I asked.

"No. They made decisions for themselves, so that, even when their liberty was taken away, their freedom was not."

"What's the difference?" I asked.

"Liberty is a person's ability to come and go as they choose. But freedom goes much deeper, and comes from within. I watched as those men, even though they had no liberty, still chose to be free. As others could only dwell on their own personal misery, those men chose happiness. Some wrote happy stories, and some wrote inspired music, even if they wrote in nothing but the dirt on the ground or scratches on the wall. Others simply chose to help others, giving of themselves and even of their meager rations when they themselves were near starvation. Those men chose not to let their captors determine their happiness or misery, nor their actions. Only they could determine what they would be, and they chose a positive attitude, even in the darkest abyss of prison and despite our inhumane treatment.

"I realized those men were truly free because their circumstances could not dictate who or what they would be. I made the determination that I also would find that freedom within myself. It was not easy, and at times, when a guard was especially vicious, I could feel myself slipping back into thoughts of revenge. But when I would realize what was happening to me, I would work to force those thoughts out of my mind, even to the point I could almost forgive the unforgivable acts done by our captors."

"That seems so impossible," I said.

"It's not easy," Max replied. "I don't think one in a thousand is able to find the fortitude to develop it in their lives. I know I never mastered it, but striving to that end did give me the strength and hope to endure, and I think it is what helped me to survive. And when the war was finally over, it helped me to be able to go on with my life and put what had happened behind me."

The three of us talked quite a while, and when I drove home that night, I thought a lot about what Cyrus and Max had said. It didn't change the fact that I wished I could get Kaylynn a wagon, but it did help me feel like I wasn't doing too bad of a job.

When I got home, I continued to think about it as I shoveled the walk. My little girls had their noses pressed against the glass window. I would throw a snowball at them, and they would jump when it splattered. They would then laugh so loudly I could hear them through the glass.

When I finished, I went inside to warm up and rest. Hannah met me as I came in. "Honey, I've got something to show you."

She held out a women's magazine that a neighbor always passed on to her. It showed an ad by a soup company. For one thousand soup can labels, plus ten dollars shipping, a person could get a wagon. It wasn't one of the small metal ones like the neighbor boy had, either. It was one of the really nice ones with the tall wooden sides.

"I think we could afford ten dollars," Hannah said.

I sighed. "But where am I going to get one thousand soup can labels? We can't afford canned soup."

She shrugged. "Well, it doesn't hurt to try. We could ask everyone we know to save them for us."

I thought about it. My dad always said that God helps those who help themselves. I had been praying for a wagon, and maybe this was the answer. Maybe I could do it if I worked at it.

I went around to everyone in the apartment building and the neighborhood – everyone except Harold. I doubted he would eat soup anyway unless it was free. Everyone I talked to agreed to save us labels. Even with all of the extra help, we still only had 12 labels by the end of the week. I figured, at that rate, Kaylynn would be married with children of her own before I'd have enough. But that night, as I took our garbage out to throw it into the dumpster, I saw something that gave me an idea. There, right on top, was a soup can. I found an old step stool and stood on it while I carefully sorted through the garbage. By the time I finished, I had 32 more labels.

When I brought them into our apartment, Hannah mentioned that there were other apartment buildings that each had a dumpster. Grabbing my step stool again, along with a flashlight, I went from one to the next, like a raccoon rummaging for food. By the end of the night I had collected dozens of labels.

The deadline to have them mailed in was two weeks before Christmas, only a couple of weeks away, but I was beginning to feel hope that I just might be able to get my little girl a wagon for Christmas.

# Chapter Twenty
# Who Is Rich And
# Who Is Poor

Even though I had told Harold that I was not expected to shovel the walks before 6:00 in the morning, whenever it snowed at night I could expect a knock on my door before 5:00. I wished I had told him 'no' that first time he had come, because he came to expect it of me. I was approaching finals and was growing tired from the long hours of study. Add to that the amount of time it was taking to collect soup can labels and shovel walks, and I hardly got any sleep at all.

One night, I stopped at some Christmas tree lots to see if they had an inexpensive tree. Most of them wanted at least ten dollars, and that was just too much on our budget. I wanted to save what little I had mostly for presents. One older gentleman seemed to realize my situation, and he directed me to some trees he had set off to the side.

"These are a little sparse on branches," he said, "and I doubt they would sell for much. I'll give you one for two dollars."

He was right about the branches, but I felt I could make one work. I chose the one that I felt was best, meaning it had one good side. We would put the tree in a corner and just keep the best side out.

When I arrived home, my little girls were standing at the window watching for my arrival. When they saw me pull the tree from the back of my pickup, I could hear their squeals of delight muffled through the glass pane.

I brought it to the apartment door but could hardly get the girls to stay out of the way so I could bring it inside. I had purchased an old, rusty stand at one of the second hand stores I had visited. It worked perfectly.

We had just set the tree in place when there was a knock at our door.

When I opened it, there stood Harold bundled up like he was heading out. I was surprised to see him, especially dressed that way, because he usually went to bed at 6:00, and it was already after 7:00. "Are you responsible for changing the light bulbs in the building?" he asked.

"Yes," I replied. "In the hallways and the outside lights."

"What about in the apartments?" he asked.

"Each person is responsible for changing their own."

Harold didn't want to spend his money, but he also didn't want to feel obligated to anyone. When Thanksgiving had come around, Hannah had felt sorry for Harold being alone and had asked me to invite him to dinner. I was sure what he would say, but I went and asked. Sure enough, just as I expected, he turned me down, saying he didn't want to owe anybody anything.

So I was not surprised when he pulled out a dime and held it out to me. "Could I pay you to change one for me?"

"No," I said. He looked disappointed, but then I continued. "But I will do it for free."

He nodded, not even smiling, and quickly pocketed his dime. I followed him up to his apartment. When he opened the door, the cold flowed out like we were walking into a freezer. I shivered. "Is your heat not working, Harold?"

"Why do you ask?"

"It is so cold," I replied.

His face showed his disgust with me. "Do you know how much it costs to heat an apartment? A person can just bundle up."

I hadn't thought I needed to bundle up to go to his apartment, so I wasn't ready for it. As I stepped through the door and flipped on the switch, the darkness didn't change.

"I can see the problem with the lights," I said. "Let's turn on the kitchen light so I can see what I'm doing."

"They won't work," he replied.

"What about the bedroom?" I asked.

"Nope," he answered.

I realized I must have misjudged him. I had thought he liked his apartment dark because he didn't want to pay the light bill. I didn't know the lights were blown.

"I can change them all," I told him.

"Oh, no, no, no," he replied. "I only want the one done in here."

"Why?" I asked.

"Why?" he repeated, as if he couldn't believe I would ask such a dumb question. "I'll tell you why. I never use those. Did you know that the biggest cost in power is when you turn a light on? So I only turn on this one in the living room when it is dark and never touch the others. It gives me enough light into the other rooms to do what I need."

"What about when you are cooking? How do you have enough light to see?" I asked.

"Then the burner is on and it gives me enough added light," Harold replied.

I was astonished at what lengths he would go to to save a penny, but thinking about cooking reminded me about the soup cans, so I asked Harold if he ever had any.

"Why would you want those?" he asked.

I explained about the wagon, and Harold just grunted. Then he spoke with great disgust. "You'll never have lots of money if you waste it on stupid things like toys for children. And if I ever do buy soup, which I seldom do, I buy the cheaper brand."

Harold found a chair for me to stand on. The only light was coming from the open door into the hallway, so I fumbled in the dark to take off the light cover. I finally was able to remove it. Even though it was a three-bulb socket, I could tell that there was only one bulb. I realized I could accidentally stick my finger in one of the open sockets if I wasn't careful.

I removed the one bulb and Harold handed me a new one. I screwed it into the socket and the room was instantly bathed in a really dim light.

"Do you want me to put bulbs in the other sockets?" I asked.

"One is more than enough," Harold replied.

I put the light cover back on and then stepped down from the chair. I picked up the blown bulb that Harold had set down. It was only 20 watts. As dim as the new bulb was, I figured it couldn't be much more than that. Harold saw me look at it and spoke as if proud of himself. "They cost one third to run compared to a 60-watt bulb."

"You know," I said jokingly, "it might be cheaper to just have a small night light plugged into a wall socket in each room. I think they are only about five watts each."

I was kidding, but Harold became excited. "I never thought of that! I have some I could use."

This man was unbelievable. Every minute I kept thinking he would say he was just kidding, but he didn't. It seemed impossible for anyone to be the way Harold was.

"Well," I said, "I had better be heading home. I promised my little girls we would decorate the Christmas tree tonight."

"Buying a Christmas tree and stuff like that is stupid," Harold said. "It's a waste of money to buy presents that you don't need. It's about as dumb of a tradition as there is."

"I disagree, Harold," I said. "Christmas trees and presents are fun. They make life happy. And it is hard to put a price on something that brings joy to those you love."

"You sound just like my stupid son," Harold said. "You remind me so much of him it makes me sick."

"You have a son?" I questioned. The thought of Harold being married or having children seemed impossible.

"I said I had a son," Harold replied, "not have."

"Oh, I'm sorry," I said. "When did he die?"

Harold rolled his eyes. "I didn't say he died."

"But you said . . ."

"What I said was I had a son. He has disowned me and wants nothing to do with me."

"I'm sorry to hear that," I said.

"I say good riddance," Harold said. "I tried to teach him thrift and frugality. I was the perfect example on how to conserve and invest. But, no, the world says a person needs to enjoy life and waste money, and he believed it, just like you do. I tried, but he wouldn't listen to me. Like you, he is always thinking that money should be spent on silly things like Christmas trees and sparkling lights. He was always upset that he couldn't have new clothes like others did, or other new things. What he had was just fine. And what I refused to let him have, he didn't need anyway. He said I cared more about my money than about anyone else, and he was leaving and never coming back. Well, whoop-dee-doo. That's just one less person I have to care about."

I was so shocked I couldn't say any more, but I was grateful I didn't have Harold as a father. I went back to our apartment, and as I shivered, trying to warm up, I told Hannah about my experience. She, too, was surprised to find out that Harold had a son.

We decorated our tree, and the whole time I watched Hannah work with our little girls making homemade stars and popcorn chains, I thought about Harold's son and how he must have felt knowing his father wouldn't even spend money on Christmas things. I wanted more than almost anything to get some nice things for my family for Christmas, but I couldn't, because I didn't have money. Harold had the money to buy his son presents, but wouldn't because he didn't want to part with his money.

When we finished, our tree looked sparse, but pretty. I had spent 80 cents on two strands of lights at a thrift store. I had checked both sets before I bought them, and they worked well. We put one around our tree and one around our window. Actually, we only made it around the top and two sides before we ran out, but it looked nice. I was the one that had the privilege of plugging in both sets of lights. When I did, Hannah and the girls clapped. As they did, I wondered how Harold couldn't feel that a moment like this was worth the small price paid for it.

We shut off the room lights, and we all sat on the couch under the red, white, blue, and green glow of the Christmas lights. We sang some Christmas songs and were just there together. I wondered if Harold's son was somewhere enjoying the Christmas season, perhaps with a little family of his own.

When it was bed time, we turned the room lights back on, helped the girls dress in their pajamas, and then I read them a story. As I tucked them into bed, I couldn't help but feel sorry for Harold. He had so little of what really mattered.

After the girls were snug in their beds, I headed out into the night to search the dumpsters for soup cans from which I could take the labels. The clouds had disappeared, leaving a beautiful, starry sky, but the temperature was dropping quickly. My hands were freezing as I touched the metal of the dumpsters and the cans. As I worked, I again thought about Harold, and I wondered what had made him the way he was.

I was soon to find out. The next morning, before 5:00, a knock came on my door. I groaned as I rolled out of bed. "It must have snowed last night," I said to Hannah.

I answered the door, and sure enough, there stood Harold. "I know," I said. "It snowed and you want me to come shovel the walk."

"No," he replied. "My water isn't working."

"I'm afraid you'll have to get hold of the maintenance man for that," I said.

"Can't you come look at it?" he asked.

I yawned and nodded. "Let me get dressed and I'll be right up."

I dressed, and then remembering how cold his apartment was when I changed the light bulb, I bundled up in my coat. When I arrived at Harold's apartment, the door was open and the room was lit with a night light. The air coming from his apartment was nearly as frigid as the outside night air. I was sure I knew what the problem was even before I checked it out. "Harold?" I called through the open door.

"In here in the kitchen," he answered.

I made my way into the kitchen and found another night light was the only source of luminescence in there. I wished I had never made that joke about night lights.

"What's the problem?" I asked.

"See for yourself," he said, turning the faucet knob and having no water come out.

"The problem is really quite obvious, Harold," I said.

"What?" he asked.

"You've let your apartment get so cold that the pipes have frozen."

"What can I do?" he asked.

"I have a little electric heater that we can plug in and thaw them out," I replied.

"Are you crazy?" he replied. "Do you know how much electricity that would use and what the cost would be?"

"Maybe a dollar," I said. "That's nothing compared to the thousands of dollars they will charge you if the pipes crack."

"How could they charge me for that?" Harold asked. "They're not my pipes."

"No, but the contract says you are responsible for any neglect or abuse to the apartment, and keeping a proper temperature is specifically mentioned."

The panicked expression on Harold's face was priceless, even in the dim light. "Well, maybe we better go ahead with the heater, then," he said.

I went down and retrieved the heater. When I came back into the kitchen, Harold asked, "Is there a way we could get an extension and plug it into the hall outlet so it won't charge my bill?"

"That is also not allowed on the contract," I replied.

Harold reluctantly plugged the heater in for me, and I positioned it under the sink. As we waited for the warmth to do its job, I decided this was a good time to find out more about him.

"Harold," I asked, "how did you get to be so . . ." I paused. I had almost said miserly, but realized that might be offensive. "How did you get to be so careful with your money?"

Harold smiled. He loved to talk about money.

"When I was a boy," he said, "it was the time of the Great Depression. We never had much. Oh, we had plenty of food and things. But if there was ever something we wanted, my dad would always say, 'Use it up, wear it out, make it do, or do without,' until I could stand it no longer. I swore to myself that I would never be poor again; I would be a millionaire someday.

"When I started working at my first job, I saved every penny I could and started investing. I learned to make a penny go farther than anybody I know. And now look at me."

He said it all so proudly, and yet I thought, "Yes, now look at you – a miserly old man." But I never said it.

It wasn't long until the water started to drip. And not long after that, we had a good stream. Harold immediately shut off the heater.

"You should make sure you keep you apartment heat above 40 degrees," I said. "You might want to keep the doors underneath the sink open to allow the heat of the room to flow in there, and if you let the water drip just a little, that will help, too."

Harold pulled a dime from his pocket. "Can I pay you?"

"No," I said. "That's what neighbors are for."

Harold looked pleased as he pocketed the dime. He had already known what I would say.

I taught a 7:00 class, so it was time to be getting to work. I hurried and stopped by to feed and check on the horses. The temperature was close to zero, the coldest it had been since the little horse had been born. Her blanket was still wrapped around her, and their barn was cozy and warm.

The next day was Saturday, and Brenda came. It was her first chance to see the baby horse, and she was immensely pleased. "You did a fine job taking care of her," she said. "I can't believe her hair is so short."

"It's already growing," I told her. "In the week and a half since she was born, I bet it has added about a quarter inch."

"Wow!" Brenda exclaimed. "She must have been almost bald."

"What are you going to name her?" I asked.

"I was thinking about calling her Blackie, since that rhymes with Jackie."

I nodded my approval. "That works well. I haven't seen a stitch of white on her."

I gave Brenda an apple to feed to Jackie, and I fed her one, too. I had stored lots of apples from an old crab tree, hoping they would last the winter. When Cashmere saw us giving apples to Jackie, he whinnied his jealousy. We moved to his pen and we each fed him one. We then stood and watched him race around his corral as fast as he could in the limited space. We each gave him another apple as a reward.

"I'll be glad when he can run in the pasture again," Brenda said.

I felt the same way.

After Brenda left, I hauled hay and did some repair work that took most of the day. It started to snow about midday, so that by the time I arrived home in the evening, the walks needed to be shoveled. I was dead tired, and the thought of that extra work was hard to face, but when I stepped from my pickup, my two little girls were standing with their faces pressed against the window, diligently watching for me to come home.

The delight I saw in their faces when they saw me lifted my spirits. I picked up some snow and crushed it into a ball and threw it at them. It hit the glass between them, and they crumpled against the window in laughter. I would shovel a while and then throw a snowball, only to have them collapse again in laughter.

Harold came home and sat in his car for a long time watching this, pretending he was listening to the radio. When I finished the walks and went into my apartment, he emerged from his car and went inside.

As soon as I came inside, Kaylynn asked, "Daddy, we play wif you?"

I was so tired, the last thing I wanted to do was to go back out, but I couldn't resist her sweet, anxious smile. I nodded. It took a while to get them bundled up, but we were finally ready. Once outside, we rolled up the three balls for a snowman. We then made a snow woman with a much better figure. Finally, we did two little snow girls.

Hannah brought out some carrots and some crab apples for the noses and eyes. She brought out our old camera and took a picture of the little girls and me with our snow family. We went inside, and I helped the little girls take their outside clothes off. Hannah went to warm some milk for hot chocolate while I went out to make another quick pass on the sidewalks.

The whole time we had been building the snow family, I had seen Harold watching us from his window. I thought he was probably disgusted with me, but as I finished the last swipe on the sidewalk, I turned to find Harold standing on the top step of the stairs leading into the apartment building.

He took a deep breath, and then spoke something that apparently had been weighing heavily on his mind. "You know, you have a sweet family. I understand you and your wife are planning on having more kids. Let me give you some advice. Don't. Children take a lot of money, and if you have more children, you'll always be concerned about having enough to take care of them. But if, instead, you don't have any more children, and learn to conserve your money, you'll have more for the family you do have, and you can be rich like me."

I knew that Harold was actually trying to be nice, and for the first time I felt he was concerned. I realized that was probably why he had been watching my family. He had grown fond of my little girls. But what he said just wasn't right, and I felt I had to respond.

"Harold, you're not rich. You're the poorest man I know," I said.

This seemed to shock him. "I'll have you know that I have millions of . . ."

I interrupted him, knowing what he was going to say. "I know you have millions of dollars. But money doesn't make you rich. It only makes you wealthy. The richness of a person's life is not measured in dollars and cents, but in the value and depth of how he lives. You may have a lot of money, but you have nothing of any real value.

"Can your money love you? Is it sitting anxiously at home with its nose pressed against the window watching and hoping for you to return? Does its eyes light up when you pull it onto your lap to read it a story? Does it laugh and play and bring you dandelions on Fathers' Day? If you were to die tomorrow, would it feel the loss of not having you there and feel like its whole world had fallen apart?

"You carefully tend your money, watch over it, and protect it. But what does it give you in return for all your love and diligence in taking care of it? It has given you nothing of lasting value, and never will, except perhaps the biggest marker in the graveyard. And that is nothing but cold, unfeeling stone."

"And just what will you have when you die that is so wonderful?" he asked.

"More important than what I will have when I die is what I am building while I live," I replied. "I am building memories of love, life, and good times together with my family. When I do pass on, my wife and my children will have those memories. I may not have the biggest marker in the graveyard. I may not be able to afford one at all. But I will have people who will be sad that I am gone. I will have people who will wish I was still around. I will have a family that misses me. But what memories will you have left?

"Will you have someone to come and kneel at your grave and miss you and leave flowers to let you know they love you? Will your son even know you are gone?"

"I will tell you what I have right now that you don't," Harold said. "I have freedom. I can buy whatever I want and do what I want. You, on the other hand, have to dig through dumpsters to find soup can labels just so you can try to buy some stupid little wagon for your daughter."

I knew he was right about me struggling because I had no money, but the contradiction of his statement was huge.

"You are not free," I said. "You are the most enslaved man I've ever met. You are a slave, and your money is your master. It is demanding, cold, uncaring, selfish, and jealous, and it has you locked in its prison and stands as the warden. I may be a prisoner of my circumstances, but yours is a prison of your own making, a prison with no bars nor walls, a prison with little air, and no light. For the love of a penny, you have built with your money a self-imposed prison where no one ever comes to visit. Your money causes you to live like an animal in a hole that is dark, dismal, and freezing to keep you from parting with one extra nickel. It forces you to leave your warm bed and face the dark and frigid temperatures of the morning just to save the cost of a ten-cent newspaper. And it has forced you to choose it over the love of your son."

"I am not a prisoner," Harold said, "because I am free to spend it, if I truly want to."

"Are you?" I asked. "Could you really bring yourself to spend it, or would it cause you distress? Just as a regular prison is built one brick, one stone, and one bar at a time, our own prisons are built by us one thought, one desire, and one action at a time, until they become the habits from which we can't escape. Those self-imposed prisons are stronger than any built of steel, cement, or stone, because we would work to flee a steel prison, and will, if we have a chance. But the ones we build for ourselves we will never leave, because we have no desire to do so. And, even though the door stands forever open, we can't bring ourselves to step through it."

"I just don't like to waste money on frivolous things," Harold said.

"I'll tell you what is frivolous," I replied. "To die and have all your money left, unused, and helping no one. That is not only frivolous, but foolish. The only thing money is good for is the joy and usefulness it can bring from its proper use. To just have it and never use it is like a person starving to death with a cupboard full of food, because they simply want to keep it and not use it. And you, Harold, are a man starving for the best parts of life. You are not living; you are merely existing. And you will never, ever experience the things that truly make life worth living, because you will be gone before you ever enjoy using your money.

"You will never know the joy of the things money can't buy, let alone what it can. You will never enjoy the delight in your son's eyes when he opens a gift of something he has always wanted, knowing it was given with all the love of the giver, something that was unneeded, but makes life better and happier."

"Is giving something that is unneeded and frivolous what it takes to show love?" Harold asked, his voice betraying his disgust.

I paused a moment and thought before I answered. "Yes, Harold," I said, now much quieter. "Yes, it is. Because if you only give what is needed, you give of necessity. But when you give something that is wanted and hoped for when it is not needed, then you give of yourself, and you give of your heart. And that is the greatest gift a man can give."

Harold was quiet, and seemed to be thinking deeply, so I continued. "I may never have as much money as you, but what I do have I use to make life better. That is the only thing it truly is good for. And the things that I do have are priceless things that money can never buy. So, in reality, I am much, much richer than you are, and I always will be."

We stood, staring at each other for a brief moment, then Harold looked down. The situation was uncomfortable, so to ease the discomfort, I took my shovel and scraped down the walk. My little girls banged on the window, so I stopped, picked up a snowball, and threw it at the window. As they burst into laughter, Harold raised his eyes once more to meet mine and spoke in a voice choked with emotion.

"Yes, you are a richer man than I am, a far richer man."

Then he quietly turned and went into the apartment building, leaving me standing alone in the cold winter air.

# Chapter Twenty-One
# A Little Red Wagon
# And An Old Scrooge

It had been a week since Harold's and my talk. The days to Christmas were getting closer, and I still didn't have the soup can labels I needed. I had gone out searching every night until the dumpsters and I were on a first name basis. I knew every inch of what was in each one of them.

The temperatures were still dropping a little colder each night, and each night after my foray, I would come back just a little colder than I had the night before. The night before the labels had to be mailed, before I set out on my rounds, I sat down to count them.

I carefully stacked them in stacks of 100 so I wouldn't get it wrong. There were 9 stacks plus 41 more. I was 59 labels short of the 1000 I needed. I counted them again, hoping that somehow I would be wrong and there would be enough, but the count came out the same.

Hannah came in and held out two more.

"Where did you get those?" I asked.

"Harold brought them," she replied.

"Harold? He bought something other than the cheap brand of soup?"

Hannah shrugged. "Something is different about him. Did you know that he has started getting the newspaper?" I shook my head, so she continued. "I noticed it the other day. The paper delivery boy went up the stairs, and he never has done that before. So after he left, I went upstairs to see why, and there was a paper leaning against Harold's door."

"Maybe it was just a sample copy," I said.

"I thought it might be, so I checked for a few more days, and there was always a paper there."

We were still talking about it, when there was a knock on the door. When I opened it, there stood Harold.

"Can you come put in some light bulbs for me?" he asked.

I nodded and reached for my coat. "Oh, you won't need that," he said.

I looked at him, and he was dressed in warm pajamas, but nothing else. The surprise must have shown in my face because he just smiled and headed back up the stairs.

I followed him, and to my surprise, I found his apartment nice and cozily warm. I was also surprised to find the one dim, twenty watt bulb still glowing. I had figured it must have burned out and needed replacing, and that was why he needed my help, but here it was, still working. He handed me a 60-watt bulb.

"Can you replace the one that is in there?"

I just nodded, too stunned to speak. I pulled over a chair and removed the light cover. I screwed the new bulb in an open socket and then unscrewed the 20-watt bulb. I handed it to Harold and was just about to put the cover back on when he stopped me.

"Would you mind putting a bulb in each of the other two sockets?" he said, holding out two more bulbs.

I tried to hide my shock and act as if everything was normal, but from the grin on his face, I must not have been succeeding.

The surprises were far from over. He also had me put bulbs in the bedroom, the kitchen, and the bathroom. When I finished the last one, I didn't think I could feel more shocked than I was, but when I stepped into the living room, I saw something I hadn't seen when I came in. There was a Christmas tree decorated with lights and everything. I couldn't believe I had missed it. But maybe it was simply because the tree lights weren't on, and I hadn't expected it, so I hadn't looked. What was even more incredulous to me was the huge pile of presents that surrounded it.

In my shock, I stood there staring, trying to take it all in, when I suddenly realized I was making a spectacle of myself. I turned to Harold, and he had a grin on his face that was even bigger still.

"Do you like my tree?" he asked. I couldn't even speak, so I just nodded as he continued. "How about the rest of the room?"

I turned and looked around and realized the whole room was decorated with tinsel, garlands, and even some homemade popcorn chains.

"It's beautiful, Harold. Did you make the popcorn chains?"

He nodded. "Took a long time, too. But heck, what else do I have to do? I've quit going to the coffee shop. I wanted it nice because my son is bringing his family to visit tomorrow night. He was 18 when he left home, and he is now almost 40. And you know what else? He is married and has two sons and three daughters. Can you believe it? I'm a grandpa. Of course, I had to have presents. I'm going to have cookies, and hot chocolate, and everything."

I finally found my voice. "That is wonderful, Harold," I said.

"Where does your son live?"

"Oh, he only lives about 20 minutes from here."

It was hard to imagine that Harold's son had lived that close, and yet they hadn't seen each other in more than 20 years.

Harold's voice grew quiet as he continued. "What you said the other night really made me think. I've decided to enjoy what life I have left. I've even paid the money for a library card. There are some books I've always wanted to read, and now I'm going to."

I smiled. A library card only cost five dollars per year, and Harold had even been too cheap for that before.

"This is all beautiful, Harold. I'm happy for you."

"I may always be conservative with my money, but I'm never going to be a slave to it again," he said. "Speaking of which, how much do I owe you for doing the lights?"

"Harold, you know I won't charge you for it."

"I thought you would say that," he said. "So I have this."

He handed me an envelope. "What's this?" I asked.

"Look inside."

I opened it, and inside I found a ten-dollar bill and three soup can labels. The money had a little note paper clipped to it. It said, "To pay the shipping for the wagon."

I caught my breath, and could hardly believe he remembered that from when I told him about the wagon. I suddenly felt an appreciation for him that I had never felt before. "Thanks, Harold," I said.

He smiled. "Thank you for helping me to understand what a fool I've been."

I nodded and left. When I opened the door to our apartment, Hannah looked up at me and smiled. But, instantly, her smile turned to a look of concern. "Are you all right? You look like you have seen a ghost."

"I almost feel like I have," I replied, "The Ghost Of Christmas Present."

I told her all about what had happened. She listened quietly, and when I finished and showed her the envelope, the shock on her face made me laugh. "I was the same way," I said.

Hannah smiled and cried at the same time. "I think I'll make some cookies to take to Harold tomorrow, for when his son's family comes," she said.

We helped our little girls into their pajamas. I read them a story and did our night time routine, and then I tucked them into bed. It was then time for me to head out to the dumpsters.

"I've got to get them now," I said. "Harold has already given me the money for the shipping, so I can't fail."

"With everyone pulling for you, I'm sure you can do it," Hannah said.

An hour or so later when I returned, I was so cold that my teeth were chattering. Hannah brought me a cup of hot chocolate while I counted what I had.

I added the three from Harold, plus the ones I was able to get, and I was disappointed to find that I was still 36 labels short.

"There weren't very many tonight," I told Hannah. "I think it was cold enough that no one brought any trash out."

"What are you going to do?" she asked. "They have to be postmarked by tomorrow."

"I am not going to get this close only to fail," I said. "There has got to be some other place I can get some soup can labels."

"There is that apartment complex over on Pine Street," Hannah said. "But you know what everyone says about the owner."

Indeed, I did know what people said, and I also knew from experience. I never went over there. It was about a quarter mile away, and the owner was a crotchety old man.

One evening, when I went there with the youth in our community to do some caroling, he yelled at us and told us to leave. He said he hated Christmas, and he hated everything to do with it.

From what the others told me about him as we left, I figured I was likely to get shot if he found me going through his dumpster. But I was not about to get this close to my goal and still fail, so I grabbed the step stool and my small flashlight and headed to the dumpster of the man everyone had nicknamed Scrooge.

# Chapter Twenty-Two
# A Man Named
# Scrooge

I made my way
through the cold, dark streets to
the apartment complex on Pine
Street. By the time I arrived, my
hand was nearly frozen to the step
stool, but I quickly and quietly
went about my work, digging
through the dumpster.

I had found 11 labels
when a loud voice behind me made me jump. "What do you think you're
doing?"

I turned to face the bright beam of a huge flashlight. Scrooge was
there, and not only did he have a flashlight in one hand, he held a baseball
bat threateningly in the other. It took all my courage to speak.

"I'm gathering soup can labels."

He looked at me like he thought I had drunk fermented eggnog.
"Why?"

I explained about my little daughter wanting a wagon, and how I
was a college student and couldn't afford one. I then told him about the
soup company promotion and how, if I could get one thousand labels, I
could get it for free.

"I didn't think anyone would care if I took them off of the cans
they had thrown away," I said.

When I finished, I was sure he was going to call the police and
have me arrested for trespassing. But instead, he just stood looking at me
for the longest time. Finally, he lowered the bat and quietly asked, "How
many do you have?"

"I have 964 at home, and I found 11 more here," I said, holding
them up to show him.

He looked at me again for a long time, until the awkwardness
made my heart pound. Finally, he turned his flashlight from shining in my
face. "You will be able to see better if you let me hold my big flashlight
for you."

With his help I eventually found another 19 labels. I still needed six more. When I finished, and climbed down from my step stool, the old man swung his light around and commanded, "Come with me."

I followed him to his house. As I expected, Christmas had skipped his little home. There was not a single Christmas decoration anywhere.

He led me into the living room and told me to take a seat. He then disappeared into the kitchen. While he was gone, I looked around the room. It was a comfortable home, but it was very strange. Everything was old fashioned, and it was like I had stepped back into the 1940's. An old grandfather clock stood in the corner and ticked loudly. There were some black and white pictures hanging on the wall. One was of a young girl, and one was of a beautiful woman. Next to them was a wedding picture.

But it wasn't just the old things. The feeling in the home was strange. I had been in homes with antiques, and I quite like antiques. But this was different. I couldn't see anything modern. There was no television, but there was an old box radio that stood to one side. It was one of the kinds I had seen in movies that people listened to when Franklin D. Roosevelt told about the bombing of Pearl Harbor.

The light switches, the light fixtures, and every piece of furniture must have been made previous to 1950. It wasn't just nostalgia. It was more than that, and it didn't seem quite right.

When he came back, he had six cans of soup. He peeled off the labels and held them out to me. "Take these."

I looked at them, almost expecting them to be from the 1940's as well, but they were new.

"But how will you remember what soup is in them?" I asked.

He shrugged, "Doesn't matter. Surprise soup is the best kind. Besides, at my age, they all taste the same."

I thanked him, and then he did something I didn't expect. He smiled and chuckled slightly. "You should have seen your face when I shined my flashlight on you. You've probably heard lots of scary stories about me, haven't you?"

I didn't know what to say, so I just shrugged and nodded.

He held out his hand. "My name is Robert Delford."

I took his hand. "Tom Johnson," I replied.

I had stood when he had come back into the room, and he motioned for me to sit again. "You're that guy over on Elm that has the two little girls and the blonde wife, aren't you?"

I nodded, so he continued. "I've seen you out playing with them, walking together to church, and going off together in your little pickup. You probably didn't even know I've been watching you, did you?"

"No, I didn't know," I replied. When we would walk to church I had seen him at times and had waved, but he had always just scowled and turned away.

"You know why I have been watching you?" he asked. I shook my head, so he continued. "It's probably because you reminded me a lot of myself when I came back from the war. Did you know that my family has lived in this house since the day I was married?"

I shook my head. "Actually, I know very little about you."

Suddenly, he became very quiet. I didn't know what to say, and the awkwardness of the situation was only compounded by the loud ticking of the grandfather clock. I was just about to excuse myself when he spoke again, quietly, and in a very sad voice.

"You probably also didn't know that I had a little girl once, did you?" I shook my head, so he continued. "I was drafted into World War II at 20 years old, and my wife, Mary, and I were married when I came home on leave after I finished basic training.

"My little Katie was born while I was in Europe. She was two by the time I got home. By the time Christmas rolled around, she was three. We didn't have a lot of money, and I wanted to do something very special for her. There was something she wanted more than anything, and I bet you can't guess what it was?"

"What?" I asked.

"You're not going to believe this, but what she wanted was a wagon, just like your little girl does now. That's why I was so shocked when you told me."

Robert paused, and I began to sense there was something deeper to the story. I just waited for him to go on, and eventually he did. "I couldn't afford one either, just like you. But I was determined she would have one for the next year, so I scraped together what little money we had, and I purchased some lumber. I made a beautiful wagon."

Once more he paused, but this time tears rolled down his face. I just waited, and finally he continued, struggling to speak. "But just before Christmas that year, she got the measles. She died on Christmas morning and never even got to use the wagon."

Suddenly, I understood more about this old man than most in the community probably ever knew, and I realized why he despised Christmas.

I didn't know what to say. I realized that my presence was bringing back painful memories for him. I thought I should leave, but before I could, he continued.

"Mary and I both had the measles, too. After Katie died, Mary seemed to lose her will to live, and I lost her only a few days later."

"I'm sorry," I said.

"I had hoped I would go, too," he said. "But I wasn't that lucky." He paused for a brief time and then spoke quietly, as if speaking to himself. "I couldn't stand the sight of the wagon, so I burned it."

He sat there silently for a while, wiping away his tears now and then. Then, suddenly, he looked up. "Heavens, where are my manners?

You must be freezing from being out there in the cold. How about some hot chocolate?"

Even though I knew I ought to get home, I felt a need to stay, so I smiled and said, "That would be nice."

He led me into a kitchen that matched the living room, with the exception of a fairly new stove. There was an old wood stove there that radiated warmth, and I moved up near it. He didn't use his new stove to make hot chocolate, but, instead, put some milk in a pan and set it on the wood stove.

We talked quite a while, drinking the hot chocolate when it was ready. "You know," he said at one point, "I don't think I've hardly talked to anyone about it since then. I guess I just locked my life and heart that Christmas and never let anything change. I mean, look around you. Even my home is still the same. I haven't even moved a piece of furniture."

I had already begun to sense that was why his home was the way it was, but as he said it, it seemed to be more of a revelation to himself than to me.

"I probably wouldn't be talking about it now, either," he said, "but the coincidence of the circumstances, the wagon for your little girl and all, it is so unusual."

We continued to visit, but when the grandfather clock in living room boomed out that it was midnight, I suddenly realized that Hannah would be worried. As I turned to leave, he asked me to wait. He retrieved an old ribbon and handed it to me. "This is the ribbon I tied on my little girl's wagon all those years ago. When you get the wagon, tell your little girls Santa sent this ribbon for it." He then smiled brightly. "Merry Christmas."

I smiled back. "Merry Christmas," I said, "and thank you for the ribbon and the soup can labels."

When I got home, Hannah was anxious about where I had been. I told Hannah the story as we packaged the labels.

She smiled. "Maybe it was more than fate that led you there."

The next day I mailed the package of labels with a check for the shipping. I knew it would be weeks before the wagon could get there, but I could feel the excitement already starting to grow.

Hannah took a huge plate of cookies to Harold to help with his party. He laughed and thanked her. "I'm very grateful. My cooking skills aren't as good as I thought."

As the appointed time drew near, we watched out the window. Finally, a car pulled in. A handsome man and a beautiful woman stepped from the car along with five children. The oldest boy was about 14. There were three girls aged from about 7 to 11 years old. Then there was a little boy who was about three. They were such a cute family.

As they started up the walk, we heard a pounding come down the stairs, and Harold rushed out the front door. His laughter was contagious, and though the others seemed somewhat reserved, they smiled. We watched until they had passed from our view into the apartment building. Then Hannah reached over and gave my hand a squeeze.

The next two weeks seemed long as we waited for the wagon. I had plenty to do to keep me busy as I finished up finals and took care of the horses, but, each day, I would rush home only to find it still hadn't come.

But, finally, on Christmas Eve, it arrived in a big box. I was glad the little girls couldn't read because it said, "One wagon, some assembly required." After we got the girls in bed, I opened the box. The pieces fell into a pile on the floor.

"Some assembly required?" I said to Hannah. "My heavens, what is their definition of some?"

We spent until 2:00 in the morning putting it together, but I thought how nice it was to be in where it was warm and not out digging through dumpsters. When it was finally assembled, I tied the old yellow ribbon on it and set it under our small tree. Then I collapsed into bed.

The sun wasn't even up the next morning when I heard Kaylynn's squeals from the other room. "Linny, he came! Santa came, and he brought us a wagon! And it is the best wagon ever!"

"I think that's our cue," Hannah said sleepily.

I had always grown up with the understanding that animals were fed first. I dressed warmly and headed off to take care of them while Hannah prepared breakfast and struggled to keep the little girls out of the presents.

As I opened the door, I almost ran right into Harold. "You're not going to the coffee shop today, are you?"

Harold snorted a disgusted snort. "Of course not. I told you I don't go there anymore. My son invited me to come over for Christmas, and I need to be there early so I can see the children open their presents. I want to see what they think of the ones from me."

I smiled. "What did you get them, Harold?"

He laughed. "Frivolous stuff. Stuff from the heart."

Even though the air was cold, thinking of Harold with his son's family made me feel warm. I made sure that the horses had a little bit extra for Christmas, and I gave them a few extra apples. Even Blackie was getting old enough she would chew on one. I'm not sure whether she ever truly ate it, though.

When I arrived home, Hannah had bacon and eggs ready. We seldom ate bacon because it was too expensive, but Christmas was the one exception. We made sure the girls had plenty of real food before we let them dive into the stockings and what candy we had been able to afford to put in them.

We enjoyed our time unwrapping presents. Kaylynn insisted on sitting in the wagon the whole time she unwrapped her presents, and

Linny wanted to join her. Once we were all finished, I announced that it was time to go for a wagon ride.

"Some place special?" Hannah asked.

I nodded. "We are going to Robert Delford's."

"The man everyone calls Scrooge?"

"Yes," I said. "The Scrooge that isn't."

"Who is he?" Kaylynn asked.

"Remember how I told you that Santa gave me the yellow ribbon to tie on your wagon?" She nodded, so I continued. "We are going to his house so he can see you with your wagon."

Everyone bundled up, and we tucked our two little girls into the wagon, wrapped in a big blanket. I fluffed up the ribbon so it showed prominently.

When we got to Robert's home, Kaylynn looked up at me. "Daddy, this couldn't be Santa's house. There are no Christmas decorations."

I just smiled and said, "Maybe Santa was too busy to decorate."

"Or," she considered, "maybe he isn't home yet from delivering presents."

We did see Robert standing in the window, and my girls waved. He smiled and waved back. I pointed at the yellow ribbon and his whole face lit up in a grin.

That night we decided to go out one more time so we could see all the Christmas lights glowing up and down the streets. Hannah and I bundled them up nice and warm in their wagon, and we headed on our way. As we were passing in front of Robert's house, we stopped. It was the house of Scrooge no more, for there was an old wreath on the door and an ancient set of lights glowing along the porch. Kaylynn smiled. "Oh, look, Daddy. Santa must have finally come home."

"Yes, Sweetheart," I said. "I think Santa has finally come home."

# Chapter Twenty-Three
# A Chicken Named Fluff

January brought even colder weather, and with it came a chicken that I called Fluff. How she got that name was purely by accident. I don't know where she came from or who owned her, and nobody else seemed to, either. One day she just showed up in the barnyard and decided she was cock of the walk. I guess she wasn't cock of the walk, being a female, so she was hen of the pen, but she sure decided she owned the place.

It all started right after the first of the year. I came to feed the horses one morning, and she was just there in the barn, and during my absence she had laid claim on it. I started to enter to get some grain for the horses, and she came at me, squawking and flapping her wings. She had no tolerance for me at all.

I backed up a step under her attack, and it made her even braver. She flew at me, pecking, squawking, and scratching. I shooed her away with my bucket. "Get away, you psycho fluff ball!" And that was how I ended up calling her Fluff. It was short for Psycho Fluff Ball.

She was red in color. Actually, she was kind of mottled, but she was mostly red. She was on the smallish side for a chicken, but what she lacked in size, she made up for in attitude.

When she wasn't occupied with trying to kill me, she was busy running here and there, bossing anyone around she thought she could. She even attacked pieces of straw that floated down out of the rafters.

Cyrus, Ernest, and Max were regulars now, showing up every Saturday when I came to work. They had commandeered some straw bales that they lined up in a row. They liked to sit there and argue over what I should do. They all saw Fluff trying to boss me around, and they each had an opinion about it.

"If that little beggar pecked me, she'd end up right in a stew pot," Max said.

Cyrus disagreed. "Aw, she's just trying to make herself a warm home away from the winter cold."

170

"Besides," Ernest added, "she wouldn't make a half cup of stew."

"And you've got to admit," Cyrus said, "she does add a layer of interest to things around here."

That was pretty much the end of the discussion. The men came to watch me because they were bored with retirement, and anything that added interest was a welcome addition. Besides, they enjoyed seeing me jump when she would get in an especially good peck.

As time went on, Fluff put up with me coming into the barn to do my chores, though she kept an eye on me and squawked warnings when she thought I was moving beyond her allowed boundaries. I asked Brenda if I could sprinkle out a little grain for her, and she allowed me to, as long as it wasn't too much. That helped Fluff tolerate me a little bit more.

It was only around three weeks after she had come that I learned the reason she was so defensive. She was still flitting around, trying to chase every leaf, twig, or creature out of the barn, when I heard some peeping sounds coming from a dark corner in the barn. Despite her acts of intimidation, curiosity got the better of me, and I inched closer. I endured her pecking at my legs until I was close enough to the sound to get a good look. Sure enough, it was full of little fluffy bundles of about every imaginable color.

"Well, Fluff," I asked, "where in the world did you find yourself a rooster?"

She looked at me sideways and squawked a long squawk as if to say it was none of my business.

I watched day by day as the little chicks grew. They doubled in size almost overnight. I planned to bring my family to see them the next Saturday if it was warm, but then, sadly, they just disappeared. But when they did, there was a trail of feathers. I knew whatever had gotten Fluff's chicks must have had a fight, because Fluff was minus lots of feathers too.

By the time Fluff was once again in her protective mood, most of her feathers had grown back. It was almost March, and when she squawked and pecked at me, I didn't miss a beat. I snuck over to the corner, and sure enough, there was a pile of eggs. I kept an eye on them, and the first day I saw part of a beak poking out of one, I rushed home to get Hannah and my little daughters. Fluff was beginning to trust me a little bit, but the others made her nervous. Still, she let us get within about

eight feet before she squawked her warning. From that distance we watched for quite a while as a little yellow chick made its way into the world.

Within a day, there was a nest full of babies for her to protect. My own girls accompanied me as often as they could, and they always wanted to see how the baby chicks were doing. The chicks grew fast, and were soon coming with Fluff to scratch for the grain I gave her. And even though she never attacked me, Fluff always kept herself between me and them.

Then, one Saturday, as I was cleaning Cashmere's stall in his barn, Fluff came flapping and squawking, pecking at my feet. I pushed her away with my foot. "Beat it, Fluff!" She attacked again, and then ran toward the other barn flapping and squawking. I went back to my work, and she attacked me again, only to run back toward her barn, flapping, squawking, and turning in circles. I watched her a minute and then said, "I could swear you are acting like you want me to follow you."

Cyrus, Ernest, and Max all smiled. "I think you have been watching too many Lassie reruns," Ernest said.

I took a step toward her, and she rushed toward the other barn, stopping to look back at me. I took a few more steps, and she went a little further. Finally I just followed her to the other barn with the three men grinning after me. As I stepped out of the bright winter light into the barn's dim interior, I could see nothing. My eyes gradually started to adjust, and as they did I realized the barn was very quiet. There were no peeping chicks – nothing.

I slipped over to the corner, and could still see the chicks. They were still there, just staying deathly still. I couldn't figure out what was going on and was about to go back to my work when Fluff rushed at something by her nest.

That was when I saw it. A giant, wild tomcat was sneaking toward the chicks. It had seen me and had held still, but Fluff knew he was there and wanted me to know.

She attacked him, pecking and beating with her wings, forcing him to give away his position. He was huge; the biggest tomcat I had ever seen. He fought back against her, unwilling to give up his predetermined meal, and, with every swipe of his claw, he sent feathers flying. I was furious. I grabbed a nearby shovel and raced toward the cat.

He saw me coming and knew the tables were turned. He ran for the door. I threw the shovel and nicked him, sending him rolling before he fled into the nearby field. Fluff lay there, bleeding and not moving. As I came closer, she tried to move to her babies, but her leg was broken.

I was afraid the cat would return, and I wasn't sure what to do. I couldn't live in the barn to protect her. Cyrus, Ernest, and Max had heard the entire ruckus and appeared at the doorway just after the cat ran out. It only took them a moment to grasp the situation, but as I picked Fluff up and they saw her, torn and bleeding in my arms, they quickly understood.

"My heck!" Max said. "She was coming to get you to help her, wasn't she?"

"I'm not sure what to do," I said. "The cat will surely come back."

"It's too bad she didn't put her nest in the stallion's stall," Cyrus said. "He hates cats. He would have stomped that cat into the dirt."

I laughed. "Cyrus, you're a genius."

He looked puzzled. "I am?" Then he, along with the others, caught on. He grinned. "Of course I am."

Ernest said he had the perfect box in his garage and left to retrieve it. As injured as Fluff was, she still squawked a warning as the others came closer to look at her and her nest. When Ernest returned, he scooped some straw into the box. I gently laid Fluff in it and then moved over to her nest. She didn't even protest, seemingly understanding I was trying to help.

I hurried to scoop the little chicks into the box, but when I got to the last two, they panicked. They took off running, and I spent fifteen minutes of futile effort chasing them, trying to catch them while the three men laughed at my expense. Finally, I paused to think. I set the box full of chicks in the area where I scattered grain for them. I put some grain in the box and scattered a little bit on the ground. Eventually, the other two chicks came, and I carefully grabbed them and put them with the others.

"You're pretty smart," Ernest said. "But I enjoyed it more when you chased them."

I cleared out one end of Cashmere's stall and put the box with Fluff and her chicks there. The only way into the barn was through the door to his pen, and I knew Cashmere would never let a cat in. I also knew he liked Fluff. She often scratched for food in his corral, and he would nuzzle her. She let him more than most, but even with him she might squawk when she had had enough.

He came over and curiously looked at me, and then at Fluff and the chicks, as if asking what was going on. "You need to take care of them," I said.

The men were all at the gate watching me. Max shook his head. "You talk to him like he is human."

Cyrus nodded his agreement. "That's true. He does. But I think the old stallion understands every word."

I got them a little pan of water and some grain. Fluff tried to stand. "You just lay there, Fluff, until you get better," I told her.

But she wouldn't lie down. She worked until she could see me, and then she clucked to me. It was a sad, soft cluck, and she looked at me with big eyes, as if she was asking me to take care of her babies. "We'll get you better, Fluff, and you can take care of them yourself," I said. The men didn't tease me this time, but, instead, stood there quietly as if they, too, thought that was what she was saying.

"Sure, we'll get her better," Cyrus said.

But the next morning, she had died. She had her babies tucked up snugly under her when she went. I returned home for Hannah and our little girls. They stood by as I dug her grave by the barn she had defended as her home. By the time I finished it, Cyrus, Ernest, and Max were there.

They even brought over their wives.

Hardly a word was spoken as I put a little straw in the hole and then laid her in it. As I did, the men doffed their hats. I felt stupid at my tears. How could I be crying over a chicken? But I realized everyone else felt the same way. She had seemed like more than just a chicken in the way she had protected and, finally, given her life for her chicks. But for me it was even more. She had trusted me to help her, and I hadn't been able to save her.

Over the next month I became mother hen to Fluff's little brood, and whenever I was working there, they followed me everywhere. The men continued to come watch me work, and they thoroughly enjoyed watching the little chicks trailing me.

"Well, don't you make the ugliest mother hen?" Max teased.

And each night when I left, I made sure they were tucked into the box in the end of Cashmere's manger.

When the chicks were a month old, I knew I needed to find a new home for them. They had outgrown their box. I found a farmer who wanted them and had a nice chicken coop. It was hard to say goodbye to my little tag-a-longs, but I knew they needed a home away from any cats.

I didn't give them all away, however. I saved the feistiest little mottled red hen and made a permanent home for her in Cashmere's manger.

I named her Fluffy.

# Chapter Twenty-Four
# Running Free Again

It was almost May by the time the pastures were clear of snow and dry enough to move the horses there for the summer pasture. Brenda had me checking them every week, and when I felt they were dry enough and the stream was flowing again, she decided it was time. She had me wait for a Saturday when she could be home.

"I want to see what Cashmere does when he is set free," she said.

I brought Hannah and the girls, and we met Brenda at the barns. I had fixed her trailer so we could haul them there in it. I loaded Jackie, letting Blackie trail behind. Blackie was quite big, and I had long before taken off the blanket, or what was left of it, anyway. She had pretty well worn it out rubbing and scratching against the fence.

As Jackie stepped into the trailer, Blackie balked. She started a panicked whinnying. Jackie joined in, and the reverberation in the trailer made my ears ring. I had a small halter on Blackie, but she would jerk away from me when I would reach for her. Finally I snagged it, but I couldn't pull her in. I put a lead rope on her and tied her to the inside of the trailer.

I got behind her, but remembering the kick I got from Splash, I used the trailer door to squeeze her into the trailer. Once she was in, she quickly moved up by her mother, and I shut the partition gate.

I had never loaded Cashmere, and I didn't know what he would do. Having learned his history, I was sure he was well trained, but I remembered the story about them loading him in California. When I led him to the trailer, he stepped in as easily as if he were walking into his barn.

Brenda laughed. "I will never get over how he acts for you. After what happened the last time we tried to load him in a trailer, I wondered if he would fight it, but I should have guessed that with you it would be different."

The pasture didn't yet have sufficient grass to support the horses, so I loaded some hay into my pickup, and then we were on our way. After we parked, I opened the trailer door and stepped inside to untie Cashmere's lead rope. I could feel him quivering with excitement. He backed out as gently as any horse ever has, but his breathing started to get stronger as his anticipation increased.

I led him into the pasture, and when I reached up to undo his halter, he leaned his head down to me. As soon as it was off, he looked at me, as if requesting permission. "Go," I said.

He didn't need to be told twice. He whirled around and headed down the fence line. He ran with his tail up and his head held high. We all just watched him, forgetting about anything else. Kaylynn clapped her hands and said, "Pretty horsey!" I smiled, remembering her words the year before.

Cashmere came thundering up to us and slid to a stop. He reached his head down to me, expecting an apple. I had brought some, of course. The ones I had stored were getting old and wrinkled, but he still loved

them. I gave him one and sent him on his way again. After he made his round and came sliding to a stop, Jackie whinnied. We had forgotten all about her and Blackie as we watched Cashmere.

I gave Cashmere another apple, and then he went for another run while I unloaded Jackie. Blackie followed her out and pranced around. Her little nose quivered at the smells of the new pasture. When Cashmere came to a stop, I gave each of the three horses an apple, and then Cashmere took off again.

Blackie took off behind him, and for a brief distance Cashmere slowed to let the little horse run with him. Blackie was fairly fast for a little horse, but, soon, Cashmere opened up his speed and left the little horse far behind. Blackie turned and trotted back to us, and reached the gate at about the same time as Cashmere.

"I only have three more apples," I told him. "One for each of you, and then you get hay."

Brenda laughed. "I think you spoil the horses."

I fed them their hay, and then I left to take Hannah and the girls home. I came back and started mending the fence. I was careful to keep my bucket of tools outside the fence where Cashmere couldn't get it, though he did get my hammer a couple of times. I had two hammers, one I would use to pull the wire tight, and one I would pound the staples with. I would put the pounding one under one arm while I stretched the wire tight. He would reach up and grab the one from under my arm and take off with it.

The first time I made the mistake of dropping the one hammer to chase after the one he stole. He ran out a distance and dropped the stolen one. While I was retrieving that one, he ran back and stole the other. With all of the precautionary measures I had to take to protect my tools, it took twice as long to fix the fence as it should have, but I finally finished.

**\*\*\*\*\*\*\*\*\*\*\*\*\*\*\*\*\*\*\*\*\*\*\*\***

The summer went by quickly. I finished my class work at the university and only needed to finish up oral exams and the thesis. I was also looking for work. When October rolled around, the cool air of autumn told me winter was right around the corner. By that time I had everything finished for my degree, and I had a teaching assignment at a college in Idaho. We would be moving there in November.

We were spending time going to Idaho to look for housing, and I was preparing for the classes I would be teaching. The thought of leaving the horses hung heavy on my heart. Would Brenda sell them? Would Cashmere always have a place to run, or would he be locked in a stall again? She hadn't bought any hay, nor given me any indication what her plans were.

A few weeks before we moved, Brenda met me at the pasture when I brought hay to supplement the horses' declining pasture. Blackie was almost as big as her mother, though she wasn't as filled out. She was going to be a very pretty horse.

Cashmere did his normal runs to earn apples. Blackie seemed to idolize him, and would trot around, following him. Cashmere would nuzzle her as if she was his own little horse.

Brenda and I leaned on the fence, and as we watched Cashmere run around the pasture, I had a million questions for her. But before I could ask, she started to answer them, as if she knew what I had on my mind.

"I bet you are wondering why I haven't had you haul any hay," she said. I nodded, so she continued. "I'm shipping the horses to California."

I guess the concern must have shown in my face, because when I turned to look at her, she laughed. "No, they won't be locked in a stall."

I smiled back, embarrassed at my obvious expression. She

continued. "I have purchased some property down there that will have enough pasture space for these three horses, plus Patches and Splash. Cashmere will be able to run forever and will never be locked up again."

Cashmere came over for an apple, and I gave him one. Brenda stroked his nose as he happily munched. "I've thought a lot about it," she said. "Without you to take care of them, and with the increase in the cost of hay, I decided to invest in some land to support them. And, most importantly, I want a place where Cashmere can run free for the rest of his life."

Brenda turned and looked at me. "I have also thought a lot about your question about why I own horses, and I have finally started to understand some things. In my job, I travel, run from place to place, living from a suitcase in hotel rooms. I realized that, in some ways, I feel overwhelmed and trapped, much as Cashmere felt in his stall.

"When I see him running, there is something that wells up inside of me from the very core of my soul, and it is as if I am on him, or I am him, free to run, to gallop and feel the grass beneath my feet and wind in my face. I suppose that is why I own horses – because it brings a measure of freedom to my heart."

She paused a moment and looked at me. "Does that sound sappy?" she asked.

"No," I replied. "I've felt the same thing, and yet, I could never quite describe it. Working out here on weekends always lifted my heart and helped me to face the challenges of school and work."

"I know that was why I bought Cashmere," Brenda said. "When I saw him locked in that stall, it was as if I was locked in there with him."

We watched Cashmere take another run, and as I thought about what Brenda had said, I could feel the exhilaration as if I was with him, running free.

"When do they go?" I asked.

"What day do you head to Idaho?" Brenda asked.

"Thursday, November 9th," I replied. "That is when our house will be ready for us."

"Then I will make sure they head out on or before that day. You will have to load him. I'm sure he won't let anyone else."

The next few weeks went by quickly as we prepared to move. When Saturday, November 4th came, I knew it would be the last Saturday I would have with the horses. I set my alarm the night before so it would wake me up while it was still dark. As I drove to the horse pasture, the moon threw out shafts of silver where it peeked from behind the clouds. The stars twinkled like fireflies, first visible, then hidden, as the clouds sailed silently with the breeze.

I arrived at the horse pasture just as the sun was throwing its light against the clouds from behind the mountain, chasing moon and stars into hiding. Cashmere came over, and I held out the bridle I had prepared for him. I had never put one on him before, but I knew he was well trained and hoped he would remember what it was. He lowered his head, and I slipped it on.

Once everything was in place, I opened the gate and led him through. Jackie and Blackie called to us. "Don't worry," I said, "we'll be back before you know it."

Since I was not going to use a saddle, I had nothing to tie things to. I had a pack, so I put it on, and then I led Cashmere to the fence and used it to climb on his back. I could feel the excitement surge through him. There was enough light so that we would be safe riding along the road. I pointed him toward the mountain, clicked my tongue, and touched him lightly with my heels.

He surged forward, wanting to run, but I held him back to a trot, wanting to save his energy. In no time at all we had gone the first mile and the road changed from gravel to light gravel over dirt. Another mile brought us to the end of the road. From there a riding and walking trail snaked in crisscrosses upward along the mountain side. I had never taken this path before, but I heard that it went up to a mountain plateau that gave a tremendous view of the valley and the other valleys lying directly north and south.

As we reached the trailhead, the sun's rays shot into the sky from behind the mountain, creating a fire of color. An early fall snow had dusted the tops of the highest peaks. The scattered clouds in the sky reflected the sun's rays and looked like a ruby tiara shimmering and dancing red, orange, and blue hues across the mountain rim above the snow.

Cashmere trembled as we turned onto the trail heading upward, and he pulled against the reins, wanting to run.

"Not yet, boy," I told him. "Let's save your energy for the mountain plateau."

I tried to pull him back to a walk, but he would have none of it. We compromised with him still trotting briskly up the trail. When we would come to segments with steep drops or tight turns, it was all I could do to force him to walk for our safety.

As the sun broke fully above the mountain rim, its light fell into the valley, lighting up what was left of the beautiful fall foliage. The trees were painted in vibrant oranges and browns with evergreens mixing in a splattering of green.

A deer darted across our path, and Cashmere lunged forward, seeming to think it was a challenge to race. I reined him back, and he snorted his disapproval as we continued to climb. The trail turned into a canyon with a stream flowing from it, the same stream that ran through the horse pasture. Even though it was starting to taper off, there was still plenty of flow for it to create a percussion ensemble as it crashed and tumbled over small waterfalls.

I looked for a pool, and when I found one, I turned Cashmere toward it and let him drink while I drank from the canteen in my pack. He drank deeply, but quickly, wanting to continue on. We traveled along the stream, crossing it a few times as we went. As we went deeper into the canyon, the valley faded from view except for small glimpses through the trees from a few high outcroppings we crossed.

We eventually reached the end of the canyon and had mountainsides all around us, except in the direction we had already come. From one hillside flowed the water for the stream from multiple springs. I chose one that was clean, pure, and had the best flow, and I filled my canteen. At that point, the trail switchbacked along the mountain.

Cashmere whinnied at me to hurry up. The many smells that

flowed on the crisp autumn air increased his excitement. I watched his nostrils flare as he took it all in. I breathed deeply and caught some of the aroma. The breeze carried the smell of water, moss, trees, and snow from a ridge of a nearby mountain peak.

I found a rock I could use to climb on Cashmere's back, and we were soon on our way. We worked our way back and forth along the mountain, and, when we came over the top, we were on the plateau I'd heard about.

It was about a mile long, gently sloping toward the valley, and was covered in a high mountain brush grass. We were above the timberline, so no trees grew there, though some gnarled ones hung tenaciously to the rock just below the plateau. This was it. This was the place I had heard of.

From there we had nearly a 360-degree view, blocked only by a few snow-covered mountain peaks. We paused briefly to look at the valleys that lay all around us, and then Cashmere shook his head up and down, pulling against the reins.

"Okay, boy," I said. "Let's go."

I let the reins loose, and leaned down as I gave him the slightest touch with my heels. He didn't need any more. Away we raced along the ridge. We were at the top of the world, and everything lay at our feet. A curious eagle came screeching down from the highest mountain peak and swooped alongside us. Cashmere stretched out his neck and raced as if he was back on the track in Germany, and the eagle was Bruin. We covered that mile distance faster than I had ever done before on a horse.

As we reached the end of the plateau, the eagle turned upward into the sky, and we circled and headed back. Once again the eagle swooped down along side us, and we raced. As we came back to where we had started, the eagle turned upward and disappeared toward his mountain home.

Cashmere would have turned and run again, but I pulled him to a stop. He was getting older, and though he didn't seem to understand that, I did. The air was also thinner, and I was having a harder time breathing, so I knew it would be harder for him, as well.

He begged and pulled on the reins, wanting to run again. "I know how you feel," I said to him. "I feel it, too."

I felt a freedom I hadn't felt in a long time. My schooling was done, and my days of struggling to take care of my family were hopefully ending. The world and nature were spread out in all of their glory before us. And best of all, we were sharing the moment together. I could sense that he felt as I did. Freedom is better when it is shared. When I rode him, he ran faster and stronger with us together, as though it gave him greater strength.

I walked him for a distance to cool down, and then I slid from his back. I pulled a lead rope from my pack and hooked it onto his halter. I held one end of the rope while I retrieved my lunch and water from my pack. He munched on the thin mountain grass while I ate peanut butter and jelly sandwiches.

After he had rested a while and had eaten, he came and nuzzled me, wanting to go for another run. I put the bridle back on him and led him to a small boulder that looked as if it had just plopped out of the sky. I climbed on it, balancing carefully, and pulled him over. As soon as I was on, we were off.

We spent a few hours there, sometimes relaxing, sometimes running, but always enjoying the feeling of no cares as the world rolled by at our feet. It felt as if there was nothing to hold us back, and, if we

wanted to, we could have swooped and soared up onto the mountain peak with the eagle.

But as the sun started its descent in the sky, I knew it was time to get back. We didn't want to break a leg trying to get off of the mountain in the dark. We raced across the mountain plateau one last time, and when I turned Cashmere for the trail, he resisted.

I felt my heart tighten even as I spoke to him. "I understand," I said. "This is our last time to run and be free together, but you will never have to worry about being locked up again."

With that, we headed down the trail toward home, and back to whatever life would bring.

## Chapter Twenty-Five
## And Walls Come Tumbling Down

Thursday came, and I was up long before the sun was. The moving van had come the day before and was already gone, but there was lots to do. What little we had left had to be loaded into our pickup, and then we had to clean our apartment.

It was already midafternoon before we packed up our final things. Friends came to say goodbye; among them was Harold. When he shook my hand, he smiled. "You may always be richer than me, but since I have my son's family in my life, I am becoming richer every day."

I nodded and smiled. I could hardly believe it when I first saw him out playing on the lawn with his grandchildren. I knew he was right.

Once we had said goodbye and had our little girls buckled in, we headed on our way to the barns. Cyrus, Max, and Ernest were there with their wives. They all hugged Hannah, Kaylynn, and Linny goodbye. Cyrus promised to put out a little grain for Fluffy now and then.

I filled some buckets with water and some with grain, and when Brenda joined us, I loaded them and the last of the hay into her pickup. The horses would need all of that for the trip. We said one last goodbye, and then we headed to the pasture.

The horse trailer wasn't yet there, and I was glad. I hoped for some time to just watch the horses before it came. Cashmere came up and wanted an apple. I told him to run first, which he did. When he finished

182

his run, I gave him his reward. Jackie and Blackie wanted some, too.

Hannah brought the girls up to the fence, and Brenda joined us, and we all watched for a while as Cashmere would run and then return for an apple. I had brought a big bag and fed him quite a few, but I didn't want him to get sick. I also wanted to give Brenda some to take to California.

As we continued to watch him run, Hannah and Brenda visited. I just quietly listened, not feeling like visiting.

When the truck with the trailer finally pulled up, I could hardly control my emotions. I loaded the water, grain, and hay into the trailer. I then loaded Jackie, with Blackie following close behind. Blackie only paused a moment at the trailer before she stepped into the stall beside her mother. She was big enough by then to have her own stall.

While I was loading them, the driver thought he'd help out and went to put a lead rope on Cashmere. When he did, Cashmere reared and snorted, and the man quickly retreated.

"There is no way you can touch that horse," Brenda told him. "He will only let Tom."

I walked out to Cashmere with the lead rope and snapped it on his halter easily, without any fuss. But then I couldn't control my emotions anymore, and I laid my head against his side. Cashmere could sense something was wrong, and he nuzzled me.

After a moment, I took some deep breaths and led him to the trailer. He seemed to sense that I wouldn't be going with him, and he balked. He whinnied to me, and I swallowed hard a couple of times before I could speak.

"It's okay, buddy," I said. "You will be free to run for the rest of your life."

I reached up and petted his nose, and he followed me into the trailer. When I shut the door, he whinnied to me, calling to me to go with him. I opened the little door on the side, and he reached his head down and nuzzled me.

"I love you, too, buddy," I said. "I love you, too."

I handed him one more apple. "You be good," I told him.

As the truck and trailer started to pull away, he called out to me. I waved. "Bye, Cashmere," I called back.

Hannah reached up and looped her arm through mine and leaned against me. Kaylynn wrapped her arms around my leg and started to cry.

Brenda gave me a hug. "I promise to take good care of him," she said.

We said our goodbyes, and then we climbed into our pickup as we watched Brenda drive away. The mood was somber as we headed to Idaho, to our new life and our new home. To ease the mood I turned on the radio. As the sun was dropping in the sky, setting on our life here in preparation for the dawn of our new life ahead, the radio announcer voice excitedly broke the silence.

"We have astonishing news from East Germany. The East Germans have said, in essence, that the Berlin Wall doesn't mean anything anymore . . . Anyone who wants to leave East Germany and go anywhere in the world is free to do so. . . The shockwaves are barely now being felt . . . In all reality, the wall has fallen down."

And he was right, except it wasn't just the Berlin Wall that had fallen. Many walls had come down – for me, for Harold, and even for Robert Delford, the man people called Scrooge. But mostly, they came down for Cashmere. For he would always be able to run and live free.

# ACKNOWLEDGMENTS

A big thanks to all of those who have helped me edit this book, especially to my wife, Donna, for all of her help editing and encouragement in writing.

## IMAGES ACKNOWLEDGMENTS

- Can Stock Photo Inc. / ebphoto: canstockphoto.com
- Shutterstock: shutterstock.com
- Yay images: yaymicro.com
- Devin Quigley
- Ioana Balcan
- Cover: Mark McKenna

Read other stories, purchase more books, or sign up for a free short story book by going to
**http://www.publishinginspiration.com**

Other books
by
Daris Howard

### Super Cowboy Rides

The first in the **Under Open Skies** series, **Super Cowboy Rides** is a humorous and inspirational story of five-year-old Tommy Johnson from his antics on the farm to the challenges of not fitting in at school. As one reader wrote: "The little boy, Tommy, reminds me of Calvin from the **Calvin and Hobbs** comic strip by Bill Watterson. It is such a fun book to read!"

This is a must read story for the whole family.

### The Three Gifts

A beautiful Christmas story about three young men who are convicted of mugging little children for their Halloween candy. Instead of sentencing them to jail, as is expected, the judge sentences them to 100 hours of community service babysitting at the Women's Crisis Center.

They were prepared for jail, but they were not prepared for what was in store for them as the children opened their eyes and hearts and changed their lives.

### The Mail-Order Bride

It was to be the big day for Eli. His fiancée, Molly, was coming in on a ship. Two years earlier, unable to find work in England, he had headed for America. His ship was caught in a storm, and he ended up, not in Pennsylvania as he planned, but in Newfoundland.

But that was all behind him now. He had written to Molly every day for the two years, and now she was coming so they could be married.

But Eli was in for a surprise. Unbeknownst to him, Molly had married. She had bought him a mail-order bride, and Eli's life was going to suddenly take an unexpected twist.

### Essence Of The Heart, The Royal Tutor

*Mystery, Intrigue, And Clean Romance!*

When he is called before the queen, Jacob, the handsome, young Captain of the Royal Guard, is sure it is to discuss the baffling increase in assassination attempts against the royal family. Instead, the queen assigns the shocked, young captain to tutor her out-of-control, tomboy daughter, Marie.

Humiliated at what he feels is a degrading and impossible assignment, especially for a military captain, he determines to train the princess like he would one of his guardsmen. He will demand strong discipline, tough academics, and sword combat training. He is sure that his rigorous approach will push the princess to complain to her mother, who will then remove him from the assignment.

But to his surprise, Marie instead responds positively to the harsh discipline, and becomes a princess like no other.

## Life's Outtakes books
### (52 humorous and inspirational Stories in each book)

**When The World Goes Crazy** - Life's Outtakes Year 1

**All's Well Here** - Life's Outtakes Year 2

**When Life Is More** Than We Dreamed - Life's Outtakes Year 3

**Nothing But A Miracle** - Life's Outtakes Year 4

**Singing To The End Of Life** - Life's Outtakes Year 5

**It's Ninety Percent Mental** - Life's Outtakes Year 6

**Angels Among Us** - Life's Outtakes Year 7

# About The Author

Daris Howard is an author and playwright who grew up on a farm in rural Idaho. He associated with many colorful characters including cowboys, farmers, lumberjacks and others. Besides his work on the farm he has worked as a cowboy and a mechanic. He was a state champion athlete and competed in college athletics. He also lived for eighteen months in New York.

Daris and his wife, Donna, have ten children and were foster parents for several years. He has also worked in scouting and cub scouts, at one time having 18 boys in his scout troop.

His plays, musicals, and books build on the characters of those he has associated with, along with his many experiences, to bring his work to life.

Daris is a math professor, and his classes are well known for the stories he tells to liven up discussion and to help bring across the points he is trying to teach. His scripts and books are much like his stories - full of humor and inspiration.

He and his family have enjoyed running a summer community theatre where he gets a chance to premiere his theatrical works and rework them to make them better. He has plays translated into German and French, and his work has been done in many countries around the world.

In the last few years, Daris has started writing books and short stories. He writes a popular news column called *Life's Outtakes*, that consists of weekly short stories and is published in various newspapers and magazines in the U.S. and Canada including **Country**, **Horizons**, and **Family Living**.